LIARLAND

MADISON RUPP

MONARCH
Publishing

NONARCH PUBLISHING
Copyright © 2024 by Madison Rupp
All rights reserved.
ISBN 979-8-9909535-0-5 (print)
ISBN 979-8-9909535-1-2 (ebook)
First Edition

Cover by Katt Phatt
Edited by Andie Smith and Rochelle Rupp

LIARLAND

To the people who make life feel like a roller coaster:
Mom, Dad, Adam, and Taylor

CHAPTER
ONE

PINELAND WAS a decent summer job until people started dying.

"Freak accidents," the folks in charge claimed. "Could've happened anywhere."

Anywhere else would've closed, even if only for a day, but not Pineland. I don't think anyone or anything could convince Marty Boone to close his beloved theme park.

"Guests visit Pineland for immersive entertainment and environmental education," he reminded the public in a carefully crafted statement. "As a portion of every ticket supports critical conservation efforts, it is vital we remain operational, for the community and the planet."

So, despite two dead employees in two weeks, I'm still expected to bike into work today, because according to my parents, I have a reputation to repair and college tuition to afford.

If I'm about to put my life on the line for some bored Midwesterners to ride janky roller coasters and rot their teeth with cotton candy, I think the least Marty Boone can do is give me some sort of hazard pay.

Though, after last night, I guess I should be thankful to still have a paying job at all.

If a freak accident doesn't take me out, my piece-of-crap bike will. The back tire wobbles. The chain clicks like a disappointed mother. My left pedal is loose, but I didn't have time to tighten it this morning after bargaining with the devil that is my snooze button.

My handlebars jerk at the sound of a car horn blaring behind me. Tightening my grip, I glance over my shoulder to find a blue truck barreling down the gravel road that careens around the back of the park. Rolling my eyes, I pick up the pace, much to my left pedal's chagrin. It jiggles, threatening to fall off as the vehicle slows beside me.

"Wanna hop in?" Dev calls through the open window, tapping the side of his truck.

Unbelievable. I pretend not to hear him. It's better for both of us this way.

"Chill, Gwen," he says. "It's just a ride to work."

It's not and we both know it. "In that gas guzzler? No, thank you."

Dev ignores the hint. "Why not?"

"You know exactly why—"

The retort vanishes with a gasp as my pedal falls off. My sneakers immediately skid over the dusty gravel, desperately slowing to a halt before I fly over the handlebars. Coughing, I wave away the cloud of dirt swirling around me, wishing I didn't already feel like a cartoon character. I haven't even clocked in yet.

"So, about that—"

"Shut up," I mutter, tossing my bike in the bed of his truck and climbing into the passenger seat with a gag. The interior reeks of eau de high school boy. Sweat, potent body spray, and more sweat.

Dev pointedly locks the doors. A silent challenge that dares me to criticize his precious, pungent truck. Frowning, I shift so the warm breeze from the open window hits my face. I can't be picky because I need this ride. Showing up late would be the final nail in my coffin.

There was a time when I'd have happily accepted any drive with Dev Vishwakarma. Then he went and ruined everything, causing us to spend the entirety of junior year pretending the other didn't exist, which was a feat considering we live a whole three houses apart.

One arm hanging out the window, Dev whistles along with the radio. I try not to think of what the wind is doing to my hair. Not that anyone will see the tangles once I don the mascot costume that I thought I'd finally escape this summer. My arms cross over my churning stomach. In all the wrong ways, this feels like old times. Like last year—or even last night—didn't happen.

At first glance, Pineland is like any other forested park in Michigan. Unpaved roads weave between ginormous maple and spruce trees. Then your eyes spot the sun-faded roller coaster tracks peeking out of the deep-green foliage and you wonder what kind of steroids this national park is on.

Reaching the employee lot at the back of the property, Dev parks, not bothering to roll up his windows before hopping out. Why bother? The only bad things that happen in this town occur inside the park.

Gravel crunches under my sneakers as I begrudgingly follow suit and we head towards Crew HQ. Compared to the immersive park, this drab, two-story employee building doesn't have to impress anybody. I have a theory that Marty Boone designed the space to be so unappealing that no one wants to hide in the back during a shift. It doesn't work much.

"Think anyone's dead today?" Dev asks far too casually.

Two weeks ago, the opening team found sixty-one-year-old crew member, Sandy Wade, slumped over a ride vehicle of the coaster, *Wolverine Racers*. Apparently, the night prior, Ms. Wade lost her inhaler while closing the ride, suffered an asthma attack, and died. During the week, Ms. Wade taught biology at Hathaway High. Our principal canceled finals because students were so distraught at the loss of their favorite teacher.

A week later, they found Ruby Cahill's body in a walk-in freezer, between boxes of peanut-butter-dipped bananas. The college student had a severe nut allergy and worked in attractions, not food. But there was a half-eaten banana near her corpse and her fanny pack was missing an EpiPen. Self-inflicted, the medical examiner proclaimed. Her confused friends were inconsolable, so Marty Boone graciously granted them a few penalty-free sick days.

Both deaths were ruled as tragic accidents. Cases closed.

"Dunno. Did you kill anyone last night?" I instantly regret mentioning yesterday, but Dev plays it off.

"Nope. Did you?"

"Not that I'm aware of." Unless killing my reputation counts...

"Impressive." He swipes a lime-green ID to unlock the main door.

"Just trying to make my parents proud," I say, sliding in after him.

"Since when?" Valerie scoffs, falling into step beside me. She's already in her pristine Park Ranger costume. An evergreen-plaid dress with a brown sash covered in embroidered park patches and glossy buttons. A matching beret is perched atop her sleek, onyx hair.

I should've anticipated Valerie waiting for me. On the rare occasion that we get into it, we always spend the following days making it up to each other. Still, the sight of her is a relief. Yesterday's fight didn't feel like something either of us could simply get over.

Judging by her hopeful grin, my best friend is more than ready to put last night behind us. To show each other—and the rest of this nosy town—that we're fine.

I should want the same, especially after a video of our fight made its rounds online. On camera, I come across as a jealous bitch. Rightly so, I guess. I was sure this would be my summer to don the role of Park Ranger, but the job went to my best friend instead.

If Valerie can move on, so can I. Without each other, we'll never survive this place. I wonder if we're going to address it outright, but she's busy skeptically eyeing the boy beside me.

She squints. "Been a minute, Vishwakarma."

"Orchestra keeps me busy," he responds easily, not taking the bait.

Valerie shoots me a look and I answer with a small shake of my head. This day doesn't need more drama. If Dev wants to play nice all of a sudden, so be it.

Crew HQ is bustling with Pineland employees relishing their final gulps of bitter coffee before prepping the park for opening. No one seems nervous clocking-in to a workplace where employees keep dying. I guess that's the consequence of living in a small town like Hathaway. People around here trust what they're told. If they say the case is closed, then it is. A tragic accident is just that.

Weston, our classmate who is a ride operator at the drop-tower, *Deciduous*, is waiting outside the locker rooms. His muscular arms stretch his mustard-yellow polo. After sparing me a disgusted scrunch of his nose, he flashes an eager smile at Valerie. "Morning, Val."

Now that she's Pineland's most iconic character, Valerie is as eye-catching as a rosy-pink crabapple tree in bloom. It's a burden she readily accepts.

"Have you seen Luca?" Valerie asks, and Weston visibly deflates like the cheap balloons sold in the park.

Dev snorts and disappears into the men's locker room.

"No, why?" Weston asks, doing his best to maintain his bravado.

"No reason," she says coyly. "We missed you at Open Season last night."

Please. Valerie was too busy flirting with Luca Mendes to notice if Weston was present at the summer kick-off event for employees.

Weston shrugs absentmindedly. "I stayed home to watch the playoffs."

My eyebrows raise at his lie. We both know I saw him here last night.

His eyes cut to me for a split second, daring me to speak up.

Not noticing, Valerie giggles, "You skipped the best party of the year for a hockey game?"

"Our shifts start soon," I say, pulling her towards the women's locker room so I can privately clue her into this boy's caginess. Weston McCray, the most aggressive guy on the school's hockey team, is not the kind of person you call out in public.

The boy squints at us. "So, you two are friends again?"

"We never stopped," Valerie snaps, "and I'm sticking with her. For all we know, there's a sick serial killer on the loose causing all these freak accidents."

"Even if that were the case," Weston chuckles, "don't you think you're safe with me?"

Smirking, she cocks her head to the side. "Not in the slightest."

"Bye, Weston!" I call over my shoulder, dragging Valerie into the locker room. When it closes, I shoot her a pained look. "You can do way better. Like Luca, who's delightful."

"Delightful is boring." She can't even finish the sentence without giggling at how ridiculous she sounds.

I'm not laughing at the prospect of someone as obnoxious as Weston hanging around us all summer. "He's shady, Val. I saw him—"

"Gwendolyn Gardner?" A far-too-chirpy voice calls down the locker bay.

Shit. It's never a good sign when you hear Hannah say

your name—especially if you're me. The woman is way too young for the number of gray hairs pulled into her bun, but that's the price you pay when you're one of the few year-round managers at Pineland.

"Oh, you're here." At the sight of me, her thin lips stretch into a smile that shoots a chill up my spine. After she kicked me out of Open Season, the last thing I'd expect Hannah Flannigan to feel is pleased that I showed up to work today.

My surprise must play across my face, because she waves her clipboard and tuts, "You forgot to clock in. Chase called out, so we'll need you to take on some extra meet-and-greets."

Of course, he did. Trying to keep my bitterness in check, I wrangle my brunette bob into the tiniest nub of a ponytail. I should be thankful they're still letting me wear the hot-and-smelly Sybil the Red Squirrel costume. As everyone's been quick to remind me, things could be way, way worse. As a favor to my father, Marty Boone didn't fire me for causing a scene in the middle of his park last night. His patience only pissed my father off more.

Dad's anger still rings in my ear. "If we lose Marty's business, it's more than your tuition we won't be able to afford."

"Sounds good!" I say to Hannah, mustering my best thanks-for-not-firing-me smile.

Feeling especially protective, Valerie isn't having it. "That's not fair. Gwen shouldn't have to work double sets because Chase is playing hooky after a late-night at Open Season."

"It's a big day for Sybil the Squirrel! Everyone wants to meet the star of our new ride."

"Have you considered that people keep dying because they're worked to the bone?"

Hannah ignores Valerie, locking eyes with me. "Welcome Show is scheduled as usual. Immediately after, report to *Sybil Saves the World* for the grand opening ceremony."

Happy for the chance to make things right, I nod eagerly. "I'll be there."

"Thanks for being a team player, Gwen," Hannah says, her voice sarcastically sweet, before she hurries away to ruin someone else's day.

Frustratedly swinging open her olive-green locker, Valerie rifles through a mess of park maps, gum wrappers, and training guides. I already know what she's hunting for—a tube of lavender-purple lipstick. Technically against the dress-code, Valerie wears it when she's in a capital-m Mood. Glossing it over her brown lips, she silently challenges anyone to pick a fight with her. It's a fierce signal that she'll give it right back.

"Hannah's taking advantage of the situation," Valerie huffs after rubbing her lips together. "One misunderstanding shouldn't ruin your summer."

My summer was ruined when I didn't get the Park Ranger role, but I'm not reopening that can of worms. I'm supposed to be over that, even if I desperately needed the job. My folks can't afford anything more than community college. But Valerie and I have our sights set on schools outside of Hathaway. Our goal is out west, so she can start her acting career and I can study environmental science. If I'm ever to escape Hathaway, I'll need every scholarship I can get. The one given to every Pineland Park Ranger would've made a world of a difference, but Valerie was selected for the role instead of me.

His way of giving back to the community, Marty fully supports the student who plays the Park Ranger after high school graduation. Scholarships, letter of recommendations, the works.

"I better get going. Need to grab my fursuit early, I guess."

"This place is bullshit," Valerie mutters before sarcastically waving good-bye. "Have a super save-the-world day!"

I offer my best scout salute before turning it into the finger, earning a snort from Valerie.

Pretending things are fine between us is comforting. I don't want to be at odds with my best friend. It would be a long summer without her.

When I exit the locker room, I force a chipper grin to stretch my lips. At least I won't have to fake it for long—the sole perk of wearing a mascot head all day.

Outside costuming, Dev waits with an enormous black bag on wheels. Hannah must've gotten to him first. He's now dressed in knee-length tan shorts and a polo that's juniper-berry blue. An acorn-shaped name tag is pinned to it. As Sybil's character attendant, he spends most shifts taking pictures for guests and waving obnoxious kids away from the squirrel's bushy tail.

"Extra sets on the first day of summer? How did we get so lucky?"

I blow out a breath. "I'm going to kill Chase."

"Pineland's gotta meet its body quota somehow," he sighs darkly.

Has the world turned upside down? I have a fight with Valerie and now Dev wants to be friendly again. He didn't say a single word to me during our shifts last weekend. What changed?

I awkwardly lead the way from HQ to the outskirts of the park. It's not much better looking out here, but the natural light and looming greenery certainly helps. Marty Boone abides by a strict if-guests-can't-see-it-who-cares-what-it-looks-like rule. Holding my breath as we pass a dumpster, Dev and I proceed around a corner and onto a completely different planet.

Pineland once claimed the title of Michigan's most-popular tourist destination for a reason. Its spotlight may be dimming, but the park is still a haven of fresh air and adventure.

Though upon closer inspection, little of Pineland is truly natural. The walkways are paved with cement. There are buildings everywhere. Sure, they may look like enormous bird-houses or log cabins, but there's nothing organic about the air conditioning pumping inside.

The biggest offender is the Great Oak—appropriately dubbed as "Fake Oak" by crew members. Pineland pretends to have built their park around the enormous tree. It's actually a sculpture with emerald leaves that never change or fall.

While the scenery may be mostly manufactured, the intent is still present. Come for a good time. Drive home knowing you donated part of your dollar to Mother Nature.

Everything is operating as usual. Birds are chirping. Rides are cycling. Crew members are hurrying to restock carts with sugar-coated almonds and sour-apple cotton candy. As sick as I am of Hathaway, it's hard to dislike Pineland moments before it opens. The calm before the storm.

Dev and I duck into the back of *Maple Marketplace* so I can pull on my costume. After padding is fastened around my hips, I step into the suit and Dev pulls the zipper up my back.

"I hate this thing," I grumble as sweat already begins to drip down my neck.

"Hey," Dev says, helping me secure the ginormous, cartoon head into place, "at least no one can stab you through all this."

"Do you not think their deaths were accidents?" My voice is muffled by the mask.

Dev winces at himself. "No, I do. Though I wonder if things would be easier to accept if we knew an outside force was at play."

I understand what he means. The sudden deaths made everything feel temporary. Dark humor helps us forget we all were ticking timers with an unknown number of minutes remaining.

"Well, even if there is a killer on the loose, I won't see 'em coming." I squint through the mesh eyeholes, which make it so I can only see a few feet ahead. And peripheral vision? Forget it.

"Gwen, I know you're not happy about it," he murmurs, "but I'm glad you're still Sybil."

Since when? It was Dev's decision to end our friendship after I broke his heart.

Or is this pity? I'm sure he's aware of my humiliating night. Maybe all this—the ride to work and the first conversation we've shared in months—is because he feels bad for me. I frown behind my mask. Nothing makes my skin crawl more than sympathy from someone I used to consider a friend.

"Better to spend the day with me than someone as obnoxious as Chase," I joke, fighting to keep my voice even.

He pretends to deliberate. "I get paid either way."

"Don't insult me like that, Dev."

His deep laugh has me wondering if I'm too pessimistic. Perhaps he truly wants to be friends again. Either way, I'm suddenly thankful for the costume that hides my warming cheeks.

Checking the time on his phone, he apologetically says, "We gotta go."

Sighing, I follow Dev out the door, exaggeratedly walking back into the park. Ahead, guests line up at turnstiles, eager to start their day of fun and thrills. There's more of them than usual—likely because of the new ride debuting.

Just within the park entrance is a roped-off platform that's made to look like a tree stump. It's tall enough that guests on the other side of the turnstiles will have a decent view of Sybil the Squirrel. Dev helps me onto the stage, before nodding to an audio technician off to the side.

The sound of jubilant trumpets ring through the forest, eliciting a cheer from the crowd. They're extra enthusiastic to see Sybil today.

"Welcome to Pineland, everyone!" In sync with Sybil's audio, I pantomime dramatically, as if I'm truly saying the words. The movements are strictly choreographed. One hand waves to the guests, the other rests on my hip. "Who's ready to go nuts about nature?"

The crowd roars as the fanfare picks up and I shimmy into a humiliating jazz square.

There's one cheer that carries over the rest. It's high-pitched and a tad overzealous.

I startle as Dev suddenly grabs my gloved hand and pulls me from the tree stump. The guests begin to quiet with confusion, but the one voice still screeches through the forest.

That's when I realize the sound isn't a cheer—it's a scream.

CHAPTER
TWO

I'm used to tuning out screams. They all become white noise when you work in a place with roller coasters, carnival games, splash pads, and street shows.

I couldn't ignore this shriek if I tried.

It's shrill and ragged. The sort of sound that sends a shooting chill up my spine. Despite my thick and furry outer layer, goosebumps rise over my skin.

"Dev, what's happening?"

"I think it's coming from the Fake Oak," he says breathlessly, dragging us from the front gate, where murmuring guests are still being held outside.

My heart seizes. Valerie hosts her first presentation on composting beneath Pineland's grand centerpiece.

Dev and I charge down the main walkway, passing brightly painted gift shops and snack carts that already smell of buttery popcorn. Past gardens growing herbs sold in the park and eerie exhibits that feature poisonous plants and insects. Crew members abandon their posts to locate the source of the scream. We're all headed in the same direction.

My heavy costume is hardly made for this sort of movement. I try not to trip over my bulky feet or bushy tail. I likely would've dropped altogether if it weren't for Dev's tight grip on my gloved hand.

He pushes us through the throng of crew members gathering beneath the Great Oak. All around us, heaving sobs interrupt horrified whispers. One stands out among the rest. I've heard Valerie cry countless times, but never like this.

"Holy shit," Dev breathes out.

"What is it? Is she okay?" I desperately try to catch sight of my friend through the mask.

Without any guests around, I hastily rip Sybil's head off mine, only to choke out a gasp.

At the base of the Great Oak is a maintenance door, which grants utility access to the top of the tree. Off the record, crew members consider the little nook a decent hideaway during dull shifts. Valerie usually ducks inside before starting her educational programs.

Visible through the open doorway, two bodies are slumped on a stairwell that winds up the cement trunk. One on top of the other.

Valerie's head shoots up, releasing a heartbroken whimper before rushing into my arms. Peering around my shaking friend, my gaze lands on the body of Luca Mendes.

Forget tragic accidents or freaky coincidences. There is nothing natural about this.

Luca's head lies in a pool of deep red blood. Dried streaks of it trail from the corners of his eyes and nose. His lips are parted with the shock of departing this world so early.

Recoiling, my eyes squeeze shut. Bile tickles my throat as I tighten my hold on a shaking Valerie.

All around us, startled crew members regain their ability to speak.

"Is that Luca Mendes?"

"Are you sure he's dead?"

"Call for help!"

"No one touch anything!"

A crackling voice over a loudspeaker silences everyone. "All crew members will report to HQ immediately."

Eyes shooting open, I find my shocked expression mirrored on my coworkers' faces. Did Marty Boone actually delay the park opening for a staff meeting?

But what alternative does he have? There's a dead teenager in the middle of the freaking park. Certainly, we'll have to close for the day. Maybe even forever.

"I'm not leaving Luca!" Valerie protests as managers begin to shuffle the crowd away from the Great Oak. Sirens begin to ring in the distance, wailing mournfully alongside the crew members.

A grim-faced Weston appears and Valerie leaves my arms for his. "They'll take care of him."

"Take care of him?" She winces, pulling back. "West, he's *dead*!"

"Clear the area!" Commands a security guard wearing a Mountie uniform. The sirens only grow louder as frantic orders blare through his radio.

"We gotta go," Dev mutters under his breath, nodding back at the stern security guard frowning at us. Best to not press our luck.

With no other choice, we numbly leave Luca. I itch to glance back for one last look at the classmate I've known all my life, but I'm no longer in control of my body. Or perhaps, that's the wisest part of my brain protecting me from further nightmares. Luca wouldn't have wanted us to remember him drenched in blood. A boy that sweet and beautiful deserves to be remembered better. With flowers and poems, not blood stains and screams.

Weston's arm protectively around her, Valerie cries the whole journey through the park. She isn't the only one in tears. Distraught employees trudge backstage like a funeral march.

I'm too shocked to emote. All I hear is a deafening heartbeat in my ears. It's dizzying, making walking in a straight line virtually impossible. Beside me, Dev is lost in a daze, those dark brows furrowed as he tries to work out what happened.

Did Luca fall? I don't remember him drinking last night. When did he go into the Fake Oak? And why? Nothing adds up as I try to piece it together. Though, I wouldn't consider my brain sharp at its current state.

I've never seen a dead body before. No matter how I try to banish the bloody image from my mind, it's no use. Every time I blink, Luca's there.

The bile threatens to rise again. *Don't you dare get sick. Be strong for Valerie.*

We were with Luca for most of last night. It was no secret he had a thing for Valerie. He spent most of Open Season with us, making his intentions clear.

Now, less than twelve hours later, he's dead?

Luca was happy, confident, and full of life. His future was set. He was already committed to playing hockey for Michigan after graduation. It would keep him busy while he studied business so he could successfully take over his family's restaurant. Now those plans are meaningless.

My stomach curdles as the reality sinks in.

This was no accident. Someone did this to him. The temperature increases inside my costume. Why would anyone hurt Luca Mendes?

My eyes dart around HQ as we enter. Only crew members had access to the park during Open Season. Each year, Marty Boone keeps Pineland open late so that his high school employees can enjoy the park before the summer season officially starts. A chance to let loose before the hard work begins.

If only crew members were here last night, that can only mean one thing: *One of us did it.*

The atrium fills with murmuring as others reach a similar conclusion.

I blink with surprise as the last face I expect to see

pushes towards us. Amanda Boone is Marty's granddaughter who lives in San Antonio. At the end of last summer, she swore that she wasn't coming back to work another season. I didn't blame her. We may work for her pain-in-the-ass grandfather, but she has to go home with him and whichever old lady he's chosen as his current sweetheart. It must be torture.

Amanda's face creases with concern at the sight of Valerie.

"Did she really find him?" Amanda whispers, and when I nod, her blue eyes begin to glisten.

Weston's nose wrinkles when he notices her. "Don't try convincing anyone to stay loyal to your grandpa's deathtrap of a park after this," he snaps, only stopping after Valerie elbows him.

"Amanda's not like that," Valerie says, her voice hoarse, giving the girl a nod. Even after they amicably broke up last summer, the girls remained close. I wonder if Valerie knew Amanda was planning to return this summer.

Amanda sets Weston with a firm stare. "You're one to talk about loyalty."

His nostrils flare, as if she doesn't have a point. Luca's body is barely cold and Weston already has his arms around Valerie. Not that anyone should be surprised. Weston's always wanted the life Luca was living. Why stop at hockey scouts and summer flings?

My mouth goes dry. How far would Weston go to have what was once Luca's?

He did lie about last night...

Stop. Don't spiral. Nothing makes sense but accepting that is better than jumping to obscene conclusions. Weston is a lot of things, but he isn't a killer. No one around me should be. This is Hathaway, for crying out loud. We're quaint. We're boring. Sure, we may have the occasional small-town scandal or freak accident, but nothing as sinister as murder.

Valerie's gaze narrows as Marty Boone appears with his

latest girlfriend, Captain Nora Pierce. "If they dare say the words 'tragic accident,' I swear to God—"

"I'm horrified by the reason we're gathered together." Marty's booming voice fills the space. He's not the sort of man to need a microphone to capture the attention of a room.

Aside from some sniffling, everyone immediately falls silent. No one dares speak over the man who single-handedly put Hathaway on the map.

"I know many of you are as confused as I am. Luca Mendes' death is a devastating loss. He was one of Pineland's finest and brightest. After an illustrious summer as last year's Park Ranger, he became the youngest crew member in Pineland history to be promoted to manager."

"Please stop talking about Pineland," Amanda groans under her breath.

"During this difficult time, safety must remain our utmost priority. As is our usual protocol, if you see anything that appears out of sort, say something. Likewise, Pineland will cooperate with Hathaway Police as they investigate this concerning incident." He nods at Captain Nora Pierce, who steps forward with her hands on her hips.

I frown at Valerie as she angrily mouths, "*Incident*?"

"The Hathaway Police Department will be increasing their presence at Pineland," Captain Pierce says solemnly.

"Nora—" Marty Boone begins to interject.

Even from the back of the room, I spy the strain between two of the most influential individuals in Hathaway.

Captain Pierce clears her throat. "I want to make it exceedingly clear that you are safe here, as are the guests. Pineland's security team is highly trained and will collaborate with HPD when necessary."

"*If* necessary," Marty corrects. "I shouldn't expect something like this to occur ever again."

"No," Nora concedes, "of course not." Fly-aways from her graying-black bun glint in the sunlight pouring into the atrium. "However, it would be wise to abide by the buddy system for the time being. At least until we have a better understanding as to what occurred."

"Nora, please," Marty says, fighting to keep his composure, "best to not scare anyone."

She ignores this, still addressing the room. "You deserve answers and will receive them in due time. However, throughout our investigation, we must prioritize the family's privacy."

My heart lurches at the thought of Luca's parents. His younger sisters. Their world just lost its orbit.

Captain Pierce continues, "If you know anything, please stop by my office in town. Together, we will get to the bottom of this unfortunate event."

"Murder," Valerie whispers, practically trembling with anger. "How can they discover what happened if they won't even call it what it is?"

I'm inclined to agree with her. They're so quick to call everything an accident around here, but what if they are wrong? What if we're all in danger?

Marty steps back in line with the Captain and she softens beside him. According to my mother, Nora Pierce was one of Marty's many school-aged flings that he rekindled later in life. Mom always said that Marty's first wife—Amanda's grandmother—never stood a chance because she didn't buy-in to the Hathaway way of life. They divorced before their only grandchild started elementary school.

Staring up at Marty and Nora now, I realize they're quite the power couple. They are Hathaway. Our security and economy rests in the palms of their hands.

"After great consideration, it's been determined that Pineland will not close today. Out of respect for the Mendes family, we ask that you do not speak of today's tragedy with our guests."

At this, all the air is sucked from the hall. I'm not sure any of us can be surprised, but that doesn't make the reality any less startling. Pineland is a fortress. Nothing—not even three bodies found on the inside—can make this place fall.

"However," Captain Pierce interrupts, "my team will be roping off the Great Oak and surrounding area for the foreseeable future."

"Please ensure any disappointed guests that the Great Oak will be available for photographs in the next day or so," Marty Boone cuts back in. "Additionally, a therapist has been contacted. If you wish to speak to someone while on break, they will be in Training Room 3."

Straightening his tan suit, he ducks his pointed chin. "Lastly, if anyone feels they must go home, you are dismissed from your shift today. Please ensure your area coordinator is aware should you plan to clock out early. However, remaining with the team will be greatly appreciated and noted."

Dev raises his eyebrows at me and I shake my head. I have to stay. Sure, some crew members only work at Pineland for the free park tickets, but most of us are here because we need something from Marty Boone. Or, in my case, owe him.

"I know today will be difficult, but please remember why we are here: for our guests and for the planet."

Amanda snorts with disgust. She's the only one who can get away with it.

There isn't a single crew member in the atrium that doesn't look terrified at what we're about to do. Go on about our day. Try to smile, wave, and entertain. Act like nothing happened.

Finally, the emotions catch up with me as my vision blurs with tears. Luca is dead. *Dead.* Maybe I should go home. Blinking the moisture from my eyes, I check on Valerie, who is releasing a disbelieving breath.

Silent, furious tears slip down her dark cheeks. Reading my mind, she says, "You know I'm not leaving." The crack in her voice gives her away.

Valerie is one of the few people at Pineland that doesn't owe Marty Boone or need anything from him. After her mother skipped town in middle school, her father poured himself into providing for Valerie. She never needed a summer job to buy a new outfit for a party or fund her college tuition. She's staying because of me. I can't afford to leave.

"I'll be okay."

"I'm not leaving you." The firmness of her voice tells me not to push it. When Valerie's mind is made up, there's no changing it.

All around us, crew members report back to their posts, traveling in groups. They spare frequent glances over their shoulder as they depart.

My gaze falls to Weston, who to my surprise, appears keen to get back to work. After hugging Valerie and promising to check-in later, he struts off alone.

I blink after him with disgust. Weston and Luca were teammates for years. They sat at the same lunch table at school. They worked out before clocking in for their shifts. Timed their breaks so they could talk hockey over lunch. And yet, Weston doesn't seem even mildly upset that his friend is dead.

It's not just disrespectful or heartless. It's unsettling—especially when I recall how pissed Weston was last night when he stormed into Crew HQ and asked me about Valerie's whereabouts. I told him that Valerie was in the park with Luca. Weston's furious response still rings in my ears:

"I'm gonna kill him."

And now, Weston is lying to everyone by saying he wasn't at Open Season.

I'm gonna kill him.

CHAPTER
THREE

I NEVER THOUGHT I'd be thankful to be trapped inside the sweaty, squirrel costume. But right now, the only thing keeping me from crumbling is hiding behind this mask.

Hopefully guests didn't notice that Sybil was twitchier than usual while posing for photos. The park mascot meets visitors in her home—a hollowed-out "tree" that's adorned with the latest in squirrel-furnishing. Pillows made from leaves, a sturdy nest, and piles upon piles of acorns. It would be far more magical and charming if the AC wasn't broken. Even so, wearing a heavy costume in this hot room isn't the reason I'm nauseous.

As I pantomime happy interactions with young visitors, I hear their parents ask Dev why the Great Oak is closed for photo ops. He fumbles the first few times, struggling to string together an acceptable reason. But by mid-morning, the excuses come easier.

"Sorry, folks! Routine cleaning is taking a bit longer than usual."

"Scheduled maintenance. You know how that goes."

"You can still snag a great photo with the tree from the front of the park."

Not that the guests have to ask for long. News about a boy found dead in the park's icon is all over the internet before noon. The comments are abuzz with speculation and questions. How did he die? Is Pineland safe?

I thought the horrific news would thin out the crowd, but it feels like the opposite occurred. The guests pretend they're around to show support for the crew members, but I see right through their "genuine intentions." They want to witness a sliver of the scandal. To later recount to their friends that they were there when *it* happened.

Dev and I hide in the back between sets with Sybil's enormous head sitting between us. The rest of the fursuit is hanging near a box fan, airing out before my next set. We're taking turns with a handheld, battery-powered fan that's barely clinging to life. After my face feels cooler, I pass it to Dev, who immediately holds it near the back of his neck, where I spy sweat slip down his umber skin.

Clicking his tongue at something on his phone, he hands it over for me to read the post.

RIDE OR DIE *@RideOrDie*

Pineland's body count rises. Hathaway High junior, Luca Mendes, found dead. When will Marty Boone accept his "planet-saving" theme park is a threat to anyone who steps foot inside?

MY MOUTH GROWS dry at the sight of the handle. Shit.

I scroll down the feed, my lips parting as I read through a slew of recent posts trashing Pineland and calling the public's safety into question.

"Guess Ride or Die got tired of humiliating everyone in Hathaway and decided to go after Pineland instead."

"Guess so," I hear myself say, while my mind whirs with confusion.

"New profile picture too."

Likely the work of AI, the picture features a neon-red mask with Xs for eyes, a menacing grin, and twisting roller coaster-track horns.

After taking his phone back, Dev continues to read the account's new posts. Excusing myself to refill my water bottle at the cooler, I use the opportunity to check my phone. Hesitantly opening the app, I attempt to toggle from my personal account to the burner shared with Valerie.

That's when my worst fears are confirmed. I'm no longer logged into Ride or Die. Attempting to enter the password, I swallow hard when I'm brought to a screen saying I used an incorrect phrase.

Oh my God.

Someone hacked Ride or Die. They're using our meager platform to come for Pineland.

There's no way Valerie would ever post about Luca's death like this. Whenever we posted from Ride or Die, it was silly gossip. Mostly harmless rumors to keep our classmates entertained. There's little else to do in a small town other than swap secrets.

"You good?" Dev asks, finally looking up from his phone.

Stuffing the device away, I squeeze my eyes shut, but find no reprieve from the anxious thoughts. Someone stole Ride or Die. Who? Do they know the account used to belong to Valerie and me?

I immediately feel guilty for my selfish fears. Luca is dead. Someone killed him. I shouldn't be worrying about something as futile as social media.

My temples throb to the beat of the chirpy theme song playing nonstop on the new ride next door. Marty Boone—or rather, his PR team—had the good sense to cancel the ribbon cutting ceremony for *Sybil Saves the World*, but that doesn't mean I'm free from its taunting.

"Save the planet, it takes us all! From Great Oak-big to squirrel-small..."

The singsong voice is high-pitched and squeaky, like Sybil is trying to permanently permeate our brains with her theme song.

Before everything went downhill at Open Season, I experienced the attraction. Marty thought it would be nice for crew members to get a sneak preview of his new dark ride. He's lucky we weren't allowed to record, otherwise, no one would have turned up for today's grand opening. There's nothing grand about the cheap animatronics with exposed wires and jerky ride vehicles that slowly move through cheap scenes.

I groan, rubbing my hands down my face. "How many more sets until break?"

"Two," Dev mumbles apologetically.

"I don't think I can go back out there."

"Do you need First Aid?" He asks dryly. Theme park employees are required to refer guests to first aid for liability reasons. It's hard not to mockingly ask the question to each other.

"I need to get out of here."

He pauses before jumping to his feet. "Screw it. Let's go."

Moments later, Dev jogs around the corner and proclaims to the line that Sybil needs to stock up on acorns and will not be meeting guests for at least an hour. He returns to our break space with a rebellious glint in his eye.

"What a rush."

I can't fight the amused grin playing on my lips. "My hero."

This makes Dev's eyebrows raise, so I clamp my mouth shut. We can't go down that road again. Not after we're finally being cordial with one another.

Together, Dev and I stuff the ripe smelling fursuit into the black duffle bag and slip out the back door.

"We're screwed if Hannah finds out," I muse as we head straight for HQ.

"I dare her to fire us. People aren't exactly lining up to work here. Especially not now."

Dev has a point. Pineland used to be Hathaway's precious group project. For generations, our community pooled together to operate the park each summer. But thanks to Wetlands, the new water park that opened across town, most of Pineland's usual employees decided that the grass was greener (albeit wetter) on the other side. At this rate, it's probably safer too.

We weave through the shaded park, dodging the warm patches of sunlight that pour through the gaps in the trees. The wildflowers lining the path are so beautifully convincing that it's difficult to decipher how many are fake. We hurry past the squeaky chair swing, *Monarch Mayhem*, and the toasty-smelling *Climate Café*, which serves pressed sandwiches. We pass through *Sapling Spring*, the crowded kiddie-area where screaming children run through a garden of sprinklers and ride miniature attractions.

It all feels horrifically normal. Like Luca's death was a fever dream.

The tension in our shoulders ease as we enter Crew HQ. Praying we don't run into Hannah, Dev and I slink through the atrium and into the break room. Fluorescent lights showcase fridges, vending machines, and scattered tables that are normally filled with chirpy crew members eager for a break. Everyone's quiet today.

Tucked into a booth in the far corner, Valerie and Amanda sit closely, their expressions grave as they converse. My heart pangs for my friend. I can't believe she stayed at work for me. I should've tried harder to convince her to leave.

Our fight last night feels so small now. Insignificant.

At least she's not on break alone. If I could pick anyone other than me to keep Valerie company, I'd choose Amanda.

When they casually dated last summer, both agreed it was nothing serious because neither wanted to do long distance come September. It was hard not to be envious of their mature, no-strings-attached happiness. It's the main reason why I don't date. Everyone around here comes with strings as thick as rope.

Valerie's shoulders sag with relief when she sees me. "Thank God, you're here."

"Dev bailed us out of jail."

"At least the boy is good for something."

"Thanks, Valerie," Dev says dryly, sliding into the booth beside me. "You two see the Ride or Die stuff?"

"Yeah, pretty interesting." Valerie's dark eyes flash.

I raise my eyebrows, covertly asking if she has any idea who did this. A minuscule jerk of her chin tells me no. Fantastic. We're both clueless. Granted, this problem is at the bottom of the mountain compared to everything else going on today.

Amanda twists her hunter-green cap backwards over her copper curls. Her nails click anxiously on the table. Only a Boone can get away with sky-blue polish at Pineland. Plus, her managers over at *Sybil Saves the World* already have their hands full with the unreliable attraction.

"Grandpa's already running with his 'freak accident' narrative," she mutters under her breath.

"Some accident," I scoff.

"That's because it wasn't," Valerie insists. "Someone killed Luca and I know why."

All our eyes widen.

Dev regains his composure first. "What do you know that we don't?"

"It's obvious, isn't it? Luca was killed to make a viral headline."

"What are you talking about?"

It's a ludicrous leap to make. I'm not confident this was an accident, but the idea that someone killed Luca for the sensation of it...

"Gwen," Valerie tacks on after noticing my skeptical expression, "we both thought it was fishy when Ruby died shortly after Ms. Wade."

"Yeah, but—"

"Do you think it's purely coincidental that Ride or Die is now spewing anti-Pineland propaganda?"

My mouth opens, then clamps shut, as I struggle to articulate my fears. It can't all add up this way.

"Are you suggesting," Amanda cuts in as she connects the dots, "that freaking account is the reason Luca died?"

Valerie nods, making my stomach drop. "Not just Luca."

When I find my voice, it's raw, the words scratching against my throat. "That's impossible."

Goosebumps prickle my skin. Was our account hacked by a murderer?

"Ride or Die has gone through quite the rebrand. Who's to say they're not behind all this?"

Dev sounds skeptical. "What kind of serial killer wants to go viral on social media?"

"One who wants to shut my grandpa's park down," Amanda breathes out.

She's never been one to give a shit about Pineland. Between it ripping her family apart and forcing her to spend every summer in the middle of nowhere, it's more of a burdening obligation than a point of pride.

"That's what's happening," Valerie says. "I'm sure of it."

Dev shakes his head. "I'm not buying it."

"Shocking," Val snaps.

My best friend's confidence has my nausea returning in full force. But now is not the time for a full-blown panic attack in the middle of the break room.

"Ms. Wade was everyone's favorite teacher," Dev tries to

reason with us. "She's the last person anyone would want to kill. Her death was a horrible accident."

"A death that made the front page," Valerie reminds him.

Though I wish I wasn't, I'm also beginning to see the bigger picture. "And Ruby Cahill comes from a long line of Hathaway legends. Her ancestors literally founded this town. Another damning front page about Pineland."

"And Luca Mendes is," Valerie winces, "*was* a Hathaway golden boy. Someone who was going to leave here and make a name for himself. All their deaths were destined to make headlines."

"A rising body count will certainly catch some negative attention," Amanda says.

"Are we sure about that?" Dev interjects. "Because the park looks pretty busy to me."

Valerie shakes her head like it's obvious. "So then the murderer will keep killing until people get the point: Pineland isn't safe. We can't stay open if no one comes."

I clear my throat. "If all of this is true, who do we think they'll go after next?"

"Isn't it obvious?" Valerie says. "Me."

CHAPTER
FOUR

WE STARE AT HER INCREDULOUSLY.

"Val," my voice shakes, "why would someone want to kill you?"

"You're still missing the point!" She groans with exasperation. "It's not that someone specifically wanted Ms. Wade, Ruby, and Luca dead. This isn't because of some vendetta against any of them or even me."

"Then why you four?" Amanda demands, tiring of Valerie drawing this out. We all know she can't help the dramatics. It's in her DNA. But now is not the time for a show.

Valerie's eyes glisten as she hands over the final piece to the puzzle. "It's about what they had in common. What *we* have in common."

My brain whirs through possibilities, coming to a stop as I put it all together. "The killer is targeting Park Rangers."

It's a ridiculous theory, but I can't deny the clear connection. None of us can.

We fall into a stunned silence, no one daring to breathe as we process. While her expression reveals nothing, when Valerie's chocolate eyes meet mine, I see them glint with terror.

And that's what sends me over the edge, because my best

friend is never scared. She's a backbone. Someone who never suffers from stage fright or self-doubt. Valerie Ross is the strongest, most determined girl I know. She survived her mother leaving and overcame the harshest rumors that Hathaway threw her way. Valerie never once allowed it to dim her light.

But, of course, none of that can compare to being up next on a hit list. I can't blame her for wavering now.

Warm, furious tears slip down my cheeks. The thought of someone stealing her from this world...

"Are you sure?" I whisper, already knowing the answer. Valerie is always sure.

"Unfortunately."

It all fits together too easily. Ms. Wade was the first Park Ranger, back before it was a role occupied by a student and held any real worth to the community. A few years ago, Ruby was the Park Ranger right before she moved away to college. Luca held the position last year. And now, it's Valerie.

My jaw sets. "We need to go to Captain Pierce. Now."

"You saw how Nora was at this morning's staff meeting," Amanda scoffs. "Grandpa has her wrapped around his finger. Do you really think she'll pursue any leads that insinuate his park is dangerous? She'd never suggest there is a serial killer hunting down crew members."

"It's her duty to keep our community safe," Dev argues. "A job she's taken seriously for over a decade."

I fight not to roll my eyes. Hathaway hasn't burned Dev yet. He still trusts this community wants the best for all its residents.

"Amanda is right," Valerie says, not denying Dev of the eye-roll he deserves. "Pierce isn't doing shit. We already know how Luca's case will go. A tragic accident. Again."

"There are loads of former Park Rangers still in Hathaway. Monica Wagner, Amir Bilal, Peter Du. Even Hannah Flannigan used to be a Ranger." Dev wields reason like it's a burning bundle of sage, but it does little to cleanse our conversation of wild conjecture.

"Only Hannah still works at Pineland," Valerie points out. "This isn't a vendetta against anyone who was ever a Park Ranger. The killer is clearly sticking to people who still work in the park because their issue is with Pineland."

"Then the killer isn't going in order; otherwise, Hannah would've come before Ruby and Luca," Dev reminds her.

Valerie's nose wrinkles. "I'm sorry our murderer isn't following the rules you made up for them."

My phone vibrates in my pocket, making me jump. Swiping it open, I read the text.

MOM

Just saw the news. I want you to come home.

Of course, she wants me to come home. There's nowhere Mom likes me more. Here, in Hathaway, for the rest of my life.

GWEN GARDNER

We both know I need to stay

MOM

Let's prioritize your safety over Marty's money.

It's all I can do not to audibly scoff. It's incredible how fast people around here—especially my mother—turn on each other. Just last week, she was lecturing me on the importance of making Marty's money so I could afford college. Besides, Dad would blow a gasket if he found out I left work early after Marty's *favor*.

Placing my phone face-down on the table, I tune back into the conversation. Dad and Marty can have what they want. The last thing I'm doing is leaving Valerie now.

"I think we all agree the killer is a crew member," Amanda is saying. "Someone who went to Open Season last night."

"Hold up—did you say killer?" Weston casually asks as he slides into our booth, forcing Amanda and Valerie to make room for him on their side.

Jeremiah and Cole, two other guys from the hockey team glumly follow in his wake. They blankly stare at Dev and I until we scooch over so they can join our side of the table. Realizing the pair take up most of the booth, Dev uncomfortably clears his throat as our sides press together.

A year ago, I'd worry this was another one of his hints I'd have to attempt to ignore. But I don't have to be oblivious now. Dev more than established any feelings he once had for me are long gone, taking our friendship along with it.

Peering around Valerie, Amanda shoots daggers at Weston. "Don't you think it's obvious that Luca is the victim of foul play?"

Fanning his glistening forehead with his hat, Weston slowly blinks his deep-blue eyes as if the idea is just dawning on him. How could he witness Luca's bloodied body and not think anything of it?

Because he did it. A little voice screams in my head.

Amanda squints frustratedly. "Try to work it out. We'll wait."

"Y'all really think someone killed Luca at Open Season?"

"Don't hurt yourself with all the thinking."

If Weston weren't an athlete, I'd wonder where he found the strength to ignore Amanda's attitude. "Guess it makes sense. Still wild."

"That's a word for it."

"I wasn't there last night," Weston goes on to say. "Anyone see something suspicious?"

The moment he finishes, he shoots me a daring look, waiting for me to out him. It has me sitting up straighter.

Was I really the only one who saw him? No one else seems

to have; otherwise, they'd say so. What happens if I tell the others?

Weston's firm gaze makes it clear that I don't want to find out.

Fine. I'll wait until I'm alone with Valerie to spill his secret. Let her decide what to do with the information.

"That's what we've been saying, man." Jeremiah pipes up, his voice hoarse. "Nothing was off last night."

I realize his eyes are ringed with red. He should've gone home when he had the chance. What could he possibly need from Pineland that made him think it was better to stay instead of mourning his friend in peace?

"We were all together," Cole adds, nodding to me and Valerie, "until pretty much the end of the night."

He's right. Valerie wanted us to meet up with Luca's crew at Open Season. We spent most of the evening together, until Valerie called me a buzzkill and I snapped.

I wince as the scene flashes through my mind.

"How long is this bad mood of yours going to last?" Valerie whined as we took a snack break in the park's main quick service dining location—a field full of food trucks and picnic tables. "All night? All summer?"

I hadn't meant to let my hurt fester for so long. There's nothing I wanted more than to get over it, but I just couldn't. I've never wanted to be the star of the show. I don't crave a spotlight. But I needed to be the Park Ranger. Without Marty Boone's scholarship and letter of recommendation, I wasn't stepping foot in California for college. I'd love to work for a national park one day. Being a Pineland Park Ranger would've been an invaluable credit on my resume.

"If you didn't want me to be in such a pissy mood—"

"Gwen, it's not my fault they gave me the role."

"It is your fault! You know how much it meant to me."

"You're not the only one who needed this job!"

"Oh, come on!" I was screaming by that point. "You're not

broke, Val. What you are is an attention whore. You weren't even planning to audition until you realized I might actually have a shot at stepping out from under your shadow. And we couldn't have that, huh?"

Valerie went to interject, but I didn't give her the chance. "I thought you were supposed to be my best friend, but you couldn't let me have this one thing. A role you know I've wanted my entire life."

That's when my grip on my chocolate milkshake started to feel a little loose.

"I'm done being your sidekick!" I shrieked, flinging the milkshake at her.

She dodged and the cup's entire contents splattered on Benji the Bunny, the rabbit mascot that Hannah was escorting to a Meet & Greet in that exact moment. Pools of milky chocolate dripped down his white fur and that's when I knew I was screwed.

Hannah was furious. So was my father after the costume was sent in for cleaning.

But worse of all, I knew I was going to lose Valerie.

You didn't, I remind myself. *She's here. She's speaking with you. Nothing's ruined.*

I still can't understand why she would ever forgive me, but she did.

"Luca didn't leave with you guys?" Valerie inquires, regaining my attention.

Jeremiah shrugs guiltily. "He said something about needing to hang back."

"But not why?"

Weston, Cole, and Jeremiah share a look that lasts for a split second before the latter shakes his head.

Not missing a trick, Valerie's eyes narrow. "And that's what you told the cops?"

"What?" I squeak. "They're questioning people about last night?"

"That's a good thing." Dev nudges me with his knee. "It means they're taking this seriously."

"That's exactly what we told HPD," Cole confirms. "What did you tell them?"

"They haven't asked me any questions yet. I wouldn't be surprised if they're interviewing as few people as possible so they can swiftly wrap up this *investigation*."

"What Nora should do is find out who else scanned their ID to unlock the door at the Fake Oak," Amanda grumbles. "Sleuthing 101."

"How do we know she isn't?" Dev pipes up.

"Because then someone would already be in cuffs!"

Suddenly, Valerie's eyes gleam the way they always do when she's laying the groundwork for one of her master plans. "Then we'll find out ourselves. The killer can't cross my name off a hit-list if I turn them into the police first."

Weston's eyebrows raise. "Hold up—what hit list?"

She doesn't bother entertaining this question. If Weston and the others want to piece the obvious together, they will on their own.

Before Valerie can divulge the rest of her plan, someone approaches our table and we all fall silent.

Unfortunately for me, that person is Hannah.

Attempting to keep my face neutral, I pretend like I'm supposed to be on break and pray she doesn't have today's entertainment schedule on her clipboard.

"Gwendolyn Gardner, Valerie Ross," she acknowledges us with a curt nod, "HPD wants to speak with both of you."

"Me?" I squeak.

"Have our parents consented to this?" Valerie retorts.

Hannah curtly nods her head. "They have."

HPD must've contacted Dad, not Mom. Of course, my father gave Captain Pierce permission to collect my statement. "Hathaways have nothing to hide," he always liked to say. "It's what makes us a community."

This town is too small for secrets. After a while, people stopped trying to keep them quiet.

I hopelessly slump in my seat. The last thing I want to do is relive last night. Besides, what do I have to add to the conversation?

I saw Weston.

Glancing around the table, I find his hard eyes are locked on me, silently pleading for me to keep my mouth shut.

What do you have to hide?

He must read this question on my face because his lips part with shock. What does he expect? I'm not one of his buddies, nor am I susceptible to his "charm." I owe him nothing.

"Wait, Hannah," Weston interjects as the others allow Valerie and I to slide from the booth, "can I come too? Luca was my best fri—"

"Sure," she hurriedly waves him along, "why not?" Under her breath, I hear her grumble, "It's not like we have a theme park to keep operating."

Dev's mouth opens and closes as Hannah starts to guide us away. He must think better than to offer some parting positivity, because he settles on an encouraging nod.

Hathaway Police Department has set up camp in an empty conference room on the second floor of Crew HQ. They've pulled a few chairs into the hall. Valerie immediately takes a seat, pulling me down into the chair beside her.

"Cool, I wanted to go first anyways," Weston says as Hannah knocks on the door. A bald officer with some serious bags under his eyes pulls it open, not saying a word as he admits Weston and closes the door after him.

Fixing the wispy flyways at the crown of her head, Hannah warily scans whatever's on her clipboard.

"You don't need to babysit us," Valerie offers with an understanding smile. "We know you're extremely busy."

If Valerie wasn't my best friend, I may have fallen for her game.

"We've had a lot of call outs," Hannah huffs, "and they have me hunting down potential witnesses instead of working to fill holes."

I nod sympathetically, immediately joining the act. "As soon as we finish sharing everything we know with the police, we'll get right back out there."

If she weren't so overwhelmed, Hannah likely would've caught on to our eager compliance. Instead, without raising her gaze from her clipboard, she nods like this suggestion is completely sincere.

"I appreciate it, girls. See you out there soon."

After Hannah rounds the corner to the stairwell, Valerie's head twists towards me, a satisfied smirk pulling at her lips.

"You know what you're gonna say?"

My stomach twists as scenes from the worst night of my life flash through my mind. It feels like Valerie and I have moved on. I don't want to rehash everything with a bunch of police officers.

"Not much to tell, is there?" I whisper back. We showed up at Open Season around eight, met up with Luca and his teammates, rode some rides, and ate some popcorn. Valerie and I tested the foundation of our friendship, I almost lost my job, and then departed alone. Surely, all that is inconsequential in the big picture of what I can only hope is a serious murder investigation.

Valerie blinks at me. "Um, the whole Ride or Die revelation? Their plot to kill Park Rangers to close Pineland? What are you planning to say about it?"

"I—"

The words fumble on my tongue as guilt seeps through me because it hadn't even occurred to me to bring it up. Even if it means I'm in trouble by association, if there's the slightest chance Valerie's right and they're going after her next, the cops need to know.

Reading my mind, she nods understandingly. "It's okay."

"It's not."

"G, I mean it," she says so sincerely that my eyes snap to her.

"Ride or Die has got to be on their radar already, but I guess we probably should mention someone hacking our account. We don't want them to think we're behi—"

"Hell no. We're not outing ourselves if we don't have to."

"That's a horrible idea."

"I could lose my Park Ranger scholarship if Marty catches wind that I've been anything but an exemplary Hathaway."

"You could lose your life if we keep quiet."

"You owe me," she cuts back.

My head rears with shock. "Really? We're going there? I thought we agreed to forget last night."

Valerie offers me an exasperated expression. "This isn't about you going berserk at Open Season."

My jaw clicks. "This is about last summer?"

She shrugs in confirmation.

Last July, Valerie decided to dip for a music festival in Chicago without telling her dad. Understandably, he lost his freaking mind and started filing a missing person report. That's when I panicked and spilled her location.

"I had no choice but to say where you were."

"I know, I know." Valerie winces apologetically. "But you have a history of stress-induced honesty."

"They thought you were missing—maybe dead!" I retort, in disbelief we're rehashing this now. How many arguments can we have in twenty-four hours?

"I swear, I'm not coming for your decision, but this is different. A lot of money is at stake here. Not to mention my future."

It should be my future.

I shake the horrible thought from my brain. More than Valerie's collegiate future could be at risk.

"None of that matters if you're in danger!"

Valerie frantically waves her hand, pleading with me to lower my voice. "If Ride or Die is behind this, we both know they didn't come to play. We may not know who hacked us, but I'm confident giving them up to the cops is dangerous, Gwen. We want to be certain Nora Pierce is taking this seriously before we ruin our lives."

"Are you su—"

We pull apart as the conference room door creaks open. Weston saunters out, offering Valerie a warm grin, before shooting me a I'm-in-the-clear wag of his eyebrows.

Does he have the balls to lie to the cops? Pretend like he didn't show up to Open Season? There may not be cameras, but his presence was still logged when he scanned his ID to unlock the HQ door.

And yet, he's walking back to the park like doesn't have a care in the world. So what if his "best friend" is dead? You'd never know from the pep in his step as he ducks into the stairwell.

"Valerie Ross?" An officer calls out the door.

She gives me a confident nod. One that says everything she can't. Keep our cards close for now. As she disappears within, I pray we're not being complete idiots. If we withhold our suspicions and something happens...

I startle as my phone vibrates. Checking the screen, I find a notification for a DM. When I see the sender, my stomach drops like I'm flying down the enormous hill on the *Lumberjack*.

Ride or Die? Why the hell is a potential serial killer sliding into my DMs?

With shaking hands, I open the message.

Despite my better judgment, I type out a response.

It's a stupid question. Of course, whoever hacked my account and possibly killed three people isn't going to fess up that easily.

Still, I brace myself for anything when I see they're typing.

The back of my neck prickles as my gaze instinctively darts around the empty hallway. I'm completely alone. I don't know if that's for the best or not.

My mouth goes dry. Valerie.

Oh my god—they're all but owning up to the murders and confirming that my best friend *is* their next target.

A chill runs down my spine. I am desperate. I'd do anything to keep Valerie safe. But how? If I trust the cops and they don't take me seriously, I jeopardize Valerie's safety. If I help Ride or Die, I might as well be riding the most dangerous roller coaster in the world. Who knows if I make it off in one piece?

Desperate people do dangerous things.

Whoever this is, they know me well. I am desperate. Now more than ever.

CHAPTER
FIVE

At the end of our shift, the locker room is completely silent. Empty tissue boxes litter the long tables. Only Valerie is bold enough to shatter the quiet.

"Do we want to drive home with Amanda or Weston?"

Valerie might sound calm, but her red eyes and nose give her away. So does the lack of mascara on her eyelashes. She must've been wiping at them all day.

"Really, Val?"

She blinks at me innocently. "Both offered us rides."

"They offered *you* a ride."

"Everyone knows we're a package deal."

More like I'm the extra baggage that comes along with Valerie. This is how it's been for as long as I can remember. Valerie is the friend who gets invited. I'm the expected plus-one.

"Amanda, obviously."

Valerie nods knowingly. "I figured as much and already turned Weston down."

"Poor boy."

"He's really not that bad."

I snort. The boy is shadier than a storm cloud, and yet, is somehow not the most alarming person we've encountered today.

Ride or Die's DMs still taunt my thoughts, making it impossible to think straight. I want to ask Valerie if she received any messages from them but know this isn't the right place.

Maybe it's the sheer guilt of not informing Captain Pierce and her colleagues about Ride or Die's threat, but I knew better when Valerie came out with her eyes flashing. She upheld her end of the agreement. I couldn't let her down again.

I told myself it was the best way to keep her safe. *Desperate people do dangerous things.*

It's obvious Ride or Die is desperate. They've killed three people. The last thing I want to do is add my best friend to that body count.

HPD didn't even mention the account. All they did was ask for me to recount my side of what occurred during Open Season. I kept it to the point, reiterating exactly what went down.

Yes, we were with Luca.

Yes, everyone was acting normal.

Yes, I left early because my manager needed to speak with me.

No, I didn't see Luca after that.

I wasn't kept long, and much to Hannah's relief, I was back onstage before anyone had the chance to complain about a missing squirrel to Guest Services.

Valerie and I fall silent as we finish fetching our things. She doesn't need to ask if I kept my mouth shut during the interrogation. My best friend knows me well enough to trust that I did.

When we're alone, I need to tell her about the DMs from

Ride or Die. I don't want to scare her, but she needs to start taking this seriously. Being on a hit list isn't a thrill, like some coaster with half-a-dozen inversions. This is life and death.

Anxiously slamming my locker closed, I fish my hand through my faded-black tote for my phone. Nagged by the impulse to check my notifications, I can't help but illuminate the screen every other second. But just like a minute ago, nothing's there. That doesn't stop me from anticipating another threat from Ride or Die. Or a furious text from my dad because I said something wrong in my interview with HPD.

For good measure, I check the screen again. All that awaits is my wallpaper—a picture of Valerie and I flying high on the chair swing. Still no new messages. I'd be relieved if I didn't already know the anxious itch to check again will return in a matter of minutes. Maybe even seconds, considering how fast I'm spiraling.

My anxiety has always been quick to get away from me. No matter how I try to control the fears that plague my thoughts, they never cease to pound in the back of my mind. What if this is the last conversation I have with my best friend? What happens if I don't do what Ride or Die wants?

Tucking my phone into a zippered pocket, I stare into my bag for a long moment. Something's missing.

Then it hits me.

"Is this a joke?" I groan under my breath, frantically searching every crevice of the bag. My fingers graze hair ties, crumpled receipts, and pen caps but not the damned plastic card I'm missing. Spinning my lock, I wrench my locker back open. My lips purse when I find it empty aside from some granola bars and a spare eyeliner.

Fan-freaking-tastic. I'm the lucky winner of another conversation with Hannah because now I need to ask for a new ID badge.

"What's wrong?" Valerie asks warily, pulling a tan purse

from her locker. Her lime-green ID is hooked to one strap, in a handy extendable holder. I'd mocked her when she bought it at a mall kiosk after we were first hired at Pineland. But like always, I'm the fool now.

"Can't find my ID."

"It's not in your bag?"

"We both know that would be too easy."

"Maybe you left it in the Caf? Let's retrace your steps, starting from there."

She's already halfway out of the locker room before I can stop her. Following her down the hall, my brain scrambles for any way to get her out of here. She shouldn't be at the park more than necessary. In fact, I should be pushing for her to quit, though I already know those attempts will be in vain with a scholarship at stake. Valerie will always prioritize her escape from Hathaway. Nothing is more important to her than getting out of here.

"I can hunt for it on my own. Go catch your ride."

"Absolutely not. We're supposed to be sticking together until the police figure out what's going on."

"It's fine. Really." For good measure, I add, "Your dad won't want you home late."

It's the only card I have to play. Valerie knows it too, but she doesn't call me out.

"Go," I insist. "The park shouldn't be completely empty yet. I'm sure the gift shops are still restocking. I won't be alone." Catching sight of Amanda waiting near the line of crew members clocking out by scanning their IDs at the main door, I jerk my chin towards her. "Seriously, you don't want to get in trouble."

Valerie's nostrils flare with frustration, but she doesn't argue. Instead, she wraps her arms around me, resting her chin on my shoulder.

"Please don't stay too late," she whispers in my ear, her voice breaking.

I release a shaky breath, squeezing her tighter. "Trust me, I won't."

"Call me when you're home safe?"

"Obviously," I say, my mouth suddenly dry. We have a lot to talk about. Weston, Ride or Die, and the awkward pain that still lingers every time I look at her. "You do the same."

"Duh." When she pulls away, her charcoal eyes are glazed over with dread. "I love you. No matter what"

God, there's nothing I want more than for things to be normal between us. But it feels like there's this bubble of pressure waiting to burst again. We didn't finish airing our grievances last night. There's still a cork in those emotions. It could fizzle over at any moment.

"Love you back," I whisper before pushing her towards Amanda.

My eyes don't leave Valerie as she hurries up the queue of crew members. Someone at the front allows her to cut the line, and with one final wave towards me, she scans her ID and is out the door. I know Amanda will get her home safe. The sooner Valerie is away from Pineland, the better.

Turning on my heel, I hurry into the break room, relieved to find it's not completely empty. Edward and Penny Cline, an older couple who have worked the ticket counter since the park opened, speak in hushed voices as they collect their lunch bags from the fridge. They fall quiet when they notice me, awkwardly nodding goodnight while ducking out the door.

I guess I can't blame them for being uncomfortable in my presence. We all know only crew members were in the park during Open Season. And after my argument with Valerie last night, I'm not exactly the calmest person in town.

Chewing the inside of my cheek, I try to ignore my sudden unease. I've been alone in this place countless times. Like when I was young and Dad had an early morning laundry delivery. Or when Valerie had a date and I didn't want to go home, so I loitered around until security kicked me out.

Captain Pierce asked us to abide by the buddy system. Am I seriously willing to risk everything over a lost ID?

Then I recall Hannah's threats last night. She swore to never write me a letter of recommendation if I didn't pull my act together. My parents repeated her sentiments when I got home. They reminded me that Marty Boone is bigger than Hathaway. He has his finger on nearly every environmental organization in the United States. If I ever wanted to make a real difference for the planet—not a phony impact like Pineland—Marty Boone is the last man I want to tick off.

So I quicken my pace and press onward.

There's nothing left on the burgundy vinyl seats of the corner booth. Praying as I bend to check below the table, I groan when I only find crumbs. If I didn't drop it here, it must be somewhere in the park.

Too frustrated to feel nervous any longer, I return to the now empty atrium and angrily shove open the door leading back into Pineland. My badge must be between here and Sybil's meet-and-greet.

Crap. I also covered Chase's Welcome Show and sprinted from the front entrance to the Fake Oak.

"Fantastic," I mutter under my breath, realizing that retracing my steps will entail scavenging half of the park.

Stepping into the warm evening air, the empty park looms ahead ominously. This is such a stupid idea. A boy died in this park last night and I'm waltzing in alone?

No one wants to kill you, I remind myself, though the act of having to do so is far from comforting. Still, it's true. I won't make headlines.

Pineland is rarely open after sunset because Marty Boone doesn't want to pay for permanent light fixtures to be installed around the park. This means the only useful light I have to guide my path is the sun, which is swiftly retreating, leaving behind shadowy shades of burning orange and plum purple.

The background music is still playing across the park from

loudspeakers cleverly camouflaged as boulders and birdhouses. Without the cheerful guests to drown it out, the outdoorsy symphonies echo throughout Little Saplings. The splash pad is off for the night, so I carelessly walk right over the rubber surface, daring the fountain to test my mood. I'd make its water boil.

Turning on my phone's flashlight, I stomp between attractions and food venues, using the faint, fluorescent glow to scour the ground for any sign of the plastic card.

Cursing the thorough efforts of the custodial team, I blink back tears at the trash-free path. Not a single napkin or straw wrapper litters the walkway, causing a worse thought to pass my mind. If someone found my ID, it wouldn't simply be tossed in the lost-and-found. Misplaced badges are directly turned into managers.

With my luck, Hannah already has it and is waiting for me to fess up.

I can already hear her pre-termination lecture about how my actions are a security risk.

Chewing my cheek as I traverse the final stretch of the park, my stomach twists into knots as tight as the park's soft pretzels when I reach Sybil's meet-and-greet location. Hopelessly, I check behind the wooden facade, where Dev and I hid between sets. Nothing.

At this point, I shouldn't be surprised. For as long as I remain in Hathaway, my life will be cursed, because nothing—absolutely nothing—good happens here. No matter how hard I try to wrench myself free, I'll always be stuck in its miserable clutches. Trapped in an endless loop of misfortune like everyone else.

My blurry gaze drifts to *Sybil Saves the World*, the park's last-ditch effort to have something shiny and new to attract guests this summer. Its glowing sign, which features a waving, neon squirrel, flashes at me mockingly.

Suddenly, the area music shuts off and an eerie silence encompasses the park. The back of my neck prickles.

I shouldn't be here.

Turning on my heel, I suck in a breath at the sight of a tall, shadowy figure staring right at me.

CHAPTER
SIX

THE SHADOW TAKES a step towards me, and when I flinch, their hands raise innocently. "Jeez, Gwen, jumpy much?"

As soon as I hear his voice, my jaw clenches. "What are you doing out here, Dev?"

"We're not supposed to be in the park alone."

Since when do you care what happens to me?

He steps into the light of the glowing attraction sign, and for a moment, I'm stunned by my relief to see him. Dev used to be as special to me as Valerie. The face I'd search for in every room. After I rejected him, he became a ghost. Sometimes, the right decision still stings. No matter how sweet his smile or soft his hair, Dev Vishwakarma and I can never be together. The consequences are too great to risk.

"Plus, your busted bike is in the back of my truck, remember?"

I hadn't, but he doesn't need to know that. "So—"

"So when I saw Valerie leave without you, I asked what was up. She said you turned back for something."

Classic, Val. Vague-as-can-be in the presence of those she deems untrustworthy, which is pretty much everyone around here.

He bats his charcoal eyes, clearly expecting me to shed a little light on what I'm doing. Unfortunately for him, Dev is the last person I want to inform about my latest mistake.

"Sorry for keeping you," I say instead. "Let me grab my bike so you can take off."

He laughs at this. "I'll obviously drive you and your bike home."

"No, it's fine." I'm tired of accepting his pity. It's almost worse than when he was completely ignoring me.

"Literally a few hours ago, you and Valerie were trying to convince us there's a serial killer on the loose."

"Yeah, one killing Park Rangers," I emphasize. "No one's after me."

"Great thinking, Gwen. You and Valerie really have this case figured out."

"Whatever," I say, mostly to shut him up, "I'll take the ride. Thanks."

"Could've been home in the time you spent arguing."

Rolling my eyes, I gloomily lumber beside him. Perhaps I'm too great a skeptic, but his sudden kindness feels highly suspicious. Why start being nice now? The only reason people do that is when they know something or want something. In this case, I'm not sure which is worse.

Still, there is a small part of me that's relieved to not be alone out here.

As we pass the Great Oak, we fall back into the uncomfortable silence that controlled us all last year. Though, this time, it's not my fault we stopped talking. I can tell from the way Dev's awkwardly averting his eyes, he's thinking of Luca.

"A shame this place is too cheap for security cameras," Dev mutters under his breath.

"Captain Pierce can take it up with her boyfriend."

"Good one."

It sucks that he's right. Like everyone else in Hathaway, Captain Pierce knows better than to give business advice to

Marty Boone. Offending the man who funds a majority of this town is the last thing anyone wants to do. Even public services, like the school district and police department, are reliant on his hefty donations.

Without saying a word, Dev and I pick up the pace, hurrying through the rest of the barren park and into HQ. Retrieving his badge from his pocket, he scans it on his way out the door. When I don't do the same, his head cocks to the side.

"Stop looking at me like that."

"Like what?" He asks innocently, crossing the empty asphalt towards his truck.

"Like I'm a massive screw up."

He stops in his tracks, turning to accost me with a disbelieving stare. "You know I don't think that."

"Don't you?" I say accusingly.

"I don't," he insists firmly, and before I can demand for him to explain his actions over the last year, he waves me on. "Come on, I need to drop you off so I can get to Jenna's."

This piques my interest as I climb up into his passenger seat.

"You're seeing Jenna?" I ask, trying to sound casual. "I heard you two broke up before finals."

Immediately, I feel guilty for allowing my old ways as a gossip monger to take control of my curiosity. Even before someone hacked Ride or Die, Valerie was the one keeping the account alive by scouring the submissions sent in and posting the juiciest drama. My interest was waning with the small-town talk. It was petty. Suffocating. All the gossip did was highlight just how trapped I was here. Who cared if so-and-so started seeing each other or if someone was cheating to get a scholarship? I certainly shouldn't.

Still, I can't help what I already know. Shortly after our falling out, Dev started dating Jenna Thatcher, a girl from the school orchestra. I figured the tip about their relationship status was true because Dev chose to spend the summer at Pineland, rather than Wetlands, which is owned by Jenna's mom.

Dev doesn't waste his breath accusing me of listening to the rumor mill. It's a curse of dating in such a small town—everyone's in your business and there's nothing you can do about it. Just one of the many reasons why I refuse to date anyone from Hathaway, no matter how much it may upset some, present company included.

"She dumped me, but we're still friends." It's impossible to glean any hints from his tone.

"Why'd she dump you?" I regret the question as soon as it leaves my lips. It's not my place to know.

Dev clicks his tongue. "Not sure. Apparently, she can't focus on a relationship with 'everything that's going on.' AKA she's pissed I'm not working at Wetlands."

I can't exactly blame Jenna for expecting her boyfriend to work at her mom's water park. It is weird he chose to stay at Pineland.

Reading this on my face, Dev clenches his jaw. "I thought we were mature enough to handle separate summer jobs."

"It's kind of an important summer for her family."

Dev shrugs. "I'm not a lifeguard kind of guy."

I stop pushing it. His business is his. It's clear he has no plans to share why he chose to stay at Pineland.

For a while, all that can be heard is the rumbling of his truck's growling engine as the park shrinks in the rearview mirror. As an olive branch, I change the subject.

"Honestly, I'm surprised Valerie doesn't just quit," I say, covertly feeling under my seat for any sign of my badge. I feel Dev's gaze flick in my direction, but he doesn't say anything as my fingertips brush against stray coins and crumpled receipts. This is starting to get ridiculous. A neon green badge doesn't simply vanish.

"And miss out on her spotlight? Valerie would never."

We pass Hathaway's only hotel, which has a decent number of cars in the parking lot. Between the grand opening of *Sybil Saves the World* and a brand-new water park, most of Michigan is starting their summer in Hathaway. Even with everything going on, the tourists are a welcome sight, especially after a few concerningly-slow seasons.

"You understand that Valerie's going through something really serious, right?"

"She sure makes it sound that way."

"Luca is literally dead and she might be next!"

Dev's lack of concern is uncomfortable. Does he assume Captain Pierce will have this solved before we clock in tomorrow?

"You two are jumping to conclusions." Before I can protest, he adds, "If Valerie was a genuine target, the cops would be all over her. Unless there's something you know that they don't..."

His voice trails off as his eyes drift towards me again.

"There's nothing," I say firmly, keeping my face even as my insides bubble. Surely, Dev doesn't know about Ride or Die's threat to Valerie's life.

My mouth grows dry when it occurs to me that anyone could have hacked the account. Even the boy driving me home. I may have known Dev my whole life, but a lot can change in a year.

Discreetly, I slide my hand towards the door handle, trying not to feel silly for potentially overreacting. We're only a few minutes from home, but if I've learned one thing from today, it's that no one is obligated to tell the truth. Around here, lies continuously roll off the tongue.

Oblivious to my subtle shift, Dev's eyes remain trained on the road. "Maybe we should trust the cops to do their jobs."

"Yeah, because we can always trust Hathaways, huh?"

"Most of us do."

The rest of the drive through town is silent as we stew—

not that this behavior is anything out of the ordinary. Dev and I have been punishing each other with the silent treatment since we were six. Back then, there were many terse afternoons of quiet Play-Doh modeling when Dev was feeling territorial over his rolling pin and I would mess with his project. In seventh grade, I ignored Dev for a full day after he "politely" asked if I'd rather sign-up for technical theatre when he heard Valerie and I rehearse our monologues for the school play. Back then, we knew the silence wasn't permanent. That isn't the case anymore.

How long are we going to pretend that I didn't break his heart last September? Acting like it never happened is almost worse than hashing it out.

Separating the residential side of town from the parks is a quaint plaza with a few boutiques, a bike shop, pizza parlor, and Lottie's—the only spot to snag a somewhat decent latte.

Soon, we pass my dad's dry cleaner. When I realize the shop is dark, my forehead creases. Despite Pineland allotting a full day for cleaning, Dad usually works overnight to have the costumes returned by morning. If he isn't at work, where is he?

On the other side of the darkened windows, I can make out the shadowy outlines of Pineland's furry mascots—Mountie the Moose, Winston the Woodpecker, and of course, Sybil the Squirrel—waiting to be cleaned and shipped back to the park. I don't see Benji the Bunny, which probably means Dad is still working on the poor creature's fur. The guilt seeps through me at such a sickeningly slow pace that I wonder if it'll ever pass. My father isn't winning any parenting awards, but after last night, I'm not up for any nominations either.

Only a few lights rest between town and the residences. The houses closer to the shops are owned by Hathaway's most successful. There's the enormous Boone and Thatcher estates, plus the multimillion-dollar-mansions that belong to various park executives and the school superintendent. The homes grow smaller the farther out you get.

Forgetting his turn signal, Dev pulls into the last subdivision on the left. Driving faster than his mom would like, he careens along a road lined with quaint houses and sturdy sweetgum trees before hurtling down our cul-de-sac. Even though his house is first, he zooms past it, heading three driveways down to pull into mine at the end of the circle.

His truck dings with protest as we both unbuckle our seatbelts and slip back into the still-too-warm air. Between the brutal winters and humid summers, Michigan can't win. Whenever the weather flips, Valerie is quick to remind me that Los Angeles might be hot, but at least it's consistent.

Not bothering to open the bed of his truck, Dev nabs my bike with an exaggerated grunt and places it on the driveway between us.

"Thanks, again," I say hesitantly, wondering if this is where his pity ends or my childhood friend reveals himself to be a psycho murderer.

One glance into his midnight eyes and I can tell he's scrutinizing me as well. It's certainly a relief he isn't making any moves to end my life, but that means we have the matter of our friendship to deal with instead.

His eyes darken and I wonder if he's recalling a certain conversation that occurred last August.

If we're talking again, does that mean he no longer has feelings for me? That he isn't going to test the boundaries of our friendship and press for something more? No matter how nice it could be, we both know it'll only end in disaster. At least, it's an inevitable conclusion I plainly see coming. The jury's still out on Dev's awareness.

His unbreakable stare has my stomach squeezing. I silently plead for him to not dredge up the spoiled conversation of "us." It's the last thing tonight needs.

Mercifully, Dev's pocket illuminates as his phone receives

a message. His eyes dart down to it before returning to me with a sheepish shrug.

Better his phone than mine. "Tell Jenna I say hi!"

"We're not getting back together," he insists.

So what if he dates Jenna Thatcher again? Maybe I would've minded a few years ago, back when I was naïve and didn't understand the dangers of crushing on your dearest friend. Long before I had firm rules against dating anyone from here. Now, I know better than to fall for anyone from Hathaway—even someone as good as Dev. I can't get stuck with a high school sweetheart. The last thing I'm going to be is trapped here.

Dev blinks, clearly waiting to see how I'll respond to his assertion. School may be out, but apparently, I'm still taking tests. Not sure of a safer response, I nod slowly.

His face remains neutral, leaving me uncertain as to if I passed or failed. Before I can find out, the driveway light flashes. Mom signaling for me to get inside. For once, I'll happily oblige.

"That's my cue," I say, trying not to sound too relieved. "Thanks again for the ride. Maybe we can do it again sometime."

"Maybe," he says with a lopsided grin that makes me momentarily forget every one of my rules.

Get a grip.

Instead of doing something I'll regret, I wave him back into his truck and dart up my front porch. The screen door squeaks as I pull it open and find the front door unlocked.

Mom pounces the instant I'm through the door. "Geez Louise, thank goodness you're home. What on earth were you doing out there for so long?" She asks, as if she wasn't watching through the window the moment Dev's headlights pulled into the driveway.

"Talking with Dev." My voice is muffled by her shoulder as

she squeezes me tight. We're both on the shorter side, with the same almond-brown hair and eyes.

She pulls back, angular eyebrows raising. While I never told her why Dev stopped coming around last fall, I know Mom heard the full story from Mrs. Vishwakarma.

"We were just catching up," I mumble, wishing my own mother hadn't picked his side. Though, I guess I shouldn't be surprised that she chose him. Dating Dev increases her chance of keeping me here.

"Is that so? I find that unwise."

"Talking to Dev?"

"Loitering outside before the police solve this tragic accident."

"What's there to sort out if you think it's an accident?"

Mom tuts as she guides me into the warm kitchen, where Dad is sitting at the table across from my ten-year-old brother, Gil. I fight to keep the surprise off my face that Dad is home at a decent time. He hates when I bring up how eager he is to work unnecessarily late, even if it is a simple fact. Pointing out the truth only leads to a lecture about how ungrateful I am.

The sad thing is I am grateful for the roof over our head and the food on our plates. But working a regular shift at his laundromat provides those essentials. No—Dad clocks additional hours so he can maintain the barely-convincing appearance that our family is just fine. Surely, the new coat of paint on the front door will prove to everyone that we're not a total mess. Who cares what goes on behind that door? No one can tell it's hiding a strained family barely keeping it together.

Jokes on Dad. The harder he tries to mask the truth, the more obvious it is. The Gardners are a mess. We always have been and always will be.

"We're having a family dinner?"

Dad sets me with a stern look. "Yes, and you're late, Gwendolyn."

That's rich coming from him.

"My bike broke. Dev gave me a ride."

His head cocks to the side. "So, you weren't pulled into Hannah Flannigan's office again?"

Classic. We're worried about our family's reputation, not my broken bike or dead classmate.

When I got home from Open Season last night, I knew it would be better for my folks to know I'd gotten in trouble at work before word began to spread. Unfortunately, I was too late to fess up because Valerie posted a video of our fight on Ride or Die. The account was a hub for scandalizing posts that exposed Hathaway secrets. Our followers knew we only shared the juiciest content and our fight certainly fit the bill.

Really, I had no one to blame for myself. I started things by taking things too far.

Valerie apologized, but the damage had already been done. My gossipy mother gets a notification whenever Ride or Die posts. She saw the video as soon as it went up.

Mom was disappointed, but Dad was pissed. Not because it meant no one would want to write me a letter of recommendation. Nor because he was going to spend hours cleaning chocolate milkshake from Benji the Bunny's fur. No—Jonah Gardner's main concern was how I'd embarrassed the family before the entire town.

Because I'm totally the reason people gossip about my family. It's not the father who has a stronger marriage to his job than the woman he's been on-and-off with since high school. Or the mother that is known to cry with regret after too many glasses of wine when out with her friends. Two years after their messy divorce, my mother suddenly got pregnant with my father's precious firstborn son. The whisperers cite Gil as the reason they got back together. By that logic, that makes me the reason they separated in the first place.

"No," I respond curtly, sliding into the chair nearest the sink. Dad is in my usual seat—not that he'd know. A plate of spaghetti greets me. My family doesn't keep food warm. If you're not home to eat it on time, that's your problem. Mom likes to gripe that Dad has a taste for lukewarm.

I'm still shocked he isn't busy scrubbing chocolate milkshake from the rabbit's fur. I offered to come in and help, but he refused, claiming I have the habit of making things worse. He had me there.

Heat sticks to the back of my neck. The AC must be acting up again, but a new one isn't in the budget. The kitchen is uncomfortably warm from Mom's efforts on the stove top, but my Dad won't let her open a window to air out the room. Opening a window shows the neighbors we have an issue and that's the last thing the Gardners want to do.

Oblivious as usual, Gil continues to furiously tap at some game on his school-administered tablet, not looking away from the screen while he shovels pasta into his mouth. Red sauce smears across his cheek, but he doesn't seem to notice. Years ago, Mom gave up asking him to keep the device away from the dinner table. She didn't even argue when Gil begged her to sign a special permission slip for him to keep his tablet over the summer. No one dares to remind him that it's supposed to be for educational programs only.

Not hungry, I aimlessly twirl noodles around my fork. Across the table, Mom shoots Dad a look, struggling to get him on the same page. Best to get ahead of what's coming.

"Before you say anything, Captain Pierce was at the park all day. Pineland and HPD are doing their due diligence to figure out what happened to Luca."

Mom's pale brow creases. "We don't want you going back there. Perhaps a job at Wetlands would be a better—safer—fit."

We? Good one.

I glance at Dad, trying to determine if he genuinely agrees with this proposition. When Wetlands was announced two years ago, he was adamant that I remain loyal to Pineland, stating the Gardners wouldn't support "greedy competitors" trying to rip this town apart.

If I've learned one thing from the years my parents spent divorced, it's to pick an ally and play to their interests.

Shifting my gaze towards Dad, I mumble, "I can't quit Pineland after they allowed me to keep my job."

His bushy mustache twitches, unknowingly confirming I picked the right side.

"She has a point, Sally," Dad mutters under his breath. "It was likely another unfortunate accident. It happens."

"Jonah—"

"Marty Boone is a reliable customer," he retorts, making Mom's coral lips purse.

"Do you really think I want to work somewhere unsafe?" I ask her. "Because, trust me, Pineland is the last place I want to die."

"Is this because you want to stay with Valerie?" Mom says curtly.

I read between the lines. Mom's never been fond of my friendship with Valerie. She figures Val is the reason I want to leave Hathaway, which couldn't be further from the truth. My mind was made up about this town long before I struck up a friendship with Valerie.

"This isn't about Valerie," I retort. "It's about what's right for our family. I screwed up at Pineland and need to make it right."

Over the table, my parents share a skeptical glance, but neither calls me out on my lie, because around here, it's our native tongue.

CHAPTER
SEVEN

EVEN AFTER TEARING my room apart, I still can't find my badge. Because I forgot to clock-in this morning, I haven't the faintest idea as to where it could be. My fear that Hannah already has it grows more valid by the minute.

Flopping onto my bed with a groan, I immediately feel like a selfish fool. It's a piece of plastic. A few neighborhoods over, Luca's family is mourning their son and brother.

I startle as my phone vibrates on my bedspread. Blood pounding in my ears, I slowly flip the screen, sighing at my reaction when I see Valerie's name. I need to chill. Ride or Die isn't blowing up my phone.

Valerie meant it when she said we needed to forget last night—and thank goodness for it. There's so much I need to warn her about.

I wish I could shake my unease with how easily we moved past our fight at Open Season. But I guess that's the best part about my friendship with Valerie. A stupid grudge won't sink us. No matter how many cannonballs Marty Boone shoots in our direction.

"You made it home quick," she observes when our video call connects and she spies the electric-blue pillow under my head. The bold bed set was a twelve-year-old Gwen decision and seventeen-year-old Gwen is paying the price. Although, it's not as bad as Valerie's fuchsia walls. Mr. Ross said he'd have them repainted this summer, but she told him not to bother. In a year's time, she'll no longer be living in her childhood bedroom.

"That's because," I clear my throat awkwardly, "Dev gave me a ride home."

There's a telling silence as Valerie blinks slowly. "Two rides in one day?"

"The world's gone upside down."

Valerie's not the type to easily let go of an uncomfortable topic. "Is there something I should know?"

"What do you mean?"

"Why are you and Dev all of a sudden talking again?"

"No clue," I say honestly. "He just started being nice, and frankly, I'm tired of giving him the cold shoulder."

"Babeeee," Valerie groans, "you're giving him an inch. A sliver of hope that something's going to happen now that he's single again."

"We've been friends since before preschool. It's good manners, not a marriage proposal. Dev's smart enough to not pull anything again."

"Is he? Because the boy still looks at you like you're a princess or something."

"He's literally with Jenna right now."

"Trust me, that's never going to happen again."

Something about the certainty in her tone has me pause. "Uh, is there something *I* should know?"

While the Venn diagram of Valerie Ross and Jenna Thatcher overlaps extensively, they're as close as the poles. Shortly after Valerie made it widely known she'd be auditioning for performance arts programs out west, Jenna made an identical declaration, and Valerie took that personally. She was convinced a homebody like Jenna never had any intentions of ever attending school outside of Michigan, but simply wanted to audition to prove that Valerie wasn't the only one capable of making it beyond Hathaway. And so, Jenna was sucked into an unspoken competition—one that will likely last long past graduation because there's nothing Valerie relishes more than a rivalry.

"Jenna may also be an orch-dork, but she's way too uptight for him," Valerie says casually. "Something tells me the boy learned that the hard way."

The pull in my gut doesn't lessen. "Okay..."

Her voice softens. "Dev's a puppy dog. Even your little black heart has a soft spot for him. Face it, Gwen, you won't want to hurt him again. I don't think you have it in you."

"I would never date Dev to make him happy."

Her manicured eyebrows quirk. "You almost did last year."

My cheeks grow warm. Valerie and I don't have secrets, but after adamantly abiding by my relationship rules, how could I ever admit there were many reasons I considered dating Dev? His happiness wasn't my only concern.

When you grow up with someone—really see them go from a scrawny kid to the brink of manhood—it's hard not to wonder what it would be like if you took things a step further. By all accounts, Dev grew up well with his thick, shaggy hair and deep-brown complexion. He stayed slender, but still thickened in all the right places. His style also developed. Now he sports a rotating assortment of button-ups and tan trousers.

In the weeks leading up to Dev suggesting we should be more than friends, the universe threw every temptation my way: Valerie skipping movie night, thus leaving Dev and I to sit alone in his dark basement. Shortly after that, Dev was suddenly reassigned to work as Sybil's character attendant.

And then, of course, that wretched August evening when we got stuck on the lift hill of *Michigan Madness* for a full hour. By the end, words were said that changed everything. Feelings were admitted that could never be hidden again.

Sometimes, the right answer doesn't come to you until you're faced with the question.

"Don't you want to give us a chance?" He had asked while we waited for the mechanics to fix the ride.

He looked so handsome, backlit by a magenta sky. On top of the world. For a moment, I almost admitted the truth.

"What if we turn out like my parents?" I uttered instead, shaking my head. "We can't do that, Dev."

"We won't."

"Please don't push it."

His heart shattered before my eyes. His eyes grew dark just as the sun set behind the trees. Our eventual return to the station was in silence. Dev nodded goodbye to me as we departed the coaster and that was the end of us. We didn't talk for the entire school year.

"Don't you think there are more important things to dissect right now?" I say to Valerie, not wanting to think about Dev any longer.

Valerie rolls onto her stomach, resting her chin in her palm. "Is it bad I don't want to talk about Luca?"

"You don't have to talk if you're not ready."

"I'm not sure I'll ever be ready."

"And that's totally okay. Maybe one day it'll be easier."

"No," Valerie shakes her head insistently, "I'll never want to talk about Luca Mendes ever again. That chapter of my life is closed. Rehashing it won't change anything."

My chin jerks back at this cold response. I guess I shouldn't be surprised. Valerie is good at moving on quickly, but after such a traumatic day, I thought this would be the exception. "Don't you want to see justice for him?"

"I'd rather make it through the summer without meeting the same fate."

"Have you mentioned the hit list theory to your dad?"

"And be forced to quit the job with a scholarship funding my higher education?"

My eyes bug out. "You realize how insane that sounds, right?"

"I know, I know," she says, her tone turning serious, "but trust me, if all goes according to plan, I'll still have my life, scholarship, and this freaking psychopath will be behind bars."

"What plan?"

"The genius one that Amanda and I hatched on the way home today."

"Please tell me it starts with going to the police."

"Great idea, Gwen. Ride or Die can kill me before the cops find their identity."

I ignore her harshness. This is how Valerie gets when she's upset.

"Then what are we doing?" I settle against a pillow, knowing it's best to get comfy and accept what's about to happen. A plan pulls at Valerie's mind like the coils of a slingshot attraction tightening before release. It's only a matter of time before she throws everything she's got into top speed action. Time to get buckled in.

"So apparently," she sets her scene, "Cole dated someone who works in park security."

"I'm shocked," I deadpan. The Hathaway High hockey team is notorious for dating around. "Do we know who?"

"Nope. He won't spill."

"You talked to Cole about this?"

"Amanda and I were chatting with the guys in the parking lot before we left—"

I immediately interject, "Does that include Weston?"

"Yes..."

"Vaaaaal," I groan. "Stay away from him. He's a liar."

"Everyone's a liar."

"Listen," I plead with her, "good people don't lie about where they were when their teammate was killed."

Finally, this makes my friend pause. "Come again?"

"Weston swears he wasn't at Open Season, but I saw him in the atrium last night."

"And did he see you?"

"Yes."

Valerie's forehead wrinkles. "Then why lie?"

"There's more. After hearing you were with Luca, Weston said he was going to kill him."

Her lips purse skeptically. "That's just a saying, G. Weston would never hurt his best friend."

"Are we sure about that?"

I can practically see the cogs in her brain turning as she evaluates this information. Then she shrugs, saying, "Yeah, it's sketchy, but right now, we need the team's help."

"You want to trust them?"

"The only person in Hathaway I trust is you," she says firmly, "and because of that, we have no choice but to make some risky alliances."

That's a horrible idea but there's no changing her mind. It'll be up to me to keep a close eye on our new allies.

"So, what are we doing in security?"

"We're going to check the Access Control Log to see whose ID was scanned into the Fake Oak during Open Season."

I clear my throat uncomfortably. "Uh, don't we think the cops will already be doing that?"

"God, I hope so, but do we think they're going to make that information public? Marty is already insisting Luca's death was a tragic accident." Her head shakes with disgust. "Like he slipped down the stairs or something ridiculous like that."

I can't keep the scariest secret inside any longer. "Did you get any scary DMs today?"

"Uh, no. Did you?"

"Ride or Die messaged me."

She takes this revelation in stride. "Anything that revealed who hacked us?"

I shake my head. "I can't think of anyone around here with the skills to steal the account."

"Neither can I," she says darkly. "And now they're using it to broadcast their crimes."

"If Hathaway PD thinks we're still tied to that account, we're in so much trouble. Everyone's going to hate us."

"Who cares? Also, we didn't do anything illegal," she says firmly. "So, what did Ride or Die say?"

I clear my throat. "Something about wanting content in exchange for compensation."

Valerie barks out a laugh. "What kind of content? Do they want you to go live while they stab me to death on *Sybil Saves the World*?"

I wince at how casually she suggests this. "They didn't say what kind of content," I explain, suddenly finding it hard to meet her gaze on the screen, "but Ride or Die insinuated if I didn't help them close Pineland, they'd come for you."

"We already know I'm their target, G."

"Then why are you taking this so lightly?" My voice raises.

"Is that what it looks like?"

I wisely bite my tongue.

"This is why I want to find out who scanned into the Fake Oak. We find this freak so I can know who to avoid until the cops get their shit together and make an arrest."

"I'm not doing what Ride or Die wants," I insist. "Why don't we lay low for a few days? We can call out and hide at my house until someone is behind bars."

"You don't have to worry about it. After we find out who hacked us, we'll call out sick."

"What's happening tomorrow morning?"

"That's when Cole's hook-up is going to sneak us into security so we can check the log."

"Who's going to be there?"

"Us, Amanda, Cole—"

"Not Weston?"

She shrugs apathetically. I choose not to push it. There are bigger fish to fry right now. But I'm only going along with this for so long. Regardless of what we discover tomorrow, Valerie can't spend any more time at Pineland than necessary.

"We're meeting in the break room two hours before the park opens."

"And after we see who else scanned into the Fake Oak during Open Season?"

"We call out sick and hide at your house."

"Promise?"

"Promise. I'm not trying to die in Pineland."

"Good to hear."

Even if the plan is stupid, it makes me feel less desperate than before. Maybe we won't even need to break into the security hub because Captain Pierce will make an arrest while we try to sleep tonight. Then we can put these horrors behind us and carry on with our summer.

CHAPTER
EIGHT

NO SUCH LUCK.

After a restless night, I wake up and immediately scroll online for any word that Ride or Die has been arrested. All I discover is they've spent the night spewing their anti-Pineland propaganda.

Pale light shines through my window, promising the day will be another scorcher. Thankfully, I have no intentions of sweating my ass off in a squirrel costume today. Determined to get this morning over with, I slip from my bedroom and creep down the stairs.

"Good to see you're going in early," Dad remarks from the kitchen table, taking a long, pointed sip from a steaming mug. While Mom prefers to let the sun fully rise before gracing us with her presence, Dad's an early bird, because apparently, there's no better time to clean clothes than the crack of dawn. "That shows initiative."

"You know me," I say, rummaging through the pantry for a microwavable cup of macaroni-and-cheese and a mini bag of barbecue potato chips before shoving both in my tote. "Full of initiative."

"I know you're hell-bent on escaping Hathaway, but one

day, you'll be thankful you took the time to mend your reputation. Coming back is easier when it's to open arms."

I don't have time to re-explain my intentions to never come back, so I let Dad have this one with a silent wave goodbye.

The last thing I want to be is late, so I skip fixing my bike and opt for swiping Gil's dusty skateboard from the garage. As far as I'm aware, his summer plans exclusively entail gaming with his friends, so he won't miss it. With the press of a button, the squeaky garage door creaks to life.

As it raises, my lips part when I spy muddy wheels resting in the driveway. Dev's casually leaning against his truck.

"What are you doing here?"

"Valerie texted me." It must be obvious this was the last thing I expected him to say because he shrugs like it makes zero sense to him either. "She said something about you needing an early ride to the park?"

"She'd say why?"

"Of course not."

And he showed up anyway. Maybe he really does want to be friends again. But as hope lifts my spirit, anxiety quickly deflates it. Should we really go down this road again?

"I'll explain on the way." There's no way Valerie intended for Dev to wake up early, drive me to Pineland, and not find out her master plan. She can't be pissed when I tell him.

"That means you're getting in?"

I clamp my jaw shut, kicking the skateboard back into the garage in response.

"Look at me, helping Hathaway avoid another unnecessary death," he jokes dryly as I climb up into the passenger side. "Skateboarding on gravel isn't your brightest idea, you know?"

"Faster than walking."

"Fast way to die too." He side-eyes me while pulling out of

my driveway. "Pretty neat how I showed up in time to save your life, huh?"

"When you think about it, I really have Valerie to thank."

Clicking his tongue, he waves me off, somehow making the stench of his truck grow even more potent.

I gag. "Don't push that smell over here!"

"I swear, I'll pull over and you can walk."

"Then you'll never find out what we're doing this morning."

"Probably be happier not knowing."

I wordlessly agree as we continue our drive through town.

All that's lit is the gas station, convenience store, and Heidi's Sweets, though even Hathaway's beloved baker doesn't anticipate patrons seeking frosted pastries and grainy loaves for a few more hours. I'm sure Dad's laundromat will be next to open up shop for the day.

I use the commute to fill Dev in on Valerie's plan. With each detail, his frown deepens, but to my surprise, he doesn't argue with a thing. He must want to discover if someone actually killed Luca. He probably plans to run straight into Hathaway Police Department with any name we find. Although, I suspect they already know if anyone went into the Fake Oak after Luca. It must be someone difficult to arrest; otherwise, they'd be behind bars.

Careening past Wetlands, neither of us can help but sneak a peek at the ginormous water slides peeking over the mesh-covered fence. Those pieces of plastic are so powerful they ripped the whole town in two. Forced everyone to reevaluate their loyalties and pick a side. I wonder, had the choice rested with me, if I would've stuck with Pineland. I've never been the biggest fan of pools, but I doubt anyone at Wetlands is sweating their butts off in a fursuit every shift.

Looming over the park is a turquoise water tower featuring a slogan scripted in tangerine letters: "Wetlands:

Slide into Adventure!" I'll never forget the day it was painted. It felt like the beginning of the end for Hathaway.

Dev clears his throat while accelerating past. I'm curious how his meeting with Jenna went last night, but I know better than to ask.

After we turn down the gravel road that leads to the crew member lot, we park between Weston's jeep and Amanda's cranberry-colored sedan. One of them must've given Valerie a ride—ideally, the latter.

I'm quick to note the lack of squad cars out front. Didn't Nora say they'd be upping their presence at the park?

"Weston and Amanda are here too?" Dev inquires. "Why?"

"Maybe you should wait in the car," I suggest as he pulls his key from the ignition. Valerie should've never roped him into this. Things were finally going back to normal.

Dev snorts as his sneakers meet gravel with a crunch.

I hurry to catch up with him as he heads for Crew HQ. "I'm serious, this idea is already bad enough. The last thing I want is to drag you into this."

Dev stops walking suddenly, turning on his heels to face me. "Gwen, I'm not waiting in the car."

Something about the firmness in his voice stops me from arguing.

When we approach the main door, Dev withdraws his wallet from his front pocket, pulling out his green ID. Noticing that I have not pulled out my own, his brows raise.

"Have you still not found it?"

My head shakes.

"Unfortunate timing."

"Isn't everything?"

The air grows still as we pointedly ignore the infinite what-ifs between us.

Suddenly, I find the ground as interesting as can be. That's how I notice a hunk of bark in the Crew HQ doorway, rendering the need for an ID to unlock the door useless. No one will know we are here.

I sense Dev trying to meet my eyes, but I refuse to look up.

We hurry through the atrium, heading straight for the break room. It's empty aside from the last possible person I want to see: Weston. He's slumped in the same corner booth we occupied yesterday, head resting face-down in his arms.

"Where's everyone else?" I demand, crossing my arms at the end of the table. All things considered, it's far more polite than demanding why he's here.

"Boys slept through their alarms."

"Don't we need Cole to get into security?"

"Nah, we're cool without him," Weston mumbles "Geez, you and Val are a high-strung pair. She lost her shit too."

"You've seen her?"

"I drove her here."

Of course, he did. If we get through this morning, I might kill Valerie myself. What is she thinking by messing around with a guy like Weston McCray? Her greatest weakness has always been a bad idea with a pretty face.

"Then where is she?"

Weston slowly blinks, making it perfectly clear it's too early for this level of questioning. "Locker room. She wanted to change into her costume before we broke into security."

"Can we not call it 'breaking in?'" Amanda begs, coming up behind me. She's also dressed in a mustard polo and shorts. I don't miss how low she's pulled the brim of her hat over her forehead.

"What?" Weston snorts. "Not like there's any security around to catch us."

So we all noticed HPD's missing presence.

Amanda bites the inside of her check. "I overheard Grandpa and Nora having it out last night. She wants a detail present twenty-four-seven. He's convinced that'll scare people and send them across the street."

"Right into Wetlands' front gate."

"They *compromised* on HPD hanging around Crew HQ an hour before the park opens and an hour after. That way, crew members can come and go safely. Some plain clothes officers will be stationed in the park during the day and one will patrol overnight."

"Sounds super safe," I scoff.

"Then where is the officer that's supposed to be on-duty now?" Dev asks.

"How am I supposed to know?" Amanda's expression grows bleak. "Let's use it to our advantage and get this over with."

"What's taking Valerie so long?" Weston questions, helplessly shaking his head at Dev. "Chicks, right?"

"You could probably spare a few extra minutes in the locker room," Amanda retorts, eyeing him up and down.

"Damn, Boone," Weston laughs, "not an early bird, eh?"

"Seriously though," I say. "What is Valerie doing?"

My ears begin to ring. Valerie is many things, but she is never ever late. Especially not for something like this.

Something's wrong.

"Who saw Valerie last?" My head snaps to Weston. "You?"

His hands raise innocently. "I mean, yeah, I drove her here. You know, wanted to make sure she arrived safely."

This makes Amanda frown.

Noticing this, Weston hurriedly adds, "But I saw her walk into the women's locker room. Somewhere you've clearly been!"

Amanda fidgets with her cap. "Valerie came in while I was changing. She dropped her bag in her locker and left to grab her costume at Wardrobe."

"See!" Weston says, "So I didn't see her last!"

I shoot him a furious look, which by some miracle, shuts him up. The idiot is missing the entire point. I march out of the break room with the others on my tail.

"Where are we going?"

"She's taking too long," I mutter, beginning to jog through the atrium. Shoving the women's locker room door open, I yell Valerie's name, cursing when she doesn't answer. Running further down the hall, Amanda scans her ID into the wardrobe facility, pushing the double doors open when they unlock.

"What the hell?"

We're met by a disaster zone. Costumes, hangers, and accessories are scattered everywhere, like the room was hit by a tornado. Long racks of uniforms stand bare and garments blanket the tile floor.

"Oh my god," Dev breathes out.

"What happened?" Amanda bends over, picking up what appears to be Valerie's Park Ranger sash. My mouth goes dry at how roughly it's been ripped. Some patches hang to the mangled fabric by threads.

At least there's no blood. But where the hell is my best friend?

"Valerie?" I cry desperately.

We immediately spread out, darting down the long rows of costumes, pushing aside hangers of polyester polos and shorts. Desperately, I search for any sign of life. Valerie. Ride or Die. Anyone.

We breathlessly regroup in the center of the room, eyes wide with horror.

"She's not here," Amanda whispers the obvious.

Wrenching my phone from my pocket, I go to call Valerie when my heart stops at a notification on my home screen.

New Direct Message from @RideOrDie.

Holy shit.

Bracing for anything, I swipe open the message. Only five words await.

My lips part as I read the message again and again.

Ride or Die has Valerie, if she's even still...

No. Do not go there.

The room begins to spin, but before I can slump to the floor, I feel an arm scoop around my waist, holding me up. I don't have to look to know it's Dev.

Even without the ability to think straight, I instinctively lock my phone, hiding the DM from view.

"Did you hear from her?" Dev whispers.

My head shakes. "She's gone. They took her."

CHAPTER
NINE

"HELP!" Amanda's scream rings through the hall as she sprints for the door. "Someone help!"

We follow at her heels, and with every frantic footfall, my heart feels like it's about to burst out of my chest. There must be some misunderstanding. A horrible prank and a coincidental DM. Valerie was *just* here.

But my best friend knows better than to make such a sick joke. Not after the last time she disappeared without a trace. Valerie swore to me she'd never do that again. Which means something horrible must have happened.

Oh God—what did Ride or Die do to her?

As the group dashes up three flights of stairs, I call her number again and again, but am sent straight to voicemail each time. When we reach our destination at the end of a long hall, everyone aside from Weston is panting and wheezing. We're outside an office I hoped to never enter. The heavy oak door is the only one in the hall fashioned without a nameplate because Marty Boone needs no introduction.

"He's here?" I ask breathlessly. Why didn't he come running at the sound of his grandchild's screams?

"He always is," Amanda growls, no bothering to knock before she shoves the door open.

Marty Boone's silver-haired head raises with a jolt. "Mandy, love? You're in early."

"You need to call Nora," Amanda demands, not wasting a single second on formalities. "Something's happened to Valerie!"

"Valerie Ross?" He asks slowly, a tired gaze taking in the rest of us. My frown deepens at his severe lack of urgency. "What do you mean?"

"Whoever killed Luca—and Ms. Wade and Ruby Cahill—attacked Valerie!"

Marty Boone shoots out of his chair, leaning over the large desk. "There's another body?"

"No, but—"

He slumps back into his seat with a relieved sigh that makes my mouth drop open.

"Mr. Boone," I pipe up, doing my absolute best to keep my tone in check, "I know something horrible happened to my best friend."

"To your employee!" Amanda cuts in. "And a minor! So maybe try caring!"

"That's enough!" The man roars, his piercing glare sucking the air from the room. To her credit, his granddaughter does not cower as she holds her gaze. It's more than I can say for the rest of us, who are all suddenly surveying our dusty sneakers.

"We'll continue this conversation in private," he continues coolly, "as this is wildly inapp—"

"I'd say it's wildly inappropriate you don't care," Weston bravely interjects, his nostrils flaring with frustration. "Valerie Ross was here this morning and now she's not. From the looks of things, she didn't leave on her own accord."

Maybe the asshole isn't that much of an asshole...

His lips may still be pinched, but it appears we've finally

gained Marty Boone's attention. Not that it should've been this hard to do, but I'm too stressed to harp on that now.

As Weston and Amanda each detail their morning sightings of Valerie, I try to stop my head from spinning, but it's no use. I'm spiraling with theories of what could've happened to her.

Why didn't I try harder to keep her home? We knew it wasn't safe. *We knew.*

If Marty Boone doesn't call the cops in five seconds, I'm dialing 911 myself. The cops need to know every detail about Ride or Die—even the ones I'm too afraid to admit. If it brings Valerie back safely, it'll be worth any and every consequence.

Why isn't Marty Boone picking up the freaking phone?

"Mr. Boone," Dev explains with more patience than I could muster, "Wardrobe shows signs of a struggle. Knowing Valerie, she didn't go down without a fight, but we can't find her anywhere."

"Did you say Wardrobe was wrecked?" Marty Boone asks, the wrinkles on his forehead growing more pronounced.

I bite my tongue, fighting to keep the most horrible accusations from rolling off it. *Really? This is what peaks his concern? A rack of costumes ripped from their hangers.*

Thank God for Amanda, who isn't afraid of her grandfather. "It's a wreck because someone—probably our prime suspect—attacked Valerie in there! They kidnapped her!"

"Kidnapped is a strong word," Marty Boone says, making me want to pull out my hair. "Did you bother to check the restrooms before running up here? The lockers? The park? Miss Ross is a Park Ranger. She's likely getting a head start on her day. All eyes are on Pineland now. Her role has never mattered more."

"Explain the war zone in Wardrobe then!"

Marty Boone pauses with a click of his tongue, delicately

picking up the phone on his desk. Those of us standing around share an uncomfortable glance as he dials.

Should we be surprised by his lack of urgency? After all, this is the man who had three employees recently die and hasn't done a thing about it aside from a few blasé public statements across the park's various social media pages. His PR team didn't even enable comments and quickly drowned the post with pictures of smiling guests having the Best Day Ever.

Whoever he's calling picks up quickly and Mr. Boone immediately speaks into the receiver. "Will you go have a look-see at Wardrobe for me, Shannon? My granddaughter claims it's in a state of disarray."

Something tells me Shannon isn't an officer with the Hathaway Police Department.

"Grandpa!" Amanda hisses.

"Oh!" Marty Boone tacks on, "And while you're in the area, will you keep an eye out for Park Ranger Valerie Ross? Mhmm, yes, her. Thanks, Shannon."

He hangs up. Hands clasping atop his desk, he studies us. "Shannon should get to the bottom of it."

"Our hero," Amanda mutters dryly.

All but the park president startles when the phone rings again.

"Yes?" His thin lips fold into a line. "I see. How disappointing."

I share an anxious glance with the others. What did Shannon discover?

"Do tell me what you find after you check the access control logs. I want a list of who scanned into Wardrobe over the last twelve hours." Marty leans back in his chair, rocking the recliner as he thinks. "And then reach out to Nathaniel so he doesn't lose his head when he clocks in and finds his costume hall a disaster. The dirtied uniforms will need to be sent to Gardner's Laundromat." The man's eyes flit up to me briefly. "See how fast he can turn them around. We don't want our crew members looking slovenly this early in the season."

"What about Valerie?"

"Ah, yes, one more thing—did you happen to see the Park Ranger about?" He pauses, nodding slowly as he listens. "That's what I thought. Thanks for everything, Shannon."

And then he hangs up.

"Well?"

"It appears you were correct about the state of Wardrobe."

"Why would we lie about that?"

Marty ignores this. "However, there is no sign of your friend."

"Of *your* underaged employee," Amanda bites back. "Haven't you been listening? We think someone kidnapped her."

"If Nora were here, she'd tell you that a missing person case isn't opened fifteen minutes after they were seen. I'm sure Valerie's around here somewhere."

"But what about the mess in costuming?" I ask desperately. "Doesn't that mean something?"

My stomach tightens as Marty Boone turns to me, his eyes hardening as he remembers how I behaved in his park two nights ago. "Logic and nature must always outweigh speculation and scandal."

What's left unsaid rings through the room. He won't lose control of this narrative for anything.

Unable to bear Marty's accusatory gaze any longer, my head droops. Dev takes a step closer to me, his arm lightly pressing against mine. I'd appreciate his attempt to quell my anxieties if I weren't already reaching rock bottom.

"I'm calling Nora," Amanda says.

"Of course. Nora's team will be briefed on the vandalism. Perhaps while they're hanging around my park, they can find our culprit."

His face is hauntingly calm; meanwhile, I'm about to puke on his desk.

We startle at the sound of a loud knock on the door.

Luther Flannigan pokes his silver-haired head inside. "Still set for our meeting, Marty?"

Marty Boone snaps his fingers. "Ah, yes. You're always timely, Luther." He returns his attention to us. "I appreciate you kids showing up to work early. Have a super save-the-world day!"

And with that, Luther waves us out of the office before closing the door on us.

"He can't be serious," Amanda mutters.

"So what? That's it?" Weston asks with disbelief.

"No body, no crime," I whisper frustratedly.

I dial Valerie again. Straight to voicemail.

"Hey," Dev says, leading us back down the hall. "Maybe he's right." When we start to protest, he hurriedly adds, "Listen! Marty would be freaking out if he thought something was truly wrong. What if Valerie's waiting for us in the break room right now?"

But as we enter the cafeteria, our feeble hopes plummet when we find it empty. Amanda immediately starts calling Nora.

That's when reality sets in and desperate tears begin to slip down my cheeks.

CHAPTER
TEN

THEIR RESPONSE IS ALMOST INSTANTANEOUS.

I grit my teeth while they continue typing.

Of course, they somehow know I'm about to meet with the Hathaway Police Department.

My mouth grows dry as I reread the threat again and again. They have her. My dearest friend's been kidnapped by a psychotic murderer, and if I tell a soul, she dies.

How am I supposed to keep a secret like this quiet? But if I don't...

Feeling dizzy with the impossible situation before me, I stuff my phone away because HPD has finally arrived to collect our statements.

It took nearly an hour for Captain Pierce to gather the four of us into the same conference room that she was posted in yesterday. It would've been faster had Marty not pulled Nora into his office for a concerningly-long conversation. When Nora finally exited, her complexion was paler than usual.

"I don't want to keep you from your shifts for long," she begins, and I can practically see Marty Boone maneuvering her mouth like a pathetic puppet.

A middle-aged man with a thick, brown mustache and badge that reads "Detective Weegan" stands in the corner of the room, notebook and pen at the ready. We all eye him with interest. Unless you're a tourist, a new face is uncommon around these parts.

Noticing our stares, Nora introduces him. "Detective Weegan is from Detroit and is here to provide any expertise on what we're dealing with."

I should be relieved that they've brought in the big guns, but it only fills me with more dread.

"We'd like to hear your account of what occurred this morning, starting with why you four and Valerie arrived at the park so early."

On the opposite side of the table, we all stiffen, despite previously agreeing to tell Captain Pierce the truth. There's nothing the others can say about Ride or Die that HPD won't already suspect.

I'm the only one not upholding the agreement to detail everything I know. Not until I have a better understanding of what Ride or Die wants. I'm not risking Valerie's life before understanding who—or what—I'm dealing with.

Amanda takes the lead, recounting Valerie's desire to see who scanned into the Great Oak because she suspected that whoever killed Luca, Sandy, and Ruby, all former Park Rangers, would come for her next because she was the current Park Ranger.

Pierce and Weegan share a look at the mention of our Park Ranger theory, and I wonder if they'd already made a similar leap. I assume so, because Weegan doesn't write this down. No one bothers to ask why we would believe Luca, Sandy, and Ruby were murdered and not indeed the victims of tragic accidents. At least not everyone's subscribing to Marty Boone's fantasy.

"We wanted to check the access control log to get an idea of who might be targeting Valerie," Amanda finishes.

The Captain's eyebrows raise at our audacity. "And how were you going to manage that?"

"Cole LeBrandt has a, um, *friend* in security."

Weston winces as Amanda throws both Cole and his security insider under the bus, but that's what Cole gets for sleeping through his alarm.

Pierce's head cocks to the side. "Don't you think we would have made an arrest if the access control log yielded a reliable lead?"

We shrug at the officers.

"You don't have any leads?" Amanda demands.

It's the adults turn to stare at us blankly.

"Other than Ride or Die," Weston points out. "That account's looking real suspicious these days. Val figured they were behind everything."

"Why would she presume that?"

It's all I can do to keep my face even. Surely, the police are familiar with Ride or Die. Everyone in Hathaway knows about it.

"Because they clearly hate Grandpa's park," Amanda says slowly, like she's spelling out the alphabet for the Captain. "They want Pineland to close! Three deaths and one missing teenager would certainly do the trick."

"Even if there was foul play afoot—serial killers don't usually post online," Weegan points out.

Amanda opens her mouth to protest, but Nora beats her to it. "If something malicious is occurring, I can assure you four that we have it covered. Hathaway might not be the biggest town, but we're not in over our heads, kids. We have a firm grasp on the situation at hand."

I might actually combust. The guilt is eating me from the inside out. It's not too late to fess up, but what happens to Valerie if I do? Will I walk into the park and find her body hanging outside a ticket booth?

Stop that. Don't let your mind go there.

"Furthermore, it's too early to consider this a missing person case." Nora clears her throat, glancing in my direction. "For all we know, Valerie Ross wanted to put some distance between herself and Hathaway again."

"She didn't run away," I snap. "Someone took her."

Captain Pierce offers me a measured look. "I guarantee that we'll find the truth by following proper procedure and protocol."

I sniff. "Try to find my friend while you're at it."

"We will," Weegan says firmly.

I hate that I don't believe in him. Detective Weegan may be new to town, but soon, he'll be like everyone else. Bound by Marty Boone's agenda.

<hr>

AFTER THE LONGEST day of my life, Dev and I finally trudge backstage. We're both silent, too tired from all the talking to maintain any sort of conversation now. He lugs my Sybil costume in the black duffel bag, while I call Valerie over and over, to no avail.

Entertainment shifts end an hour before the park closes, so the attractions are still running at full force, aiming to empty their queues in a timely manner. Between the glowing landscape and technicolor lights illuminating every ride, golden hour at Pineland is always striking. But not even the buttery smell from the final batch of popcorn of the night or the cooling breeze blowing through the park could lift my spirits.

All day long, I foolishly hoped Valerie would appear with some silly story about how she had to run home because she forgot to turn her straightener off. We'd realize the mess with Wardrobe was a prank from the Wetlands employees. Then I'd check my phone and discern the Ride or Die messages were all some misunderstanding.

It was dumb to think everything would work out. Nothing ever does around here.

I haven't heard back from Ride or Die and there's no news on HPD's investigation. It's like being stuck at the top of a roller coaster lift hill. You're left to wait for something to happen. Maybe an employee will come evacuate you or the coaster will start moving with little warning.

"Sup, squirrels?"

Dev and I startle, our heads snapping around to find the last person I want to speak with right now. Back in his street clothes, Chase Renner falls in line with us. A backwards cap covers little of his shoulder-length, auburn locks.

"The day's done, Gwen. No need to be all twitchy."

"Your last Sybil the Squirrel set was an hour ago," Dev points out. "Why are you still here?"

Chase's crooked smile gleams. "Went to meet Mia over by the Old Wheel. You know how it is, boss."

"Actually, I don't," Dev hastily disputes.

"Same," I say, even though Chase was clearly not addressing me.

Not that I mind. It means my No-Hathaway-Boys rule precedes me. I'm the last person anyone expects to sneak off to the Old Wheel for some alone time.

Pineland may be the only theme park in the world with two Ferris Wheels: a brand-spanking-new one at the front of the park and another they'd do anything to forget. Marty Boone was too cheap to tear the Old Wheel down, so it looms in the back of the wooded property, drowning in vines and rust. The retired relic serves as a reminder to everyone that no matter how hard those who hate Pineland may try to close the park, it's not going anywhere.

Some would do well to heed the reminder.

Chase sheepishly stuffs his hands into the pockets of his cargo shorts. "I was supposed to meet Mia yesterday, but I slept through my alarm. Seeing as I'd already earned a point on my record card for being late to my shift, I figured I'd make the most of it and stay home for the day." He wags his eyebrows. "Had to make it up to her today."

"Okay?" Dev says, uncomfortably glancing at me as we veer backstage. Chase is a talkative dude, but even this is starting to border T-M-I.

"Seems like I picked a good day to skip though," Chase tacks on. "A full staff meeting? That sucks."

"There was a staff meeting because Luca was found dead," I say roughly.

Chase's pale eyebrows raise. "Chill, Gardner."

"*Chill*?" I freeze in the doorway to Crew HQ.

"Not cool, man," Dev interjects, guiding me inside before I absolutely lose it. "If you're not going to have a heart, at least use your brain and read the room."

Chase rolls his eyes, muttering something about people wound too tight as he heads through the atrium towards the parking lot.

"God, he's such a dick," I say loudly after him.

"Gwendolyn Gardner?" A judgmental voice comes from our right. I immediately regret yelling "dick" backstage when I spy Ryan Vale, Marty Boone's ever-pressed assistant. "Do you mind coming with me?"

"Uh, sure," I breathe out, because what other choice do I have?

Brow scrunched, Dev is as puzzled as I am. "I can return your Sybil suit for you."

"Thanks," I mumble before following the slender man towards the elevator. Like Hannah, he's far too young for the gray strands woven between his short, black hair, but it seems to be the price you pay when working closely with Marty Boone.

As soon as the doors close after us and we're alone, I immediately ask, "Do you know what this is about? Have they heard from Valerie?"

"I'm not sure why he wants to speak with you," Ryan responds in a tone that makes it quite clear he doesn't think I should even be allowed in the park, let alone anywhere near his boss.

My head whirs with possibilities, each more concerning than the last. Is it about this morning? Or am I finally getting fired after causing a scene at Open Season?

The space falls silent, aside from the humming from the elevator as it slowly creaks upwards. We avoid making eye contact. Ryan scrolls on his phone while I stare at the crack between the doors, willing Valerie to appear on the other side. I wilt when they pull apart with a ding and the hallway is empty.

Ryan peels down the hall and smartly raps on the park president's door.

"Send her in."

Marty Boone's tone is unreadable, which only makes my fears heighten as I hesitantly push open the door.

His office is seriously creepy after sunset. Neon-colored bulbs from the attractions below scatter the walls with ominously twinkling lights. Artifacts from Pineland's decades of operation decorate every free space, casting unfamiliar shadows. A prototype of a Sybil the Squirrel animatronic stands motionless on a side table, staring unblinkingly at whoever dares cross the threshold of the office. An old test seat from the park's first roller coaster rests in the corner, looking concerningly-close to a torture device.

Marty Boone motions for me to sit in the small chair across from his desk. His face gives no hints as to why he's asked me here.

Is this about Valerie?

Did they find her?

Is she...

Suddenly, I'm praying I'm about to be fired for my reckless representation of the company during Open Season.

"Good evening, Miss Gardner," he says. His pale eyes reflect the dim lamp on his desk.

I nod in greeting, too nervous I'll be sick all over his desk if I dare open my mouth.

"Allow me to get directly to the point. Valerie Ross was a no-call-no-show for her shift today."

My breath hitches as I brace for the worst.

"That kind of behavior is not befitting of a Park Ranger. We understand circumstances beyond our control arise, but not alerting the entertainment team of her absence is inexcusable."

My lips part. He can't be serious. "Of course, she didn't show up for her shift. She's been kidnapped!"

"It's not my job to speculate or investigate. I'll leave that to the fine officers in the Hathaway Police Department. I'm merely in charge of keeping this theme park running. However, between us, you should know that your friend is not missing," he drawls, dragging his wire-rimmed glasses down his nose and cleaning the lenses with a tan cloth from his pocket.

"How can you be sure?" My voice is barely louder than a whisper.

"According to the access control log," Marty explains,

"Valerie Ross was the first person to enter costuming this morning. No one else set foot inside until ten minutes later, when my granddaughter scanned in."

What? That's impossible. Someone had to have followed Valerie inside. Maybe they were already waiting for her.

"So, you think Valerie showed up for work this morning, tore up the wardrobe warehouse, and then skipped out on her shift?"

"I don't know what to think," Marty says, returning the glasses to his face. Finally, there's a hint of humanity in his tone. His lips purse with confusion as he ponders his next words. "I'll leave those questions to Captain Pierce and her team."

My leg begins to bounce anxiously as I wait for him to say more.

"Regardless of what is determined, Pineland must continue to operate in a manner which best serves our guests. And there is absolutely no reason to believe that my employees are in any danger. The tragedies that have plagued this park are likely unfortunate coincidences, not a string of crimes. I'm confident the police will reach a similar conclusion."

My brow furrows. *Where is he going with this?*

"And Pineland needs a Park Ranger."

My eyes widen.

Marty Boone nods, confirming my suspicions.

My best friend goes missing and Marty Boone wants me to take her job?

Before I can utter a word, Marty says, "The Ranger is a symbol of our commitment to our community and the planet. Without that reminder, those who do not understand us, will do everything they can to bury us."

"I can't—"

"You will," he says firmly. "Despite your previous transgressions, you still showed up. I am a forgiving man, Miss Gardner."

"But—"

"You may go," Marty Boone concludes, jutting his head towards the door. "Don't be late tomorrow. It's time for a fresh start."

I should've puked on his desk when I had the chance, I think while retreating from the office. This asshole doesn't care about anyone or anything but his stupid theme park.

I jump when Dev rushes to me as soon as I close the door. "What happened?"

"Enough loitering. Your friend is out," Ryan snaps from his desk in the hall. "Both of you. Go."

He doesn't have to tell us twice. We hurry to the elevator where we can converse in private. The moment we're alone inside, I let it all out in a furious whisper.

Dev's lips part with horror when I'm finished.

"Absolutely not, Gwen. No way. You can't be a Park Ranger! If Valerie's correct about all this, you now have a target on your back!"

This had yet to occur to me. Am I in danger now? Ride or Die is already in my DMs.

Without Valerie here, I'm desperate to tell someone about the account. But trusting Dev with this information invites a conversation I'm not ready to face yet. A truth that can never be taken back once uttered.

Plus, how can I be certain of who stole the account from me? With Valerie gone, there's not a soul in Hathaway I can completely trust.

"So what if there's a target on my back?" I say, ignoring the ludicrous expression on Dev's face. "Maybe that's the key to finding this freak. The way to save Valerie."

"I know you're not suggesting—"

I cut him off. "That's exactly what I'm suggesting."

Screw Ride or Die. If they have my best friend, I'll do whatever it takes to find her. I'll work with a target on my back. I'll relive every horrible detail of Open Season and continue Valerie's hunt to discover what happened to Luca because it must be connected. I'll even play along with Ride or Die's insane demand for "content." If it gets me closer to whoever's on the other side of the screen, it'll be worth it.

I will do whatever it takes to find them because it's the only way my best friend makes it home safe.

CHAPTER
ELEVEN

MOM'S VOICE is distant at first, but the more panicked it becomes, the faster I wake up. "Gwendolyn?"

"What?" I ask groggily, startling away as she begins shaking me. "Whoa, what is it?"

"Mr. Ross is here," she whispers fiercely. "Valerie is missing again?"

I curse, not caring if my mother can hear and she doesn't bother correcting my language.

"Get dressed quickly. He wants to ask you some questions."

"I already told the police everything I know!"

Mother offers me a pained look. "He's hurting. Go speak with him."

Before I even push the comforter off me, Mom is out of the room.

After dressing, I hurry down the stairs, finding Mr. Ross at the dining table. His bald head is neatly shaved and his black beard is speckled with hints of silver. His walking stick is resting against his chair as he stares deeply into his mug of steaming coffee.

"Hey, Mr. Ross," I say, realizing it's been a few months

since I've laid eyes on the man. Valerie rarely has me come over if he's home, which is fine by me, because Mr. Ross usually makes a big fuss trying to convince us that California is too far from home.

"Hey, kid," he responds slowly, dragging his eyes up from the cup to bore into me. I shiver at how petrified he looks.

"Listen," I say, wanting to be done with this conversation as fast as possible, "I've already told the police everything I know."

Mr. Ross bristles. "And what would that be?"

I blink at him. Is this a trap? Is he trying to see if my story matches what I told the police?

I begin carefully. "That something happened to Valerie at Pineland. She went into the Wardrobe facility alone and disappeared."

"Why did you let her go in there alone when there's a supposed murderer on the loose?"

"She got there before me," I bite back. "She drove over with Weston McCray instead."

"Why is it that whenever you two aren't glued at the hip, my daughter disappears?"

I gape at his accusation. I've never encountered this side of Mr. Ross. He's usually so passive. Content with his quaint life —despite all the curveballs thrown in his family's direction. That sweetness is nowhere to be found now.

"Don't blame Gwendolyn for Valerie's poor choices," my father interjects, coming to stand behind my shoulder.

"All that matters is finding her." My voice raises. "I'm certain she is in grave danger."

Mr. Ross deflates. "You're confident of that?"

"She didn't run away again," I insist, reading between the lines.

"How can you be so sure?"

"We tell each other everything," I state firmly. "If Valerie was planning to run away again, I'd know."

"You think someone took her?" My mom whispers, her eyes damp with concern.

Even though I told my parents all of this last night, they were also skeptical considering Valerie's history as a runaway. Even after I told them Captain Pierce's team brought in a fancy detective from the city, they didn't seem too concerned.

I guess they changed their minds and decided to worry about their eldest child for once. I should feel relieved, but I'm more annoyed that it took so long.

Just like before, Ride or Die's threat on Valerie's life plays at the back of my mind. I recount everything that I told the cops.

Her father still doesn't look like he believes me. "They say only Valerie's ID was used to scan into Wardrobe. Unless an assailant walked in with her—"

"She didn't run away again, Mr. Ross," I say firmly.

"She better not have." Mr. Ross nabs his cane and rises from his seat. From his back pocket, he pulls out some folded papers. He drops them on the table before me. "Hang a few of these when you get the chance," he mutters before heading for the door.

"We'll do anything we can to help," my mother says as she warily motions our guest from the kitchen.

I'm too busy staring at the MISSING PERSON flyer with Valerie's face on it. She would've been pissed that her father used a candid photo from homecoming instead of her theatrical headshot. Gazing into the shining eyes of my best friend, my thoughts grow fuzzy.

Where are you? What happened?

When our family is alone again, I hesitantly glance up at my parents. Dad's face may not give away much, but I know him well enough to tell he is absolutely pissed.

"Are you telling the truth or did you help that girl run away again?"

"I'm not lying!"

"Gwendolyn Ann Gardner—"

"I swear, Dad. I would never do that again."

"Don't swear."

"How else are you going to believe me?"

"I'd be more inclined to believe you if your actions matched your words."

"Dad," I say as seriously as I can muster, "this is real."

"You're absolutely positive she's not out seeing that girl in Chicago?" Mom asks as she reenters the kitchen. Thankfully, she looks more worried than skeptical.

"Valerie and Maya broke up ages ago."

"Maybe they decided to rekindle?"

"With her phone turned off? Valerie would never go this long without contacting me." My eyes begin to gloss over. I hate crying in front of my parents, but now that the tears have started, I can't seem to stop. "I know you have no reason to believe me, but please try. Something is seriously wrong. I have no clue where she could be. I can't track her location on her phone. I didn't even see her that morning. There were no cries for help, nor any signs that anyone else was present. Nothing makes sense, but that doesn't erase the fact that she's gone."

As I sniffle, my parents share a look, debating whether to trust my word. I shake my head with heartbroken frustration, rising from my seat.

"I'm going to be late for my shift."

"You're going to work today?" My mom's voice raises.

"I thought you wanted me to repair my reputation?"

"Not if that park isn't safe!"

"Well, which is it? Valerie ran away or something messed up is actually happening at the park?"

"Don't take a tone with your mother," Dad warns.

I clamp my mouth shut, truly not wanting to cause more trouble. Only after I see the fire in his eyes start to calm, do I have the nerve to continue.

"Besides, I'm the Park Ranger now. You don't want me to disappoint Marty Boone any more than I already have, right?"

Their jaws fall open at this news. It completely slipped my mind to bring it up last night. For the longest time, it's all I ever wanted. Now, it's a cruel reminder that my best friend isn't here to do the job instead.

I watch them fumble with their words, deciding if they should congratulate me or apologize for the horrible reason that I came about the position in the first place. They decide on silence instead.

I take this as a signal that I'm clear to go. As I finish my morning routine and pack my lunch, my parents speak in hushed whispers in the living room. Finally, when I'm tugging on my sneakers, they reappear.

"Your father needs the car to make deliveries." My mother's words are clipped, so I assume they fought about taking a detour to drive me to and from work.

"Sorry, kid, but timely deliveries pay the bills. I'm already running behind as it is."

"It's okay. I can bike."

My mother bites back the words on her mind, choosing to shoot my father a look instead. He pretends he doesn't see.

"We want you to come home straight after work. No going in early or staying late. Stick with a group of crew members. Don't go off on your own."

"Deal," I say, shoving my lunch in my bag. "I'll see you soon."

Mom squeezes me tight. Not a typical part of my morning, I hug her back, letting out a deep breath.

"I'm so sorry, sweetheart," she whispers. "They'll find her."

Trying to catch my breath, I pull my mother closer. People starting to take this seriously makes it feel even more real. Valerie is gone and we have absolutely no idea where to find her. Or if she'll even come home.

Don't think like that.

No one knows Valerie like I do. I'll find her.

Even if that means striking up a deal with a serial killer. Once I'm away from my parents' watchful eyes, I pull out my phone and send a message.

@GWENSGARDEN

I thought you wanted to work together

It takes a few moments, but Ride or Die is still prompt in their reply.

@RIDEORDIE

How eager. You can start by making it abundantly clear Luca, Sandy, and Ruby were murdered.

@GWENSGARDEN

How do you want me to do that?

@RIDEORDIE

By any means necessary.

101

CHAPTER
TWELVE

I shouldn't be surprised to find Dev and his truck waiting in front of my house.

Glancing down the road, I see Mr. Ross' sedan pulling out of Dev's driveway. "Why was your interrogation so much shorter than mine?"

Dev shrugs like it's obvious. "My parents said the only people I would be talking to were the police or our family lawyer."

"Do we need lawyers?"

"Not unless we're being charged with a crime. And we didn't do anything wrong, Gwen. We're only witnesses."

My stomach squeezes. I'm sort of withholding information from the cops. But they already know Ride or Die is suspicious. I just have confirmation of threats to Valerie's life.

I need to find out who hacked my account. Maybe Captain Pierce will be forgiving if she understands my hands were tied.

Dev spies the MISSING PERSON posters clutched in my hands. "It's all over the news too."

"What?"

As soon as I'm settled in the passenger seat, I unlock my

phone and search for the news. I don't have to scroll far. An article by the *Hathaway Harold* pops up immediately. My mouth growing dry, I click into the link.

POLICE SEEK MISSING 17-YEAR-OLD GIRL FROM HATHAWAY

HATHAWAY, Mi. — The Hathaway Police Department is seeking the public's aid relating to the whereabouts of a missing girl in Hathaway, MI. Police say Valerie Ross was last seen at Pineland theme park on the morning of June 2nd.

She is described as black with waist-length, straight black hair and brown eyes. She stands five-foot-six-inches tall and weighs 115 pounds. She is possibly wearing a green Pineland uniform.

Any information regarding her whereabouts is asked to contact the Hathaway Police Department.

SUDDENLY FINDING it impossible to breathe, I place my phone face-down in my lap.

"You okay?" Dev asks. Before I can respond, he shakes his head and says, "Don't answer that. Of course, you're not."

"Definitely not."

I've never felt so alone. Helpless. The only person in this entire town I trusted completely was Valerie. She was my anchor. The one who kept me from sailing off into the abyss. Despite what I yelled at her during Open Season, I never minded being her sidekick. Out of the two of us, she was the natural leader. Someone I could rely on to set my pace. Help me find my way. Without her, I'm completely and utterly lost.

If it were the other way around, I'm sure Valerie would've found me by now.

So it's up to me to do whatever it takes to rescue her. Starting with an ally. But if that's going to be the boy behind the wheel, he needs to give me some answers of his own. We can't go any farther until we address the elephant in the room.

"Why do you suddenly want to be friends again?"

Taken off guard, Dev glances over. "What?"

"We just spent the last year ignoring each other."

"After you made it unbelievably clear you want nothing to do with anyone from Hathaway because you're so determined to leave. Can you really blame me for pulling away?"

"I never meant to—"

"Reject me? Well, you did, Gwen."

"You know my rule about Hathaway boys," I respond coolly.

I can't get stuck here—not even with someone as good as Dev. This isn't new information, no matter how much he might have liked to be the exception.

"Well Gwen, after you didn't get the role of Park Ranger and then got into a massive fight with your best friend at Open Season, I figured you could use a friend."

"You saw?"

"Ride or Die made sure everyone saw."

She sure did. It was the last secret Valerie ever spilled on the account before it was hacked.

"I don't need your pity, Dev."

Swerving into a parking spot, Dev frustratedly throws his truck into park and yanks the keys from the ignition.

Not finished, I angrily tack on, "Just admit it. You only want to be friends again because all your other ones are working at Wetlands with your ex-girlfriend. Why would you even choose to stay working at Pineland? You knew it would make Jenna dump you."

Dev laughs dryly. "Where'd you hear that?"

Valerie—but I'm not about to admit that to him. I can tell by the obnoxious look in his eyes he already knows.

"You have it all wrong, Gwen."

"It doesn't matter, Dev. Thanks for the ride, but I think I'll walk home."

"Try not to die today," Dev mutters under his breath from the driver's seat.

I set him with a furious glare before slamming the door shut.

This snaps him out of it. "Wait, Gwen, I didn't mean that."

"Whatever, Dev. Enjoy your shift with Chase."

With that, I head into the atrium alone, ignoring the tears blurring my vision. Reaching the door, it strikes me I still don't have a way in without my ID.

"Seriously?" I breathe out. There's no way I'm waiting for Dev to unlock the door for me.

My lips part when someone shoves it open from the inside.

"We need to talk," Amanda says with a stone-cold expression.

"I have training soon."

"If you get in trouble, I'll put in a good word with the boss," she says curtly.

Unable to argue with that, I follow her into the stairwell beside the elevator shaft. The one place that's destined to be empty. Her arms cross the instant we're alone, her eyes darting down to the stack of flyers in my hands.

"Don't bother hanging those up around here. Grandpa will have them ripped right back down."

I should've figured as much.

She continues, "I'm just thankful Nora and her team are starting to take this seriously."

I sense she's not finished. "But?"

"But we both know it's not enough. They're too busy struggling to figure out who killed Luca."

Her pale eyes meet mine. They're the same striking shade of blue as her grandfather, but that's the last comparison I'd ever make aloud.

"Fair. We can't sit here and wait for them to focus on Valerie's case, so I'm going to continue Valerie's search and discover Ride or Die's identity myself."

Amanda's eyebrows raise. "Don't you think that's a little dangerous?"

"I think it's the only way we're going to save Valerie."

I'm not revealing my entire hand, but Amanda doesn't need to know I'm in contact with Ride or Die. I can't do anything that'll put Valerie's life at risk. Ride or Die is clearly all about a spectacle. If they didn't get the reception they wanted with Ms. Wade, Ruby, or Luca, they'll only go to greater lengths to gain the public's attention. I wouldn't be surprised if they leaked the story about Valerie's disappearance to the news themselves to capture the town's eyes.

I'm confident Valerie's still out there. Time hasn't run out yet.

"It's going to take some substantial evidence for anyone to connect the dots."

"So let's connect the dots for them."

"Whatever it takes," Amanda says firmly. "Let's regroup after work. Meet me at the Old Wheel once the park closes?" Sensing my hesitation, she adds, "It's the only place in this freaking town where we can actually have some privacy."

"Just you and me?"

"All of us," she says, like it's obvious. "Weston and Dev are the only ones who believe something bad happened to Valerie."

"Yeah, but—"

"I think we need to keep them close," she says meaning-fully. "I get that Weston's a chronically chill guy, but you'd think a dead teammate would rattle him a teensy bit."

"Agreed," I say, relieved to hear someone else say it. "It's like he doesn't care."

"And Dev's got that 'nice guy' act on lock," Amanda

continues, sounding wildly similar to Valerie, "but when does a guy like that not have an ulterior motive..."

She trails off, allowing a slew of awful new fears to permeate my thoughts. What if Dev's sudden interest in rekindling our friendship isn't motivated by pity? The notion that Dev could be connected to any of this feels ridiculous, but now that the seed of doubt has been planted, I'm beginning to question everything.

Why did he choose to work at Pineland instead of Wetlands?

Why was he roaming the park after it closed yesterday?

Why be so nice all of a sudden?

The Dev I knew would never put a toe out of line, but a person can change a lot over a year.

I finally find my voice. "Okay, we keep a close eye on them. I can't stay long, though. My parents will lose it if I'm home late."

Amanda nods, her ginger curls flying as she hurriedly turns to leave. "Hey, good luck today. Keep an eye out, yeah?"

She's gone before I can respond.

Granting myself a moment to steady my pounding heart in the stairwell, I duck back into the atrium, keeping my head down all the way to pick up my costume. I'm not sure I can handle anyone asking about Valerie.

Hathaway may thrive on gossip, but I refuse to allow my best friend's disappearance to become the next small-town scandal because that's exactly what Ride or Die wants. However, if faulty attractions and freak accidents don't stop the people from buying Pineland park tickets, I'm not sure anything will.

I slow down when I spy a large man outside of Wardrobe. He sports a tan uniform bearing a badge embroidered with a ginormous tree stitched over the left breast. Even indoors, he wears a Mountie hat. Apparently, Marty Boone wanted to tighten security backstage, but not enough to station a real officer here. Instead, a minimum-wage security guard is serving as lookout.

My one saving grace is that the security guard, Simon, is not checking IDs at the door. Instead, he's searching for names on a checklist, ensuring everyone walking into costuming is scheduled to work today. Judging by the way he's scrutinizing the co-workers he's known for decades, the power has gone to Simon's head.

"You're not due in for another hour, Linda," he chastises the retired pediatric nurse who works in a gift shop to stay occupied. "Go wait in the cafeteria."

"Back when he wore diapers, I never made him wait," Linda mutters as she shuffles away.

"Gwendolyn Gardner," I say once it's my turn.

"Role?"

"Simon, you've played cards with my Dad since I was six."

"Sorry kid, but the boss expects me to do the job right."

I sigh. "Entertainment."

He scans the clipboard, snorting when he reaches my name. "So, you're the new Park Ranger?"

A few heads in line crane to get a look at me, making my pulse spike. "Yes."

"Mr. Boone must have a wicked sense of humor." He opens the door for me. "Have a good shift, kid."

I slide past him, awkwardly mumbling, "Thanks?"

What else am I supposed to say?

Considering the state we found Wardrobe in yesterday, they sure cleaned it up quickly. Still, an ominous aura has filled the space. You can hear a pin drop inside. Instead of loitering among the hangers, crew members are grabbing their uniform and exiting as swiftly as possible. It seems everyone's heard where Valerie disappeared.

Ducking near the last row, I head towards the end of the long rack of blouses and trousers until I reach a small supply of

Park Ranger uniforms. It's far too hot this time of year to go for the trouser option, so I opt for the dress instead. Snagging a sash and beret from an accessory drawer, I clutch the costume close.

A few days ago, I would've done anything to don this costume. Now, it's the reason my best friend is missing and three people have died. If I wasn't so confident in being the one Park Ranger incapable of making a headline, I'd be worried I'm up next. But I have a feeling Ride or Die has a different sort of terror in store for me.

My skin crawling, I retreat to the locker room, where I change as quickly as possible. The patch-covered sash drapes over my right shoulder. My brass name tag is pinned on the opposite side. Finally, I position the chocolate-colored beret atop my head, jumping when I feel a hand brush my arm.

Cindy, who's been working snack carts at Pineland for as long as I've been alive, gives me a gentle squeeze while passing through the locker bay. "You poor girl. What a special way to honor your friend."

Her choice in words has me frowning after her. "Valerie isn't dead."

"Of course not," she responds sadly.

I need to get out of here before I snap. These people are already planning my best friend's funeral.

Ignoring everyone's eyes boring into the back of my skull as I escape the locker room and hurry through the atrium, I opt to reach the second floor via the stairwell. The last thing I want is to be stuck in an elevator full of nosy employees.

Still, the empty space has the hairs on my arms standing on end. Whoever is behind this could be anywhere. Wishing I had something to protect myself, I sprint up the stairs as fast as I can. When I reach the top unscathed and out of breath, I try not to feel silly.

The second floor is home to the executive offices, sched-uling, training, and a few decently sized conference rooms. I duck my head into the first meeting room on my right, chewing the inside of my cheek when I find it empty.

I know for a fact that Hannah trained Valerie in this exact room because she recounted every detail of that day to me. Poking my head through every doorway down the hall, I find each one vacant.

"Hannah?" I ask aloud. No one answers.

Defeated, I turn on my heel and head for the scheduling office.

Finally, a sign of life. A cheery woman sits behind a neat desk, surrounded by park memorabilia and pictures of her grandchildren. Nicolette Pfister has been creating Pineland's schedules since the park's inception. No one gets spoiled around here like Nicolette—and for good reason. Aside from Marty Boone, Mrs. Pfister is the most powerful person in Pineland because she's the one with the power to choose if you get a day off. Have a birthday coming up? Buy the woman some new yarn for her elaborate crochet projects. Don't want to miss your family's 4th of July cookout? Promise her a slice of blueberry pie. If you're going to suck up to anyone around here, it should be the woman before me.

Pulling out my phone, I open my work schedule before knocking on the door. "Excuse me, Mrs. Pfister?

"Good morning, Miss Gardner." Something about the unamused look on her face tells me I'm going to be working a full schedule every week this summer. I probably deserve it.

Clearing my throat, I hesitantly ask, "Have you seen Hannah Flannigan? We had a training session scheduled for now."

Mrs. Pfister rifles through some papers, murmuring to herself.

"Sorry?"

The woman clicks her tongue, leaning back in her seat. "Oopsie! I didn't update your schedule, did I?" She shakes her head at herself. "Hannah quit this morning," she tacks on with a sniff. "Didn't even give two weeks. I was told to take her off the schedule immediately."

My lips part. "She quit?"

Though Nicolette Pfister may not say, we both know why Hannah quit in such a hurry. She put two-and-two together about the other bodies and didn't want to be next.

I'm surprised her father didn't leave with her. Mr. Flannigan, the head of Pineland public relations, has one of the hardest jobs in the joint. It's a tricky task to cover up horror story after horror story.

Mrs. Pfister's body cracks as she rises from the desk, motioning for me to vacate her dominion. "Seeing as our designated Park Ranger trainer is no longer available, you'll have to spend the morning reviewing the materials independently."

There's a sudden lump in my throat. "I thought crew members weren't supposed to be alone right now?"

"Please," Mrs. Pfister tuts, "if someone comes after you, scream. One of us will hear."

That's far from comforting. As far as I'm aware, the only people working up here are over the age of fifty-five and live behind a desk.

Helplessly, I follow her into an office, which appears semi-vacated with drawers left half-open and papers scattered everywhere. Peeking at the door, my eyes widen when I see a plaque with "HANNAH FLANNIGAN" on the front. Poor girl left in a hurry.

Mrs. Pfister delicately pulls open a filing cabinet and withdraws a thick, white binder. Everything one needs to know about being a Park Ranger is encased within. "Probably for the best you watch the onboarding VHS again too. Reignite your Pineland spirit."

"The onboarding what?" At this, Nicolette offers me a pained expression and I hurriedly add, "Kidding, kidding. Ms. Lawson still uses VHSes at school."

Nicolette Pfister is not amused in the slightest. "There's a TV with a player in Conference 2."

"Gotcha. Thanks for your help with all this, Mrs. Pfister."

Before she can set me with any more scathing looks, I retreat to the second conference room. The space is still empty, aside from rows of long tables lined with uncomfortable, folding chairs. Instinctively, I scan for my exits, finding a second door to the hall in the back of the room.

I need to chill out. There's nowhere for a serial killer to hide.

Closing the door after me, I wheel the television stand to rest before the chair nearest the window. Below, the park operates like nothing bad ever happened. *Sapling Spring* is closest in view. Young guests dart through the splash pad, while others stand in shaded queues for a carousel, potato-sack slide, and the *Wittle Willow*, a miniature chair swing.

Popping the VHS into the video player, the TV automatically turns on. Settling back into the creaking chair, I try to get comfortable as I watch the most outdated piece of Pineland propaganda in existence. Though the outfits are amusing, the cheesy script and rough camera quality leaves anything to be desired. Despite her enormous, fluffy hair, I quickly recognize a young Ms. Wade in her Park Ranger uniform, stiffly walking through the empty park as she recites the company's vision: Encouraging guests to create lasting memories while engaging with conservation efforts.

As tempting as it is to pull out my phone, I know the moment I do, Nicolette Pfister will come check on me. I resolve to zone out instead. Aside from a few rides and restaurants, nothing has changed since this video was made. Barely anything's even been repainted. Why should Marty Boone waste money on maintaining his park? The guests will come regardless. Though, perhaps the pressure will be on with a new water park across the street. We all know that's why he scrambled to throw together a cheap, new dark ride before the start of the summer season.

Unable to wait twenty minutes for the video to end, I begin leafing through the binder.

The first section reiterates the purpose of the Park Ranger. Some nonsense narrative about the park needing an ambassador. Someone to educate guests and serve as a face for the brand's environmental efforts.

The following few sections are scripts for the various Park Ranger programs. There's the morning show about Pineland's commitment to conservation. The afternoon sessions focus on topics like the wildlife native to Michigan (most notably—the squirrel) and the various types of trees in the park (excluding the fake one in the middle). I won't be needing the scripts. I've had these programs memorized since I was a kid.

Finally, I reach the end of the binder, where each page features a different letter of encouragement from a past Park Ranger. Turning to the first letter from Sandy, my brow furrows when I see her signature crossed out with a black marker.

Flipping to the next page—a letter from Arden Singh, someone who moved out of Hathaway ages ago—I find his name left untouched. So is Hannah's and the other Rangers who no longer work for the company. But a few pages later, Ruby Cahill's name is scratched out. Frantically, I turn to Luca's page, finding his name X'd out too.

"What the hell?"

His page should be the last one in the binder, but there's one more. Heart pounding, I find one of Valerie's missing person flyers. Her eyes have been X'd out and a large question mark is scratched over her face. Flipping it, I find a message written in purple lipstick.

Do what they say or I die

CHAPTER
THIRTEEN

Thanks to an afternoon of independent training, I had plenty of time to work out how I'd make it abundantly clear that Luca and the others were murdered. I guess I should be thankful there aren't any cameras backstage; otherwise, I'd definitely be fired.

I started with the men's locker room. Covering my eyes, I hesitantly pushed open the door and asked if anyone was inside. Just as I suspected, I found it empty. No one wants to waste their lunch break in the locker room. Still, I had to be quick. It was easy to locate Luca's old locker, thanks to it being plastered with Park Ranger and hockey stickers. It was likely already emptied, but that didn't matter.

Using a pen, I scratched the words LUCA WAS KILLED onto a clear spot of the olive-colored locker. It doesn't get much more straight-forward than that. Before leaving, I snapped a picture.

Ruby and Sandy's lockers got the same treatment. As I head out, I make an executive decision to vandalize Valerie's locker as well. However, instead, I engrave it with a single word.

NEXT?

It won't matter if my work is immediately cleaned up. The pictures will last forever. I send the four images to Ride or Die. Surely, this will appease them. I try not to think about how far they'll want me to go in exchange for Valerie's safety.

A moment later, I receive a response.

My brow furrows. Does Ride or Die know that I'm in here right now? Or are they taking a lucky guess? Still my hand feels under the bench that stretches down the middle of the locker bay, my heart skipping when I feel an envelope taped beneath the wood.

The envelope is full of cash. My pulse quickens as I quickly count $500. I blink with shock. It's more money than I'll make this week at work. It could make a serious difference to my college fund. I could put it towards a car or a lease on an apartment.

No. This is wrong. Ride or Die thinks I need to be bought, but this isn't the reward I want. I'm not doing this for compensation from a serial killer. I'm playing along to keep Valerie alive.

I return the bills to the envelope and tape it back to the bottom of the bench. Ride or Die will get the message. They have me all wrong. This isn't about money. I leave it behind without a second thought.

It's not until the end of my shift, when I'm walking to meet the others at the Old Wheel, that Ride or Die shares the photos online.

RIDE OR DIE *@RideOrDie*
Keep going to Pineland and you could be next.

. . .

THEY POSTED every photo I took, including the one of Valerie's locker.

Guilt seeps through me, but I do my best to ignore it. This is for Valerie. To keep her safe until the cops can find out who's behind all this.

Without a doubt, the Old Wheel is the creepiest place in Pineland, especially at twilight. Fenced away from the public, the path to the decrepit attraction is overgrown and wild, but it's nothing compared to the Ferris Wheel itself. The earth has reclaimed the ginormous wheel. Ropes of ivy weave through the weathered spokes and cables. Fallen branches from unpruned trees droop precariously over the rusting cabins.

Thanks to its heavy rebranding as the local make-out spot, barely anyone remembers a kid died here.

In the nineties, Marty Boone was under fire for falsely claiming Pineland benefited the environment. Conservation organizations grew desperate for justice, doing everything they could to close the park down. They dug up pollution models, forest clearing records, and identified all the animals who lost their habitats for the park to be built. They even went as far as to bribe crew members to unearth damning evidence against the place.

Walker Andrews, a sixteen-year-old employee, snuck into the park after hours to climb to the top of the park's Ferris Wheel. His goal? Retrieving photographic evidence that an osprey was attempting to build a nest on the attraction. As a protected species, Pineland would need to cease operation of the Ferris Wheel immediately.

The boy never made it to the top. He wasn't the only one buried that summer. Also laid to rest was Pineland's first PR scandal. To no one's surprise, after the accident, the activists backed off.

Nowadays, I suspect that Walter Andrews falling to his death is far from anyone's minds when they cozy up under the Old Wheel with their crush.

Nearing the ride, I'm struck by the eerie similarities between the activists' methods and Ride or Die's. Bribery. Deceit. I think of the note burning a hole in my bag. I know Valerie's handwriting. Her shade of purple. This note came from her—but how is that possible? Did Ride or Die force her to write it?

"Surprised you're not strutting around in Valerie's costume," Weston notes bitterly as I wade through the tall grass to join him, Amanda, and Dev under the ride.

"Are you sure you want to go there?"

Weston shrugs. "It's hard to miss how you're benefiting from her disappearance."

"It was also hard to ignore you making a move on Valerie before Luca's body was carried out of the park. Funny timing considering you said you wanted to *kill* Luca at Open Season."

The group gasps at this revelation and Weston's face turns red.

"You said what?" Dev demands. "I thought you weren't at Open Season."

"I didn't mean it!" The boy sputters. "You know, I didn't."

Dev blinks at him. "Do I?"

"You think I'd kill my best friend over a girl? I was pissed, but I'd never ever hurt him." Weston hisses, his eyes growing wet as he appeals to the others. "I was supposed to spend Open Season with Valerie, but when I heard she was with Luca, I left. You gotta believe me."

"Of course, we believe you," Amanda intervenes, shooting Dev and I an exasperated look. "We're supposed to be on the same side, not tearing each other apart."

Weston rolls his eyes. "Is there a reason we're all here now?"

"To find Valerie!" Amanda hisses with frustration. "Kidnapping victims are usually killed within three days of their disappearance. Nora's team needs all the help they can get."

"You want to try to find Valerie without the cops?" Dev asks.

"Would you rather sit around and hope it all works out?" I jump in before Amanda blows a fuse. "We're not doing this without the cops. We're just keeping an eye out for anything that might help their search for Valerie."

"We start by figuring out who scanned into the Great Oak after Luca," Amanda says.

"Wait," Dev interjects suddenly, "wouldn't our culprit have scanned their ID at costuming before or after Valerie entered?

A detail pops into my brain. "They're saying Valerie's ID was the only one scanned into Wardrobe the morning she went missing."

"What?" Weston blinks slowly as he processes this. "Are you saying whoever took Valerie—"

"—walked in with her," Amanda finishes with horror.

"But we didn't see anyone else that morning!"

"Doesn't matter if we saw them," I assert. "They were there. The same person that scanned into the Fake Oak and killed Luca."

Amanda mutters, "Unless they walked in with Luca too. Could explain why HPD hasn't made an arrest."

"That, or they're using someone else's ID. Someone who's ruled out as a suspect." Dev's dark eyes meet mine and I'm surprised to find they're like saucers.

We're both thinking the same thing. What if someone nefarious uses my ID? Surely, I'd know if I was being framed as a suspect, right?

I do have an alibi. Hannah sent me home from Open Season. I spent the rest of the night getting chewed out by my parents. Still, I'm not about to take the fall for a murderer.

"Can Cole's ex still get us into security?" I urgently ask Weston.

His lips pinch. "Cole's folks made him quit this morning. They said he could get a job at Wetlands instead."

Wind rustles through the forest, making the wheel woefully creak alongside the branches. I wonder if everyone else is questioning their decision to stay with Pineland.

"I can get us into security," Amanda mutters, not making eye contact with any of us. "Give me a little bit to make it happen."

Lucky for her, I'm not one to pry when there's an offer on the table.

Someone's name must be tied to all this and there's no way I'm going to let it be mine.

In the distance, the park's background audio loop—a chirpy orchestral arrangement of classical western pieces—shuts off. The sudden silence makes the hair on my arms stand on end.

"We should get out of here," Weston says, clearing his throat.

This is something we can agree on. No one dares utter a word as we slip through the bent bars in the tall, wrought iron fence that surrounds the current property line.

"Guests cleared out fast," Dev remarks, glancing around the darkened park. Peering through windows, I spy a few crew members still cleaning counters and restocking shelves. Pale work lights glow over roller coaster tracks as employees do their final walks of the night. It's hard to miss that the task is now completed in pairs.

"More like security had their most efficient sweep ever. Can you blame them with Grandpa breathing down their necks?"

Ducking backstage and through the quiet atrium, we head straight for the parking lot. Squinting through the dim lighting, Dev sighs. "This'll be good."

Peering past him, my brows raise at the sight of Jenna

Thatcher and her squad of lifeguards, still sporting their lobster-red swimsuits under denim shorts.

"What are they passing out?"

I don't have to wait long for an answer, because the instant her eyes clap onto Dev, Jenna scampers up to hand each of us a flyer. Her bleached blonde hair is trimmed in a short pixie cut, and although summer just began, her skin is already perfectly tanned.

Glancing down at the paper, I scoff, "Wetlands is hosting a vigil?"

Jenna doesn't answer my question, instead grabbing my hand and squeezing it. "Oh, Gwen, I'm so sorry to hear about Valerie. Is there any news?"

I stiffen at her sudden care for my best friend. "No, they haven't located her yet."

"Have they tried Chicago?" A lifeguard named Delilah asks with such genuine sincerity that the flyer creases in my tightening grip.

"Have you tried—"

Jenna cuts Weston off, "Wetlands Water Park is holding a candlelight vigil on Saturday night to honor the members of our community that recently passed."

Amanda's jaw clenches. "It's not your place to do that, Jenna."

"I agree! It's pretty sad that my mom is stepping up to support our community when your grandfather won't."

Another lifeguard, this one a scrawny sophomore boy at Hathaway High, pipes up. "Ruby used to babysit me. Luca was our classmate. Ms. Wade was our teacher."

Weston scoffs. "You got into AP Bio, Bradley?"

"They each touched so many lives in our community. Of course it is our place to do something." Jenna says with a pitiful shrug of her shoulders. "Hathaway deserves the opportunity to pay our respects. Mom is closing Wetlands early so we can begin right at dusk."

"How charitable of her," quips Amanda. "Anything to put Wetlands back in the headlines!"

Jenna's eyes narrow. "My mother would never cash in on a tragedy. She's doing this because she actually cares. "

"We'll be there," I cut in, ignoring the surprised looks from the others.

"Good. On behalf of the Wetlands team, we can't wait to welcome you, even under such horrible circumstances," Jenna says, with a sympathetic nod of her head.

I used to think Jenna was cool, but right now, I'm starting to understand why Dev didn't take a job at Wetlands. That water park is starting to go to her head. You'd think she was the daughter of a dignitary.

Offering Dev a grim smile that doesn't reach her eyes, Jenna finally departs to continue handing flyers to other Pineland crew members trickling out of the atrium.

"If Grandpa weren't such a coward, he would be hosting this vigil." Amanda trembles with anger. "Are all the adults in this town heartless? Does everyone need an incentive to do the right thing?"

"Seriously, Gwen?" Dev groans, "I don't want to step foot in Wetlands."

"Wendy Thatcher sure was quick to insert herself into this narrative," I say while studying the lifeguards as the pass out flyers. "Think about it. She's spent the last year recruiting Pineland employees to work at her water park. Why not steal all of Pineland's guests by closing down the park?"

"By *killing* people?" Dev asks incredulously. "That's such a leap."

"The only time Pineland almost closed was after Walker Andrews fell off the Old Wheel and died."

"But that was an accident."

"We're not dealing with accidents anymore," Weston pipes up, setting his steely-blue eyes on me. "You really think Jenna's mom is behind all this?"

I hold up the vigil flyer. "We're sure as hell going to find out."

CHAPTER
FOURTEEN

"Will you just accept the ride home?"

"Thanks, but I'd rather walk."

Dev groans from his truck, which is inching along beside me as I stomp through the parking lot. "Gwen, there's a killer on the loose who's obsessed with Park Rangers."

"I'll take my chances."

"You're unbelievable."

Still, the truck pulls away. My brow furrows as it makes a U-turn up ahead, tires growling over the gravel. I squint against the bright headlights as Dev drives back into the parking lot.

What is he doing now?

Realizing I shouldn't care, I turn back around and continue walking.

"Wait up!"

I freeze at his call, turning to find him jogging up the path.

"Really?" I scoff as he approaches. "You are relentless."

"We aren't freaking kids anymore. There's some serious stuff going on. Let's not be stupid and stop talking again, yeah?"

After the day I had, our argument this morning feels totally inconsequential.

Blinking hopefully, his face basks in the yellow streetlight. I need an ally—now more than ever. I want that to be Dev, but there is a year's worth of silence between us we cannot gloss over.

Dev must realize this too, because he goes on to say, "I really am sorry about the last year. I needed to heal and that wasn't going to happen if I had to look at you every day."

I swallow as a thousand fears, regrets, and what-ifs scatter around my brain like ants when their hill is dislodged.

There are times when I wonder if I should accept defeat and throw my arms around him. Risk everything for the chance to know what it would feel like to have his lips pressed against mine.

Lock it down, Gwen.

I can't give in to temptation. Getting trapped in Hathaway like my parents is not an option. A future with Dev only ends in heartbreak. He loves it here too much.

"I'm sorry for hurting you," I finally mumble, nervous that this will fully reopen the conversation about my dating rules and his sound argument as to why I should break them.

"I shouldn't have put you in that position when I knew why you'd said 'no.'"

"Then why did you ask?" The question slips out of my mouth before I can consider the consequences.

Surprised by my brazenness, Dev ponders his response. When it finally comes, it's in the form of a sheepish shrug. "Probably for the best we don't get into that."

He's right. It was foolish to probe.

"Chill, Gwen," he says, reading my mind. "It's no biggie. We're past it."

When our eyes meet, I can tell he means it. The feelings he once had for me are long gone—and there's a horrible part of me mourning that. In another life, one where Hathaway was

Heaven, I'd say yes to anything, and we'd be having all sorts of fun.

But that's not our reality.

A sideways grin pulls at his lips. "So can we walk home already?"

I can't help but mimic the expression. "Yeah, let's get out of here."

And with that, the chasm between us begins to dissipate as we walk through the glowing town. The streets of Hathaway are well lit with golden streetlights. Walking beneath them is the only time I'm tall enough to cast a long shadow.

Pineland sets the operating hours for most of Hathaway, so pretty much everything is closed for the evening. Late night hangout spots are limited to a greasy pizza parlor and the parking lot of a gas station.

As we cross through town, heading towards the neighborhoods on the other side, Dev breaks the finally comfortable silence. "About what you suggested earlier? Jenna's mom is obviously not a murderer. Our prime suspect is a crew member who was at Open Season, not an ambitious water park owner."

I think of Wendy Thatcher, who is as much a type-A, boss lady as her daughter. The single mother was a proud product of Hathaway, born and raised. Ms. Thatcher grew up with my folks, and from how they remember her, she was going to make something of herself one way or another.

Before I can answer, my phone buzzes. I hate how my heart no longer flutters with hope. Valerie isn't contacting me.

Expecting to see the screen illuminated with a message from my mom asking where I am, my stomach clenches when I see it's a DM notification.

Dev respectfully pulls out his own phone while I shakily unlock mine.

These dramatic pauses might genuinely hospitalize me.

I swiftly click the screen off, focusing on controlling my breathing so I don't puke on the side of the road.

"Was that your mom?" Dev asks innocently.

"You really believe Ride or Die is behind this?" I respond, knowing his answer can be the last plank in the bridge we're rebuilding.

"I do," he responds without hesitation and a swell of relief washes over me.

"There's something I have to tell you." I stop walking outside the entrance to our neighborhood. Dev's face glows under the sole streetlight as he comes to stand before me expectantly.

"What is it?"

"Ride or Die's been messaging me," I reveal after a deep breath.

His lips part. "Since when?"

"Since right before Valerie went missing."

"What the hell?" He hisses. "Do the cops know this?"

One look at my face and he has his answer.

"Jesus, Gwen."

"I think it's obvious Ride or Die isn't to be messed with. I'm not taking any risks here."

"Why are they messaging you?"

I unlock my phone and hand it to him. As he scrolls, the concerned creases on his brow only grow more pronounced.

Dev mutters my name under his breath like a curse.

"It's not much of anything. Yet."

He tears his eyes away from the screen. "Not much of anything? Most of Hathaway depends on Pineland to make a living. If the park closes, the whole town will go under."

"We're going to find Valerie before that happens."

"Wait, were you the one who vandalized those lockers?"

"They're threatening her life, Dev! What do you want me to do?"

He's silent for a long while because he knows my hands are tied. Finally, he says, "I still think it's a bad idea to keep this from the cops."

"If Ride or Die is holding Valerie hostage, the last thing I am going to do is put her in danger by running to Captain Pierce."

My phone lights up again. Another DM.

"Shit," Dev breathes out, leaning in to read over my shoulder as my thumb shakily opens the message. It's not a text, but rather, an image of a piece of paper lying flat on a metal desk. Some sort of report.

Squinting, I zoom in and try to read the minuscule words: *Chief Medical Examiner, cause of death, Luca Samuel Mendes.*

Dev catches on faster than I do. "This is Luca's autopsy report!"

My heart pounds. "Do we think it's real?"

"If it is, how did Ride or Die get a hold of it?"

Dev squints at my screen as he reads. "The medical examiner says Luca died due to blunt trauma to the back of his head. I bet they think he fell down the stairs."

"Or was pushed."

Our eyes skeptically meet, but only for a second, because another message appears and the screen immediately regains our attention.

@RIDEORDIE

Leak it. @ch6abigailherron

I click the linked handle, which brings me to a profile for Abigail Herron, a reporter for Channel 6 News. "She's based in Ann Arbor," I say, reading her bio.

"But look," Dev points out a string of recent posts, "she's been in Hathaway, reporting on everything that's going on."

He's right. Abigail Herron is live at the scene, detailing the "unfolding situation" occurring at Pineland. From the looks of it, Abigail doesn't believe the claim of natural causes either. She could do some real damage with this shoddy autopsy in her hands.

"This is stupid dangerous, Gwen."

"Then don't let me die, Dev."

CHAPTER
FIFTEEN

IT SHOULD DEFINITELY BE HARDER to get in contact with trusted news sources.

A few DMs later, Abigail Herron is eager to meet me at Lottie's, the local Hathaway coffee shop.

Owned by a proper anglophile, Lottie's has an embarrassingly stereotypical British theme. The walls are covered in bunting and Union Jacks, while all drinks are served in ornate teacups. Between the Beatles blaring on a loop and hissing espresso machines, it's the perfect setting for a private conversation.

Abigail is a lot older in person than she appears on TV, with gray streaks in her ginger hair and bags under her hazel eyes. Sipping from a teacup decorated with blackberries and thistles, she waits at a table in the back.

"I wasn't expecting there to be two of you," Abigail says, as Dev pulls over a chair.

Dev had some choice words for me when I suggested going alone. It was easier to concede than get into it with him. One rarely wins a debate with Dev Vishwakarma.

The woman shakes her head. "I guess it doesn't matter. I'm glad you could take the time to meet with me, Jenna."

My chin jerks back with surprise. "Excuse me?"

Abigail's blinks rapidly. "Are you not Jenna?"

"Definitely not," Dev says, eyeing the reporter with confusion.

"You must be Gwen," Abigail hastily amends. "Slip of the tongue. I apologize for the confusion."

What would Jenna want with a reporter? From the grave look on the woman's face, I'm not going to learn. That was a one-time blunder and it will be strictly business from here on out.

"I looked you up," Abigail says. "Your online profiles show you were close friends with Valerie Ross."

She waits for me to acknowledge this is true, and when I don't, her head cocks to the side as she continues. "I hope they find your friend. You must be tremendously worried."

Again, I don't take the bait. This woman won't get a tip out of me. Ride or Die didn't ask me to fan the flame on Valerie's disappearance. I'm here to brighten Luca's spotlight. I know better than to go off-book and potentially anger the maniac holding her hostage.

Abigail doesn't seem to mind. "You alluded to having something to share with me?"

"Yeah." I nod at Dev. He downloaded the picture last night and printed it so we wouldn't have to show the reporter my chain of messages with Ride or Die. He slides the folded paper over to her.

Brows raised as she glances between us, Abigail carefully unfolds the paper and scans down the page. She sucks in a breath when she reaches the bottom. "How did you get Luca Mendes' autopsy?"

"We can't answer that."

"But you can guarantee it's real?"

We also can't answer this, but we do know the response Ride or Die would want us to give. "Yes."

Abigail glances at the paper again. "How does an athletic

boy like Luca Mendes slip down a flight of stairs?" She points to a section. "They claim natural causes but note there were scratches on his neck?"

"That's a great question," I say, meeting her eyes. "We're hoping you ask it publicly."

"I'll have to confirm this is real with some additional sources," Abigail says, refolding the paper, "but once I do, I'll run with it. People are growing weary of 'natural causes.' They deserve to know if they're in danger."

"We agree."

She glances between us again. "Is there anything else you want to share?"

I shake my head immediately. "That's all we've got."

Her eyes bore into mine, clearly expecting me to bring up Valerie. When I don't, she finally concedes. "Very well. Thanks for the tip."

"Just doing our civic duty," Dev says, earning a look from both of us, which causes him to clamp his mouth shut.

"We have work soon," I say, wanting to get out of the coffee shop before Dev can wow us all with another impressively stupid remark.

"And I have another appointment," Abigail says, raising the teacup to her lips and taking a delicate sip. "Thanks again."

"Our pleasure," I say, immediately wincing because sharing Luca's autopsy is certainly not a pleasure. In fact, it feels pretty messed up, but if there's a chance it'll help Valerie, whatever her current state, I know it's worth the risk.

Dev and I grab our iced coffees, which we wisely ordered in to-go cups, and with a final nod at Abigail, we scooch our chairs from the table. Before leaving, however, I pull one of Valerie's Missing Person flyers and tack it to the center of the bulletin board featuring local events and businesses. After staring at her smiling face for a moment, I swallow hard and follow Dev out of the shop.

"We've officially reached a new low," Dev grumbles as soon as the door closes behind us.

My jaw clenches. I've already accepted my fate on this level.

"And why on earth does Jenna have a meeting with that woman?" He continues hotly. "Maybe it's for an interview about the Wetlands opening?"

"No offense to the Thatchers, but Wetlands isn't exactly the headline at the moment."

Not sure how to respond, Dev takes an anxious sip of coffee as we begin our trek to Pineland. Summer heat pricks the back of my neck. I'm going to be dripping with sweat by the time we finish walking to work. With Dev's truck left in the parking lot last night, we had no alternative method of transportation.

Our trek is quiet as we attempt to process the morning's events. I'm not sure how much more my brain can comprehend. Not waiting for the crosswalk to change before passing through an intersection, we ignore the honking tourist.

Reaching the other side of town, we veer towards the park. Up ahead a ginormous, rectangular sign proclaims, "WELCOME TO PINELAND," and below in smaller, gold lettering, it says, "Curing the World, One Coaster at a Time!" Like a postcard from a National Park, the sign's background is painted with a dense pine forest and coaster tracks sloping in and out of the trees.

Instead of passing the sign and heading towards the front entrance, we curve around the back of the property. Cement sidewalks disappear into the gravel road as we clomp to work. The idea of going through the motions of the day feels nearly impossible, but I have to be here. My presence keeps my line of contact open with Ride or Die. It's what keeps me close to Valerie.

"You suck it up and ask for a new ID yet?"

One look at my face and he knows the truth.

"Gwen, if you're worried someone took it…"

"It's just lost. No one took it."

Another look at my face and I can tell he doesn't buy this either. "It's better to get ahead of signaling it's lost before—"

"Before we find my name on the scan-in log tonight?"

When Valerie first suggested we break into security, I thought she was out of her mind. I get it now. Taking any kind of action is comforting. Far better than sitting around and hoping Pierce's department does their job.

"Hannah's not around to yell at you."

"I don't want anyone getting the wrong idea," I mumble.

"They definitely will when you don't clock in for the fourth day in a row."

"I can mention it to Amanda's contact in security. Maybe they can get me a new one under the radar."

"You didn't do anything wrong, Gwen."

"Yeah, except crew members keep turning up dead, a killer is bribing me to do their bidding, and people think I'm benefitting from my best friend going missing."

Dev winces but doesn't disagree. "Ask tonight. It won't be a big deal."

"Because nothing's a big deal nowadays."

I don't need to check my phone to know we better pick up the pace. The crew member lot is almost full.

Pointedly ignoring the you-can't-keep-doing-this look on Dev's face after he scans his ID on the door into Crew HQ, I slip in behind him. Our eyes meet briefly before we separate. Silently telling the other to stay safe.

He heads into the locker room, whereas I keep walking towards Wardrobe. There's still a security guard out front, checking a schedule to ensure everyone entering is supposed to be here. I give it another day before Marty cuts it. We all know this safety measure is a complete show.

I keep my head down, grabbing my costume and accessories, before hurrying into my own locker room. The women who are still inside are surprisingly quiet. It sends a hopeless chill down my spine as I shrug on my uniform and fix the beret atop my head.

Swinging open my locker, my heart stops when I see it.

A tube of lipstick that certainly isn't mine.

I already know what the color will be. A rich shade of lavender-plum that perfectly suits my best friend. As my breathing spikes, I hesitantly pick it up and inspect the tube. The tip's been smashed in.

A thousand questions race through my mind. How did it get in here? Why would anyone leave this for me? Who could be so cruel?

Unless...

Ever since we were assigned our first lockers in sixth grade, Valerie and I have shared our combinations with each other. Initially, it was so she could borrow my calculator or because I needed to check my eyeliner in the magnifying mirror inside hers. Then it was so we could leave each other notes. There's no better way to trust a person than to give them your secrets in writing. Sure, screenshots are forever, but nothing validates a friendship more than physical, handwritten proof. It's how she explained why she ran away to Chicago and I confessed my horrible wish that my parents never got back together. My middle-school crush on Dev exists in a scribbled note, as does my insistence we'll never be anything more than friends.

Turning on my heel, I face Locker 2286. Valerie's.

I swivel her code as easily as if it were my own. 94-11-38. Swinging it open, my heart clenches at the folded paper resting on the cool metal.

Unfolding it, my eyes frantically skim the familiar scrawl in purple lipstick.

Never trust a boy

Which boy is Valerie referring to now?

As I crumple the secret in my hand, my stomach churns with confusion. Why is Ride or Die having Valerie play games with me? Who don't they want me to trust?

Another envelope rests at the bottom of her locker, stuffed with more twenty-dollar bills than I've seen in my life. There's over a thousand dollars, I suspect.

No matter how tempting it may be, I don't take the envelope. I don't want this blood money. I want my best friend back.

CHAPTER
SIXTEEN

My first day presenting as a Park Ranger is anything but glamorous. For one, the guests couldn't care less about me. Sure, they feign interest while I explain the different kinds of trees in the park, which ones are native to Michigan, and the ones that grew from saplings straight from Yellowstone. But I can tell something is off by how they're glancing around and refreshing their phone screens. It isn't until my first break that I discover why.

Ride or Die @RideOrDie
People are finally waking up to LIARLAND'S bullshit. How many others need to disappear or die before Marty Boone caves and closes his deathtrap.

Below is a picture of about twelve protestors standing out front of the ticket kiosk. One glance at their crude posters and their message is apparent. Marty Boone and Pineland need to be held accountable for everything happening in the park. One sign lists the names of those who died. A few wave

Valerie's Missing Person poster. Many feature the same word Ride or Die used: *Liarland*.

Off to the side of the picture, I notice Luca's sisters in the crowd, holding a framed picture of their lost brother as they speak into Abigail Herron's microphone. Judging by the anger and desperation on sisters' faces, they're clearly demanding action. It looks like the Mendes family will grant Abigail permission to run with the autopsy.

Ride or Die has nearly tripled in followers. They're closing in on fifteen thousand. That means their reach has expanded well beyond Hathaway's city limits. The outside world is starting to tune in to our scandalous little theme park.

A quick scroll down my feed reveals the protestors were removed from the Pineland ticket booths by Hathaway PD. They relocated just off property, standing on the opposite side of the road as the park's welcome sign.

"Hey." Dev slides into the booth seat across from me, rolling his eyes when Chase gestures for him to scooch over and make room for the both of them.

Not settled until his ginger hair is mussed into place, Chase finally leans back with relief. "I'm gonna lose ten pounds sweating inside that freaking squirrel."

Chase is the kind of guy who doesn't require a sturdy build to establish his dominance at Hathaway. He's a whiz with a computer, but he rarely uses his powers for good. Known for trolling the school's official website, Chase has a fondness for adding pages the district's tech team must frantically take down. The pages often feature campaigns for underdogs who should win prom queen or links to unlisted YouTube montages of the hockey team eating ice.

If anyone has the skills to hack Ride or Die, it would be the boy sitting across from me.

Suddenly, I find myself sitting straighter. Is the killer on break with us? Sitting at our very table?

Never trust a boy.

Chase blows out a hot breath, fanning his strawberry-colored face. "Digging the new look, G."

Judging by his frown, Dev most definitely does not. He circles a finger around his lips. "What's that about?"

One of my thumbs absentmindedly touches my bottom lip, which is presently glossed with lavender-plum lipstick. If Valerie is somewhere around here, somehow watching, I want her to know the message was received.

Maybe Chase can deliver the message.

"Figured it a fitting tribute," I say, fighting to keep my voice even. "A protest of my own."

"Gettum, G," Chase agrees casually before opening a Tupperware of cold spaghetti dusted with parmesan and parsley. He shovels a forkful into his mouth before nodding to my phone. "We could all learn a lesson or two from that brilliant asshole."

"Who?"

"Ride or Die," he says casually. "They rebranded into a boss. Now nobody's buying that BS narrative from the big guy."

"Ride or Die is a mindless troll," Dev shoots back. "They're the last person any of us should be taking cues from."

"A mindless troll?" Chase laughs, slapping the table like this is the funniest thing he's ever heard. "Careful with your insults, Vishwakarma. You never know where Ride or Die has ears."

"You think Ride or Die is in the break room?"

"They're one of us." Chase shrugs. "A wolf dressed in sheep's clothing."

Something about the way he innocently blinks in my direction has me breathing sharply. I have no proof—other than the intuition pounding at the back of my mind—but I'm confident Chase knows more than he's letting on.

But how do I prove it?

Chase must sense my discomfort because he casually changes the subject. "So, y'all going to the vigil tonight?"

Dev and I both nod.

"Scary stuff, huh?" Chase clicks his tongue. "Some people think the tree huggers are at it again, but this is way bigger than what happened to that Walker kid. One body's an accident. More than that? Well, crying 'coincidence' gets harder and harder."

"You don't think these are freak accidents?"

"Do you, Gwen?"

When I don't answer, Chase goes on to say, "Hard thing is —why would anyone want to hurt sweet people like Ruby, Luca, Valerie?"

"And Ms. Sandy," Dev adds.

Chase's eye flicks to the boy beside him. "I said 'sweet people,' my dude."

"You didn't like Ms. Sandy?"

The whole school did. She made a class as tough as bio bearable with her lively lectures and zany experiments. One of the worst parts about junior year was realizing she only taught sophomores and seniors.

I guess I shouldn't be surprised Chase had issues with everyone's favorite biology teacher. After spending most of last summer together, I heard plenty of horror stories from his freshman year. Chase butted heads with nearly every adult in the building.

"She gave me an F and tried to have me retake her class next year," Chase scoffs, shaking his head. "I hope she rests in peace, but damn, that doesn't mean she wasn't a bitch."

Dev and I are rendered speechless. From the sounds of it, Chase is halfway to a confession.

"Don't worry. I wound up getting a C, not that I would be seeing her next year anyways now." Chase wrinkles his nose. "That sounded way worse than I meant it."

Something on Chase's phone distracts him. Is it the Ride

or Die account? With the boy's attention captured, Dev and I share a concerned look.

Suddenly, Chase slaps his palms on the table, making me jump.

"Everything okay?" I dare ask.

"People are really trying my patience today. What's new?"

"Who?"

Chase's jaw clenches. "Hannah's not even our boss anymore and she's still finding ways to make my life miserable."

His choice of words makes me feel squeamish. "What's Hannah want?"

"Power really goes to people's heads, huh? She quits and still thinks she can make demands?"

Dev shoots a curious look in my direction before reiterating my question. "Yeah, but what does she want from you?"

"Nothing she's gonna get." Crumpling up the remains of his lunch, he slides out of the booth. "Gotta pee," he mutters under his breath as he leaves.

"Nothing suspicious about that," Dev says as soon as Chase is out of earshot. "Does everyone around here have some secret agenda?"

"Probably."

"That doesn't make me feel better."

"I should've messaged Ride or Die while Chase was still here."

"You think it's him?"

I shrug. Who isn't a suspect at this point?

Glancing back up, I find Dev staring at my lips. He averts his eyes when he realizes I've caught him. "What's really up with the new makeup? Not that it doesn't suit you, but—"

"I think Valerie is closer than we think," I whisper.

Digging into my pocket, I carefully withdraw the piece of paper and pass it to him under the table. I know I can show

Dev. There's no way he's included in the long list of boys I'm not supposed to trust.

He unfolds it, leaning back slightly so he can read the note while it's still below the table. "Where did you find this?"

As quietly as possible, I recount the morning's events in the locker room. The folds in Dev's brow deepen when I finish.

"What's the point of this? If Ride or Die wanted to send you a message, they'd just DM you."

"Wait," I say slowly, "do you think Ride or Die knows Valerie left this message? How could she if they're holding her hostage?"

Dev shrugs, just as confused as I am.

Stuffing the note deep into my pocket, I shake my head, at a loss for what to think. Nothing makes sense.

Sure, everyone in Hathaway has their secrets, but Valerie and I never kept them. Not until now.

CHAPTER
SEVENTEEN

DEV SLIDES his phone across the break-room table, an article illuminated on the screen.

DESPITE MULTIPLE BODIES FOUND ON PREMISES, TICKET SALES SKYROCKET AT LOCAL THEME PARK

Abigail Herron, Reporter, Channel 6 News

HATHAWAY, Mi. – After the bodies of Sandy Wade (61), Ruby Cahill (21), and Luca Mendes (17) were discovered at Pineland park, families and locals are calling for the park to shutter their gates. On Saturday, June 4, protestors gathered in front of Pineland, an environmental theme park that opened thirty-minutes outside of Ann Arbor in 1983. Their main demand is for Pineland to reevaluate the safety of their operations (**Recommended Read: Sparks Fly at New Squirrel Ride at Pineland**). Some protestors go as far as to insist the property close, claiming the park "too haunting" to remain open after the string of recent tragedies. This includes Liliana

Mendes (13) and Sofia Mendes (15), sisters of the recently deceased Luca Mendes.

The Mendes family insist their son, honor student and captain of the Hathaway High hockey team, did not die of natural causes. An autopsy report cites Mendes died due to blunt trauma to the head on the night of Tuesday, May 31, during the park's annual end-of-school celebration for student employees. He was found dead the following morning. The Mendes family are confident their son's fall was not accidental. It is their hope detectives at the Hathaway Police Department will unearth the truth about who ended their son's life and bring closure.

According to Luther Flannigan, a spokesperson from Pineland, the park remains committed to the safety of their crew members and guests. They are cooperating with Hathaway Police Department's investigation but have no intentions of closing the park. "Ticket sales have reached an all-time high because our guests know that safety is our top priority at Pineland," the representative confirms. "Conservation funds rely on proceeds from our ticket sales. People want to come to Pineland, and we won't withhold them from that opportunity."

RIDE OR DIE got their wish. With the autopsy results out in the open, the public will draw their own conclusion. Luca was murdered in Pineland and his killer remains at large.

Amanda reclaims my attention. "Is everyone clear on how this is going to go?"

Even if one of us did have a question, her no-nonsense expression would have anyone biting their tongue.

After changing out of our uniforms, we reconvened in the cafeteria, waiting for the chattier crew members to finally take their leave. If there wasn't a town wide event occurring in less than an hour, it would've taken way longer for the crew to clear out. Not that I would ever consider a vigil a blessing.

We reached the general consensus that whatever information we find tonight will already have been found by the police. Perhaps there won't be a name, but we'd like a look at whatever puzzle Captain Pierce is slowly piecing together.

Dev nudges my knee and I realize everyone is staring at me. "Sorry, what was that?"

"You'll go into the back office with Weston?"

"I thought Dev was going in with me?"

Amanda blinks frustratedly. "Have you not been listening at all?"

"I legit just said I have mad computer skills," Weston says, obnoxiously shaking his bangs. "Keep up, Gwen."

"Having a basic ass PC setup does not make you a computer whiz."

"Please," Weston laughs, "I learned straight from a pro. Hathaway's favorite hacker is the reason my stats look pretty on the team's site. Gotta impress those scouts, yeah?"

"Chase taught you?" I ask skeptically. When it comes to computers, Chase is like a magician. He never reveals his secrets, otherwise, why would anyone need him?

"He didn't teach me, per say, but I was watching over his shoulder while he worked his magic."

"My friend in security is leaving the computer unlocked for us," Amanda interjects frustratedly. "All you have to do is scroll to the correct date and time."

"So then why can't Dev come back with me?"

"Apparently Amanda's friend is taking summer classes for college credit," Dev says.

It all makes sense now. "Let me guess—classic lit?"

Dev's parents are English professors. Their students are always DMing Dev for tips on how to get an A.

"Ding, ding," Dev says dryly. "I wish I could go back there

with you, but I need to stay with this security guard and give them dirt on how to pass a class."

"And I'm on lookout," Amanda finishes, locking eyes with each of us to ensure we're all listening this time. "We get in, we get out. Deal?"

"Deal," we all mutter. No one wants to look more suspicious than they already do. Getting caught is not an option.

The overhead lights in the cafeteria flicker ominously, causing a hush to fall over the space. Then, as if nothing had happened at all, the fluorescent bulbs return at full force.

Weston clears his throat. "That's not creepy at all."

"Power surge?" Amanda wonders aloud.

"Let's hope," Weston scoffs morbidly.

We all know what he's thinking. Pineland has all the right ingredients for a thorough haunting.

"Ghosts aren't real," Dev pointedly reminds us.

Still, the eerie scene encourages the last pair of crew members—an old married couple who drive up from Ohio to work at the park every summer—to vacate the cafeteria. Dev slides out of the booth, poking his head into the atrium, and after he confirms it's also empty, he waves us over.

"Let's do this," Weston says by way of motivational speech.

Security is located in the basement of the same building, sharing the floor with maintenance. Together, the two departments have claimed the space as forbidden territory to any outsiders. Honestly, I'm not confident Marty Boone himself could waltz in without an invitation.

"So, who's your in with security?" Weston asks, wagging his eyebrows as we slink down the stairwell. The lighting grows less-and-less as we traverse downwards. God, basements give me the creeps. "Dating an older lady?"

Amanda frowns at his suggestion. "Ew, that's illegal."

"We're breaking into security."

"That's against the rules, not the law, idiot." Still, no one speaks up, forcing Amanda to elaborate. "Don't y'all go to school with Milly Dillard?"

We all freeze with surprise. Milly Dillard is the mayor's daughter. A rising junior, she's known for having unbelievably high standards in the people she dates, stating she requires someone who can keep up with her online demands as an influencer.

Weston regains his voice first. "Hold up! Milly D? You pulled Milly freaking Dillard?"

"It was a few years ago. What's the big deal?" Amanda asks coyly, knowing full well what the big deal is.

"Milly D always says she doesn't have time to date."

"Maybe she says that to you."

Weston lets out a low whistle, offering the girl an impressed nod.

"Since when did Milly work at Pineland?" Dev asks. "And how did she get a job with security?"

It's a fair question. I've never seen the mayor's daughter around the park. She wasn't at Open Season. Yet if she was one of Amanda's flings from a few years ago, Milly's been around.

"Hold up," I interject with a more pressing concern, "are we seriously about to trust Milly Dillard with our plan?"

"She doesn't know what we're looking up," Amanda says defensively.

"But she knows we're after something. I'm not sure—"

"We can trust her."

"You can trust her," I clarify.

"Do you want to see the access control system or not?"

My jaw clamps shut. I don't have a choice because we've reached the bottom of the stairs.

Sparing me an annoyed glance, Amanda begins fixing her curls, ensuring they fall over her shoulder just so before turning out of the stairwell and greeting her ex.

"Hi Mills!" She coos, grinning wildly.

Milly Dillard sits with her feet resting on a heavy desk.

She's tall and curvy with long, black-and-flamingo-pink hair that split into two tight braids.

The light of half-a-dozen screens illuminates her umber face. I assume each shows a view from one of the few security cameras hoisted around the park. Gnawing on a piece of gum, she finishes whatever she's typing on her phone before glancing up and grinning. "Hey, babe! You been good?"

"As good as I can be up there," Amanda laughs, her previous seriousness now vanished.

"Yo, Milly D!" Weston croons. "Since when have you been trapped down here?"

Milly cocks her head to the side. "I'm not sure that's anyone's business. Do you want people to know you're down here, McCray? Imagine a hockey scout finds out you're partaking in sketchy extracurriculars."

"Please, scouts will be eating out of my hand this season."

"Luca—may he rest in peace—might not be around, but that doesn't mean what was once his is automatically yours."

"That's not why—you know what, whatever," Weston scoffs, but I can tell he's uncomfortable with what she's insinuating. That's Milly's style. Humbling others is her specialty.

"I expect you all to keep it quiet that I'm down here," she says firmly, meeting each of our eyes.

"Okay, but why?" Dev can't help asking the question the rest of us are afraid to vocalize.

Milly's eyes snap to Dev, sizing him up. Deeming him harmless, she finally says, "Apparently being a self-employed content creator with astronomical engagement isn't a 'real enough' job for my dad. I agreed to take a position that won't impact my real job," she says, wagging her phone, "and Daddy made it happen."

It's at this moment I realize Milly is barely in the security uniform. She's wearing the tan blouse, but it's unbuttoned, revealing a black tank beneath it. Instead of the long matching pants, she's in jean shorts. Apparently, she has no intention of stepping foot in the park. I doubt she even watches the security monitors.

"Aren't you afraid to work down here alone with everything going on?"

Milly laughs. "Please, after the Luca stuff, HPD has an officer in here with me. And I'm not the overnight guard, obviously. I'm only here for the last few hours of operation and a bit into the night."

"Where's the officer?"

"I sent them into the park to grab us ice cream bars." Milly clicks her gum, still eyeing Dev. "Anyways, I'm trying to graduate high school with my AA, not lose all my brain cells over-analyzing ancient books. Your mom doesn't believe in blow-off classes, does she?"

Dev laughs under his breath, "Definitely not."

"Use Topher's computer." Milly flicks her hand towards the open door behind her, which has Amanda waving for Weston and me to get going.

After sparing the stairwell a quick glance, I follow Weston into what appears to be a computer lab from the nineties. The room is ringed with long tables, each supporting a humming computer. They've constructed dividers between each set up, though calling each desk space a cubicle would be a stretch.

Weston shakes his head at the ancient equipment tasked with keeping the park safe. "God, Marty Boone is such a cheapskate. It's terrifying."

Almost as terrifying as it is to be alone with someone I trust as little as Weston. At least Dev is right outside. I know Weston isn't going to kill me or anything, but it's unnerving to think he may be hiding the strength to do so. Not the physical strength required—I can confirm he possesses that with one glance at the veiny arms hanging out of his black muscle tank. No, killing someone requires a mental fortitude that I think— or hope—few are capable of.

On the far wall is another display of security feeds. I count only five in total. The expected angles that feature the front entrance and main gift shop. But there are a few surprises, as well.

"I didn't realize there was a camera positioned outside Marty's office," I say, frowning at the screens.

"Is that the Old Wheel?"

I nod, staring at the shadowy, lime-green outline of the abandoned Ferris Wheel on the night vision camera.

"That's so wrong," I mutter, thinking of all the teens who think they've found a moment of privacy, but are being watched by some creep in security.

"Marty probably wants to save his ass just in case some kid decides to jump again."

"Walker didn't jump. He fell."

"That's what they want you to think," Weston says, batting his bright blue eyes. "Who knows what happened that night? Maybe he was pushed."

Goosebumps prickle my skin at the idea. Weston has a point—who knows what happens around here at night? Nothing good, that's for sure.

"Found Topher's computer," he says, focusing back on the task at hand. Pulling my attention away from the security feeds, I join Weston at a computer on the far wall.

Despite the fact they work in a literal black hole, the security team seems to have tried to spruce up their cubicles with some personality. Most sport blue-and-maize decorations, alongside pictures of family. I recognize a good many of the faces from town.

Topher Hill's desk looks much like the others. College football pride, photographs of his twin daughters at a lake, and certificates for milestone anniversaries at Pineland. It's the only computer that's lit up. I wonder if he's aware that Milly Dillard knows his password.

"Hacker voice: I'm in," Weston says, setting himself in the swivel chair.

"Hacker voice: hurry up."

"I'm going, I'm going," he says, clicking the mouse. "You're uptight, you know that?"

"I'm sorry for not being calm while my best friend is missing and I try to figure out what happened to her."

"Damn, Gwen, you know what I meant."

"I don't but whatever." Who cares if Weston almost dated my friend? The patience I have for this boy is waning.

Weston obnoxiously releases a breath, double clicking the icon that features the same security logo on the scanners at all the doors: a green circle with a red pinprick in the center and the company name, VivID. The same green-and-red light that flashes when you press your badge to the scanner.

I won't relish asking Milly for a new ID. Something tells me her kindness has been tested enough tonight. I can hear her grilling Dev in the hall about Dr. Vishwakarma's questioning style and leniency with grading—two things I'm confident Dev knows nothing about.

It takes approximately an eon for the window to open on the computer. Its internal fan is breathing heavier than a kid who just rode *Climate Coaster* for the first time. Finally, the screen flashes white, taking a long second to display a spread-sheet-looking application that logs every scan-in from the day. The most recent scans are at the top of the screen, and as Weston scrolls down, the later entries appear. Each row lists the crew member's name, the time they scanned, the location, and their 12-digit work ID number.

Most scans take place in chunks, like when the staff clocks-in around 8:30 am. Throughout the day, people scan to enter merchandise stock rooms and kitchens. At every attraction, control booth operators rotate every thirty-minutes. It appears a member of the security team is manually entering who walks into Wardrobe because these scans are missing the long identi-fication number. Noticeably, there aren't any recent scans into the Great Oak. The caution tape may be gone, but everyone's giving the tree a wide berth.

"Looks like I can search for a specific date," Weston says, more to himself than me, while typing into a search bar at the top of the screen.

The evening of Open Season appears at the top of the page, ending with a security crew member doing some basic rounds throughout the park, ensuring no high schoolers were loitering after Open Season concluded. It's a shame the security guard on duty didn't swing by the Great Oak. It might not have been too late.

Scanning the window, my heart pounds as I point to the entry on the screen:

MENDES, *Luca*
   11:02 pm
   GRT OAK

THERE'S an entry of another name scanning in right after Luca. The name of someone I knew to suspect all along.

"What the hell?"

MCCRAY, *Weston*
   11:06 pm
   GRT OAK

CHAPTER
EIGHTEEN

Everyone wanted to trust Weston, but he's been lying to us the entire time.

"That's impossible?" Weston gasps as I slowly back away from the screen. He blinks at the monitor for another long moment before raising his gaze to meet mine.

A chill runs up my spine at the fury in his eyes. No wonder he didn't want anyone to know he was at Open Season.

Weston killed Luca. He's Ride or Die.

"Show me your phone," I demand.

He waves it in the air, making me flinch. "You think I'm freaking Ride or Die? Really?"

"Fine, you can show the cops instead," I cry, dashing for the door.

Dev races to me the moment I make it out, grasping my arms while he asks frantically, "Who was it?"

"Weston," I barely manage to say before the boy in question barrels out of the door.

"The computer is wrong!" He yells, pulling at the ends of his sandy-blonde locks. "I swear to God, I wasn't in the Great Oak that night!"

"You lied about being at Open Season!" I argue from Dev's arms. "I saw you there!"

"I saw you in the *atrium* and left immediately after!"

"Security logs don't lie, Weston!"

"This one does! I wasn't there!"

Amanda and Milly dash into the security dungeon, cursing at what they see inside. Dev moves in front of me, but that doesn't stop me from peering around the side of him, "You're going to jail."

"The cops have already seen this! If they thought I was a suspect, they would have pulled me in for additional questioning."

"Have they?"

"No!"

"How do we know you aren't lying?" I bellow.

"Because I'm not! This is a set-up. I didn't kill Luca!" Weston wails, still gripping his hair madly. "You know what? Screw this. If none of you want to believe me, I'm out of here."

And with that, he storms back up the stairwell.

Amanda and Milly return, their jaws agape.

"Holy shit," Milly breaks the stunned silence, moving to pick up her radio, "we need to call 911."

"We can't yet," Dev says, causing me to pull away from his grasp. "We can't be sure Weston did it."

"*We're not sure?* Are you kidding, his name is on the computer! I saw him storm into Open Season, wanting to know where he could find Valerie. You should've seen his face when I told him she was with Luca."

"So, he went into the Great Oak and killed Luca?" Dev asks. "That sounds insane."

"So is Weston! Jealousy makes you do crazy things." I shake my head with disbelief. "Why are you defending him?"

"Didn't you see his face? Weston looked terrified.

Confused." Dev shrugs. "He'd be in custody if HPD had any reason to believe he was involved."

"Marty Boone and Captain Pierce were down here the morning Valerie found Luca," Milly offers. "I swapped shifts with someone so I could go to a media event. They definitely checked the logs."

"And yet, Weston is still walking free?"

"Bet 'natural causes' is the hold up," Amanda says bitterly. "There's nothing Grandpa likes more than a sound excuse."

"Have you seen the news today?" Dev points out. "I'm not sure excuses are going to cut it much longer." He pauses, taking a deep breath before meeting my eyes again. "I don't know, Gwen. Something feels wrong about this."

"His name is on the log."

"I know, I know," Dev sighs, scratching the back of his head. "Or maybe I don't know."

"Maybe y'all have no idea what you're doing," Milly coos, leaning back to perch on her desk.

Something about her tone has our heads snapping in her direction. "Is there something you want to share with the class?"

Her head cocks to the side. "I'll share if you do."

My eyes narrow.

Milly D is the opposite of low profile. She can't go thirty-minutes without posting a life update online. The girl live streams for hours on end.

As if she read my mind, Milly puts her phone face-down on the desk, resting her hands behind her head as she leans back. "Obviously there's a psychopath running around Pineland, and as much as I'd like to believe that's Weston, I don't think he's our culprit."

"Why not?" Dev asks.

"Because I've seen the killers," Milly admits casually, sucking all the air from the room.

"Killers? Plural?" I breathe out.

"How?" Amanda asks simultaneously.

Dev is a statue, those doe eyes silently urging the girl to explain herself.

"You all better hope Officer Barnes is taking the long way through the park."

Hopping off the desk, Milly waves for us to follow her behind it. We do so immediately, no one daring to speak, lest we spoil Milly's cooperative spirit. The shortest of the lot, I claim the spot behind the desk chair, with Amanda and Dev peering over my shoulders.

Security feeds display various angles of an empty Pineland basked in lime-green light. I'm shocked Marty Boone shelled out for night-vision. We only have a second to look at them before Milly minimizes the screen.

Opening another application on her desktop, she impatiently taps her manicured finger on the mouse while waiting for the window to load. "Night shifts are the best. After Pineland closes, barely anyone is here aside from a few maintenance workers who are still tinkering with *Sybil Saves the World*. It's easy to spot someone who shouldn't be here."

"There are a million dead-zones in the park," Amanda points out. "Pretty easy to stay off-camera if you know what you're doing."

"This is true."

"And everyone knows where the cameras are located."

"Do they?"

"The camera at the Old Wheel." Turning to the others, I explain, "I saw the feed in the back."

The screen flashes with the loaded application. A handful of search bars offer different ways to locate footage from a desired time or date.

Milly allows the others to ponder this revelation while she clicks a tab to change the search from date-and-time to footage logged by each specific camera. No one dares to breathe as a rainbow pinwheel spins on the screen, loading the feed.

Why add a camera to the Old Wheel when there's clearly a need for security footage elsewhere? Ride stations, the back-rooms of quick service restaurants, inside the Fake Oak, and Wardrobe all pop into mind. If there had only been cameras there, we'd know who was behind all this. Valerie and the others would still be with us.

"At first," Milly says while the screen still loads, "I thought it was to catch the kinky freaks who sneak back there. But trust me, that's not the case."

"How do you know?"

"Because security has been instructed to report anyone that we see sneak back there. So far, we've caught Chase and Mia hooking up. Abraham made out with Cooper. Simone got with Ray." She counts the couples on her fingers. "Then, of course, you four went back there the other day. But not a single one of you has been fired."

We all share a concerned glance. Marty and Captain Pierce know we met at the Old Wheel, but said nothing?

A feed of the Old Wheel appears. The camera is clearly positioned atop a tall tree because a corner of the footage is masked by a shadowy green foliage. Though there's no mistaking the enormous wheel taking up a majority of the frame. There's a perfect, albeit eerie, view of the large spokes, tattered cabins, and sinking loading platform.

"What are they watching for?"

Dev asks, "Or who?"

Milly doesn't answer right away, because she's scrolling back through hours of video footage. I stare at the Old Wheel, not daring to blink as the footage rewinds. Flipping from dark-to-light, clouds dart across the top of the screen, trees sway mechanically, and as promised, a few parties do appear for brief moments at a time. But this isn't what Milly is looking for as she scrolls back to Friday morning.

"Wait, is that Nora?" Amanda asks, recognizing the woman instantly. The usual bitterness that comes with the name is replaced with pure confusion.

A tall man accompanies her. "She's with that detective."

Milly stops scrolling to allow the feed to play out. Captain Nora and Detective Weegan survey the Old Wheel, prowling around the perimeter and peeking into some of the cabins. They spend a long while studying one cabin that's on the right side of the wheel, hanging a few feet in the air, stuck in a perpetual ascension.

"What are they looking for?"

"Just wait."

As soon as the captain and detective leave the screen, Milly scrolls again, bringing them back into frame for a moment before blue skies give way to electric-green night. Suddenly, she stops and grants the feed an opportunity to play again.

I didn't even notice the figure when Milly was scrolling backwards, they blended so well into the shadows. But a hooded shape runs to the base of the Old Wheel, pausing with their hands on their hips. The only distinguishable feature of their identity is that this individual is of medium height and build.

Is this Ride or Die?

Milly freezes the footage, zooming in on the hazy figure as far as her system will allow. She waits for us to make out the blurred image on the back of the figure's hoodie. Dev and I recognize our high school's shield instantly: open hands hoisting an evergreen tree. Below is the phrase, *ex semine crescit silva*. "The forest grows from a seed."

"They're one of us," Dev mutters, shaking his head with disgust. "A student in Hathaway."

"It's not done," Milly says, drawing our attention back to the monitor.

Holding my breath, I brace for something to happen.

My stomach drops when a second figure appears, poking

their hooded head out of the same cabin Pierce and Weegan were investigating. The station must've seen this footage and gone to check for the hidden figure the following morning.

Dev and I share a horrified glance, thinking the same. *There are two of them.*

Amanda gasps, "Who is that?"

"I can't tell." Squinting, Dev cranes to get a better look at the footage.

Unable to peel my gaze from this second individual, my mouth goes dry.

While I can't make out what's on the back of their sweatshirt, I'd bet almost anything it's not another Hathaway High hoodie. Crawling out of the cabin, the pair disappears from view, blending into a shadow.

Milly shrugs, leaning back in her seat. "The police have seen this footage. If they could identify those figures, don't you think we'd have two classmates on their way to juvie?"

We quiet again as the figures step out of the shadows. Whatever they were talking about, they're clearly done now. They stand beneath the wheel for a long moment, both with their backs to the camera as they stare upwards.

My forehead scrunches. "What are they looking at?"

"Stargazing?"

"Praying for forgiveness?"

Finally, one figure carefully steps back into the Ferris Wheel's cabin, while the other jogs back out of view.

"Can we see that again?"

Milly scrolls back and replays the interaction. We study the screen, but there's nothing new to glean. Both figures are similar in size and appear comfortable in the park.

Even after Milly pauses the footage, I can't stop staring at the cabin hiding the second figure. Are they sleeping there? Hiding out?

I might not be able to see their face, but that doesn't mean there aren't any tells revealing their identity. There's something about the delicacy of their maneuvering. The confidence as they climbed back into their hiding spot.

Valerie certainly doesn't look like she's being held hostage.

CHAPTER
NINETEEN

THE LONGER I stare at the screen, the more worried I grow that I might get carsick in the back of Amanda's car. Milly, who declared that she wasn't missing the vigil for anything, called her manager and faked a stomach bug. Apparently, she didn't care that she'd likely run into the security manager at the vigil.

"Y'all get the car started while I close up shop," Milly had said, frantically clicking away at the computer.

We were halfway up the stairs when we heard her call after us, "Shotgun, bitches!"

Fine by me. Disassociating in the backseat was exactly what I needed.

I don't even want to fathom how Ride or Die knew we were in security. Somehow, they're aware that we saw Weston's name on the log. The hairs on the back of my neck prickle. Ride or Die is watching, but how closely?

Dev blinks at my phone, his face equally as horrified. We're in the backseat of Amanda's car as she drives us to the vigil.

160

Clicking the screen off, I slide it under my leg, wishing it would all disappear. The threats. The pompous all-knowingness. They aren't bringing me any closer to my best friend.

If Ride or Die knows about the note Valerie left in my locker, that must mean they do have her. Maybe, in my desperation to find my friend, I incorrectly assumed the identity of the shadowy figure on some far away surveillance footage.

But I know my best friend. The way she moves. How she carries herself. If that figure wasn't Valerie, then perhaps I know nothing at all.

I'm tempted to message Ride or Die back. I'll do anything for evidence that Valerie's alive.

All I know is a piece of me withers away for every hour she's gone. I've always felt helpless in Hathaway, but never like this. Before now, I never had to endure it alone.

My phone buzzes again, and immediately, Dev leans back across the seat. His lips purse when he sees the sender.

With Amanda's attention on the road and Milly scrolling on her phone, I hesitantly open my DMs.

@RIDEORDIE

Can Valerie trust you to keep her safe?

My thumbs type out a message on their own accord. Dev elbows me, but it's too late. I've already pressed "send."

@GWENSGARDEN

what do you want me to do next

Their response is instantaneous.

@RIDEORDIE

Locker 8663. 43-9-16. You'll know what to take when you see it.

My mouth goes dry as my gaze hesitantly raises to Dev. First, I'm leaking information. Now I'm stealing?

But I don't even have proof Ride or Die actually has her.

Either way, I'm gambling, and whichever bet I take feels like the losing one.

"Whose locker is that?" Dev mouths at me.

I shrug, trying to think of which locker bay hosts 8663. It's nowhere near mine. Of course, Ride or Die would send this message as soon as we leave the empty park.

Out the window, we pass tall fields of corn, standing like shadowy statues in tight, neat lines. While we don't have to drive through town to reach Wetlands, I know it would be just as dark. When the community rallies together, whether it be for a Friday night football game or candlelit gathering at the water park, everyone closes shop early.

The brand-new park glows in the distance. Each colorful water slide has an impressive lighting package, illuminating their steep drops and curves. It's great advertising. While the park usually closes at sunset, it remains in view.

A ginormous water tower shines bright, like a Christmas bauble, welcoming the line of cars driving towards it. Lifeguards are in the crowded lot, helping direct traffic. It's all so orderly. Is this how everything operates at Wetlands?

We all jump as someone raps loudly on Amanda's window.

Peering out of the glass, my jaw drops at the sight of Marty Boone on the other side. He is the last person I expected to see here.

Apparently, Amanda has the same thought.

"Grandpa?"

"Best to not be late," Marty says, his voice muffled on the other side of the glass.

"I guess not," she grumbles as we all climb out of her car.

The Pineland president must have made a pit-stop at home before heading over to Wetlands because he's not in his usual work uniform of a smartly pressed suit. Instead, he's in jeans and a black collared shirt. The sight is almost as shocking as his presence. I'm not sure I've ever seen Marty Boone in jeans before.

Surveying our crew, Marty waves us on. "You kids go on ahead. I need to have a brief word with my granddaughter."

Amanda frowns, her leg bouncing anxiously.

But one does not simply ignore Marty Boone's request, so with a guilty, "See you in there," we leave her behind as we wind through the grid of parked cars towards the water tower.

"Is anyone else shocked that he's here?" I whisper.

"It would be tacky if he didn't show." Milly's nose wrinkles. "Though that outfit is quite the statement. Anyone know where we're going?"

"I do," Dev mutters, his jaw clenched as he leads us towards the front entrance.

Tall grasses line the edge of the parking lot, where an abandoned security check awaits. The Wetlands difference is already apparent as we pass fancy airport style bag scanners. At Pineland, we rely on a few crew members with wooden rods to rifle through bags.

Ahead, an enormous blue heron stretches its silvery wings over the main entrance turnstiles. To our left, neat, white huts bear signs listing ticket pricing and dining plans. Under different circumstances, we'd be a lot nosier in the new park, but now is not the time for that.

Joining the throng of people heading into the property, we follow waving lifeguards who direct us through the unlocked turnstiles. I recognize mostly everyone, even the employees from neighboring suburbs. It's the honor students, musicians, and youth group kids. People that Jenna's mom would consider the cream of the crop. I recall a slogan on a job fair flyer: "The best attracts the best."

Even in the dark, it would be impossible to ignore the park's beauty. Manicured horticulture and well-lit walkways snake away from the entrance. Neatly painted signs guide guests towards a wave pool, various slides, and water fountains. An acoustic guitar plays softly from speakers made to look like boulders. The familiar smell of sunscreen lingers, mingling in the air with fresh paint and chlorine.

Bright blue inner tubes are stacked below a large slide called the "Crazy Crane," and as we pass, we all admire the digital wait time board out front, which is currently posting 0 minutes. Pineland crew members have to make educated guesses when manually adjusting an attraction's wait time sign.

"Dang," Milly mumbles.

"You haven't been over here yet?"

She sniffs. "No, thank you. Water parks are like communal baths."

"This way," Dev says, guiding us towards the heart of the park, where everyone appears to be gathering.

The wave pool is made to look like the park's namesake feature. Lily pads and patches of submerged grasses ring the zero-depth-entry edges, which gives way to the triangular pool. Tall, thick cattails line the far end, where waves are manually pushed towards swimmers. All around us, people are pausing where cement-meets-sand, collectively deciding to go barefoot.

"Didn't realize we'd be walking in sand," Milly huffs, tugging off her high-top sneakers. I follow suit with my sandals, stuffing them in my tote bag. Dev doesn't bother, something I'm sure he'll regret later.

Lounge chairs and inner tubes are stacked in the back, so everyone can congregate at the water's edge, where a small platform and podium has been set-up. Portraits of Ms. Sandy, Ruby, and Luca rest on easels. Valerie is noticeably absent, and for once, I'm relieved. That means there's still hope for her.

I instantly recognize the families of the deceased, sitting in a long row of chairs before the stage. They lean on each other's shoulders, and even from back here, I can hear their soft cries and sniffles.

Lifeguards wave everyone forward, pulling candles stuck in

paper cups from large tubs. Jenna is one of them, soberly nodding at each individual passing through her line.

"They're so prepared," I observe as we join the queue.

Milly peers around me. "Looks like they borrowed from Trinity Lutheran's Christmas Eve supply."

"Hey," Jenna says as we reach the front of the line. Her tone is soft and sad, like she's speaking to a sniffling child. "I'm glad you could make it."

Dev clears his throat. "Yeah, us too."

"Can't believe this is what got you back in the park," she says to him. "Although, I guess it was Gwen's idea."

I swallow uncomfortably.

Not afraid of anything awkward, Milly wiggles her fingers. "Don't worry, I'm here too."

Jenna's pale eyebrows raise. "Quite the eclectic group."

She's not wrong. Literally less than a week ago, Dev Vishwakarma and Milly Dillard were the last people you'd catch me alongside.

But summer is a time for resetting. An opportunity to switch stuff up without the whole school watching. Without Valerie, I've had to find my own way.

"Quite!" Milly chirps, sliding herself to the front. "We don't want to hold up the line."

"Of course," Jenna says, sparing Dev one final look. It's one I can't read. Does she loathe him? Still love him? Pity him? Miss him?

Why do I care so much?

Dev must not be able to decipher it either, because with a jerky nod of his head, he's moving on. Jenna's attention snaps to me.

She lowers her voice, "Is he okay?"

My brow furrows. "I think so."

"I wish he'd quit that place already," she mutters under her breath, before glancing back up at me. "You all should."

My head explodes with questions I can't ask. What was she

doing at Open Season? Why did she meet with Abigail? How could she dump a guy like Dev over a summer job?

Reading my mind, Jenna grimaces. "I'm not sure what he's told you, but he didn't do anything wrong."

"He didn't really say anything."

"Dev's a good guy," Jenna says quietly. "Too good for a girl like me."

"What are you talking about?" Jenna's Miss Perfect of Hathaway High. Always behaved, good grades, from a successful family.

Jenna just shrugs, fighting to keep the bitterness off her face. "Be good to him, Gwen. He deserves it."

All I can do is nod and hurry away, but no distance is enough to keep Jenna's words from echoing around my brain.

"Too good for a girl like me."

I know what kind of girl Jenna is—or at least, I thought I did. But apparently, she seems to think differently. *A girl like me.*

What did Jenna do?

CHAPTER
TWENTY

THE COOL SAND squishes between my toes as the rest of my skin prickles in the still-hot summer air. Heading down the shore towards the wave pool, we pass a sign asking attendees to silence their cellphones. The crowd stands soberly behind the line of chairs, sniffing quietly as they pass the flame around the crowd, lighting each other's candles.

"Geez," Milly mutters quietly to Dev, "could the poor girl be more awkward?"

"It's only been a week since we broke up." Even after everything, he's still granting Jenna grace. Dev's a better person than me.

"That's like an eternity in summer," Milly says with a pitying shake of her head. "Either get back together or stop wasting energy on each other. You're both too cute to be wallowing."

"She's right," I add, earning a surprised glance from Dev. "There's too much going on to be hung up on what-ifs."

Scanning the crowd, I spot my parents and Gil towards the back. I should go stand with them, but it feels better to stick with Dev.

"Valerie's picture should be up there," Milly says, nodding towards the pictures up front.

"She's not dead," I say firmly.

Candlelight flickers across her sad expression.

"She's not," I say again, more confident than ever in this truth. If she was gone, Ride or Die would've used her body as a piece in their game by now.

Regardless, half of Hathaway must agree with Milly, because as they pass me in the crowd, they rub my arm, whispering their condolences. It's easy to remain positive at first, but by the fifth sympathetic squeeze, my resolve begins to waver. Everyone's given up on her. No one believes she's coming home.

"Her Dad's here," Dev observes, his brow creasing.

My head snaps up to see Mr. Ross traversing slowly through the sand. His cane sinks with every step. Keeping his head down, he finds a place off to the side to stand. I wonder if we should go be with him, but something holds me back. Valerie might be my best friend, but she's always kept her home life out of view. I think it's because she feels guilty. She has everything she could want while my family struggles for anything.

If I was Mr. Ross, I'd be ticked Captain Pierce and her entire crew were here instead of searching for my daughter.

Suddenly, the area music is shut off and the park grows eerily quiet, aside from the soft sobs coming from up front. Wendy Thatcher steps up to the podium, flanked by Captain Pierce and Mayor Dillard.

"One of the things I love most about Hathaway," Jenna's mother begins, "is our strong community. Nothing displays that strength more than when tragedy strikes. I'm heartbroken that for many of you, this is your first visit to Wetlands, but as the community's newest attraction, we felt it was our duty to make our values known. We will always put Hathaway first.

We do hope your next visit will be under happier circumstances."

"Is this a vigil or a commercial?" Milly asks under her breath.

"Like many of you, I'm devastated by the reason we are all gathered today. To lose not one, not two, but three brilliant members of our community in such a short period of time is as confusing as it is upsetting. Their loss will be felt around Hathaway for years to come. To speak on the incredible impact these individuals made on our community, allow me to introduce Mayor Dillard."

No one claps as Milly's dad takes the podium. The heavyset man with a thick mustache clears his throat while pulling a folded paper from his pocket. "We're gathered here today—"

"Good Lord." Milly winces at her father's predictability.

Maybe coming to this was a mistake. It's not like Jenna or her mom are going to confess to sabotaging Pineland by killing three beloved citizens. This isn't how I want to mourn. Staring down at my candle flickering in the breeze, I tune out.

This feels like an alternative reality. It's the first Saturday night of summer. I should be clocking out with Valerie and stopping by Stu's Barn for a scoop of ice cream on our way to a party in a field. It was the sort of weekend engagement we loved to loathe. We'd ditch early, taking the long way home so we could dream up plans of what we'll do after we finally escape Hathaway.

Instead, I'm stuck here, wondering where she is and what's stopping her from coming home.

The sniffing around us grows louder, and it isn't until a hand slides around mine that I realize I'm to blame. Blinking away my blurring vision, I glance down to find Dev's fingers interlocked with mine.

"Wanna go?" He mouths.

Up on the platform, Mayor Dillard is still speaking about Ms. Sandy's impact on the school system. I haven't been paying close attention, but I don't think he's even gotten to Ruby or Luca yet.

Lips pinching, I nod. I'm not sure I can keep it together if he mentions Valerie.

"We're ducking out," Dev whispers to Milly. "Coming?"

She frustratedly twists one of her braids. "He'll kill me if I leave during his speech." Wincing at her choice of words, she hastily adds, "Sorry. You two go."

Without a moment of hesitation, Dev begins to pull me through the crowd. Despite keeping my head down, people still squeeze me as we pass. They all know why I'm leaving early.

As soon as we're off the beach, we extinguish our candles, dropping them—melting wax and all—into the empty bins left on the cement path. My feet are too sandy to put my sandals back on, but the cement walkway is cool enough to manage barefoot.

Dev guides us down the dimly lit path, his grip still tight around my hand.

We've only held hands once prior, a few days before I set rules against such an action. It was winter break during eighth grade, and we were in his basement, watching some crappy true crime documentary on Netflix. Valerie always spent her breaks in Boca with her grandparents, so winter breaks were always just Dev and me.

Out of nowhere—not even during a vaguely sentimental or semi-scary scene—Dev reached across the couch and grasped my hand. We sat there awkwardly, the air around us going completely still while we waited for something to happen. Neither of us dared to scooch closer or sneak a peek at the other.

My eyes were locked on the TV, but I wasn't watching a thing. I was too busy envisioning going on my first ever date with Dev, tackling high school as a couple, senior prom, a joint graduation party...and that's when I hit the roadblock. What would happen after that? Dev loved Hathaway and Michigan. He made it clear he was content to spend the rest of his life in the mild Midwest. Even then, it was the last place I wanted to be stuck. We'd have to break up and that would ruin everything.

So, I refused to move closer or look his way. I allowed my heart to race and imagination to play pretend until the end of the documentary. That's when I faked a yawn and politely pulled my hand from his.

After that, he never tried to take my hand again. I wondered—and worried—if he'd ever shoot another shot. Make a move that was harder to ignore, like lean in while we're on Pineland's poor excuse for a Tunnel of Love or ask me to be his date to a school dance.

My mind is too numb for imagination right now, but that doesn't keep my heart from skipping with what I hope are nerves and nothing more.

Be good to him.

Dev mumbles something under his breath.

"What was that?" I hear myself ask.

Dev halts in the middle of the path, and I barely stop in time, narrowly avoiding running into him.

"This park was not built for the dark and the signs are absolute garbage," he mutters, shaking his head with frustration. "We're lost."

I may not be capable of noticing much at the moment, but I'm keenly aware of his hand still wrapped about mine. Even now, he doesn't let go.

My heart clenches. I should pull away.

Trying to be useful, I glance around, but of course, I've never been here before. "You're the Wetlands expert."

"Ex-expert," he reminds me. "I've only been here a few times—and that was during broad daylight."

"You don't recognize anything?"

We seem to have stumbled into a corner of the park that

offers basic facilities. First Aid, changing rooms, and a closed gift shop selling water park necessities like sunscreen, goggles, and flip flops.

Dev shakes his head with frustration. "I'm pretty sure we're on the opposite side of the park than we want to be."

"Classic," I say, though I'm not fully mad about the situation. My brain is beginning to work again. This might prove to be an excellent opportunity. "Say, have you ever been backstage at Wetlands?"

Dev shakes his head again. "Nope," he says with a pop of his lips. "Ms. Thatcher always wanted us to come in from the front. She didn't want anyone backstage until they were an official employee."

"And that wasn't you?"

"It could have been." He finally turns to me, still not letting go of my hand. I'm beginning to wonder which of us will do it first. It should be me. I have rules that make it me. I can't get his hopes up.

And yet—I don't seem to have the willpower to be the one to do it. For the first time in days, I feel like I can finally catch my breath. For once, the fog that's been clouding around my brain is beginning to clear and I can properly think.

I wonder if Dev's head has calmed too, because he's stopped frantically searching for a way out of the park and has resolved to simply wander around. We'll find our way out eventually.

It's tempting to prod more about why Dev refused a job at Wetlands, but I prefer this lulling quiet instead. After hours and hours of stress, my head finally feels calm.

I'm not sure where she found the money to do it, but Wendy Thatcher truly went all out with her park. Signs shaped as winged birds point guests in the direction of various slides. The walkways are lined with cattails and tall grasses so vibrant that I question if they are real.

We must reach the edge of the park because there's a

planked barrier bearing a sign that reads, "Wetlands Employees Only." Their backstage must be on the other side.

For some reason, I'm compelled to keep walking, beginning to round the off-limits barrier.

This startles Dev out of his daze as he pulls me back. "Do you want to get arrested?"

"All the cops are on the beach."

"This isn't Pineland, Gwen. Mrs. Thatcher paid for actual security cameras. She probably has eyes on us right now."

"What's the worst that can happen?"

"Do you really want me to answer that?"

Still, he doesn't stop me as I guide us backstage. Perhaps it's because he also wants to check out the surely impressive accommodations for lifeguards or maybe he just doesn't want to let go. Regardless of his reasoning, we swiftly find ourselves striding down an open walkway that leads towards a moderately-sized building. I clock a camera outside the door but am confident no one will go back to watch this footage. Keeping our heads down, we creep up the ramp and push open the door.

My jaw drops at the facility. It feels wrong to label such a place as a break room.

Clean, circular tables with padded seats fill the center of the room. Against enormous windows are vinyl booths that aren't ripped or worn. I bet the Wetlands lifeguards don't claim an entire side for a depression nap while on lunch. How could they with so much food available? There are fancy vending machines with credit card readers and a neat cafeteria which also features a sandwich station, smoothie bar, grab-and-go cooler, and popsicle freezer. The back wall is lined with compact lockers painted a sky-blue color. Small enough to store a fanny pack or lunch sack. Numerous TVs hang from the ceiling—and I'd be willing to bet that Wendy Thatcher shills for more than basic cable too.

"Dang," I breathe out. "Why'd you stay at Pineland again?"

"I wanted to—"

I wave him off. "Excuses, excuses."

There's nothing he can say to rationalize his decision. If I weren't indebted to Marty Boone, I'd be filling out an application on Monday morning.

As we take our final glances of the glorious space, I wonder if he's filled with as much regret as I am. This is where we should be spending our summer. Sunburned, well paid, and not living in fear of being the next casualty of a "freak accident."

"We don't belong back here," Dev murmurs.

I'm about to disagree when I see it.

"Oh my God—"

Dev's grip on my hand tightens. "What is it?"

I point to the locker straight ahead of us numbered 8663.

How could Ride or Die know we'd wander back here?

Perhaps they safely assumed I'd figure out the locker's location after ruling out Pineland and school. However, I'm not comforted by the reality that they clearly know me well enough to trust I'd wind up in the correct spot.

"You think—" Dev starts to say, but when he sees me spinning the dial, the sentence shifts on his tongue. "Gwen, wait!"

I freeze at the urgency in his voice. "For what?"

"This is someone else's property."

My mouth falls agape with disgust. "Valerie's life is at stake and you want to be worried about breaking-and-entering into some lifeguard's locker?"

Dev clamps his jaw shut. His nostrils may flare with frustration, but he knows me well enough to know I'm going to open this locker.

I return to the task at hand, spinning the dial right to 43, left to 9, and right again, stopping at 16. The locker clicks, and when I lift the latch, it swings open.

My eyes immediately dart around the cube-shaped space, desperately taking it all in. *You'll know what to take when you see it.*

There's not space for much of anything. Aside from the expected items—a bottle of sunscreen, sunglasses, and a beaded lanyard with a whistle—there's not much else that fits. I spy a reusable container half-full of pretzels, an aluminum water bottle plastered with stickers, and a drawstring bag that Hathaway High gave out to members of Student Council.

Reaching for the bag, I wait for Dev to protest, and when he doesn't, I glance over my shoulder. Immediately, my brow furrows at the expression on his face. "What's wrong?"

Chewing on his bottom lip, Dev's head shakes for a moment before he finally answers. "This is Jenna's locker."

My lips part. "What? How do you know?"

"The water bottle," he mutters. "I'd recognize those manatee stickers anywhere."

Why does Ride or Die want us breaking into Jenna's locker?

A girl like me.

Hesitantly, I reach for the bag. There's nothing else in here that Ride or Die would want—so whatever it is, I'll likely find it inside the satchel.

Carefully opening the drawstring bag, a gasp escapes my lips because I immediately recognize what's inside: an evergreen Park Ranger beret.

With a shaking hand, I drag it from the bag. It still smells of her mango shampoo.

Dev's eyes have glossed over as he stares at the accessory, unable to find a voice to utter the curses surely echoing around his head. Meanwhile, mine is plagued by a thousand questions.

What the hell is Jenna doing with this? And why does Ride or Die want such damning evidence back? Are they trying to protect Jenna? Will they use it to frame someone else? Or is this just another ploy to confuse me?

Dev finally discovers his voice. "We need to get out of here."

"Wait," I say before he can pull me away from the locker. Frantically, I stuff the bag back inside, hoping it rumples in a similar fashion before slamming the door shut.

Who cares about the camera at the door? What's Jenna going to do? Report she's missing a beret that belonged to the missing Pineland Park Ranger?

Dev's expression is unreadable as he grapples with his ex-girlfriend's involvement in this case. Has she had contact with Valerie? Does Jenna know where my best friend is?

This rules out Jenna as Ride or Die. They wouldn't have me steal something from their own locker. But that doesn't mean she's innocent, either.

Before I can ponder this further, Dev reaches for my free hand again and pulls me through the break room. "Get that out of sight, will you?"

I immediately stuff the beret in my tote bag as Dev guides us back into the cool night. As blood pounds in my ears, I allow him to steer me through the park. We're not blissfully lost anymore. I can tell he wants to find the exit just as fast as I do.

We pass by the wave pool, where Hathaway still mournfully gathers at the beach. Skirting around the back of the crowd, we follow the winged signage pointing to the park exit.

It isn't until we reach the parking lot that I remember to breathe. Whipping out my phone, I swiftly type out a message with one hand. The other is still in Dev's grasp, and after everything, I'm not sure I can stand without his help.

@GWENSGARDEN

Got it

I'm surprised when the response is almost instantaneous.

Keep it safe. I'll need it soon.

This is the last thing I want to do. Valerie was wearing this when she went missing. Holding onto something that could be used to find her feels like the worst omen possible.

"They responded quickly."

"Too quick." My lips parting, I look up to my friend. "I thought the whole town was in Wetlands right now. With their phones off."

As soon as it dawns on me, I stop in my tracks. The security footage of the hooded figures looking up plays on a loop in my mind. "If you were trying to get away with something under the radar and avoid the scrutinizing eye of security, now would be the time—"

Dev finishes for me, "Because everyone else is preoccupied."

"We need to go to the Old Wheel."

I know he understands the reason behind our visit, but the way Dev's face illuminates makes my heart sink. How many times has he thought about us sneaking off to the Old Wheel? The spot where moves are made and summer flings are established.

I can't hurt him again.

And so, despite feeling like I'm about to lose my tether and float away, I gently pull my hand from his.

CHAPTER
TWENTY-ONE

I CAN COUNT on one hand the number of times I've been to the Old Wheel.

The first occasion was with Valerie, back when we were eleven, and growing out of Pineland's day camp. Most children aged seven-to-twelve are shipped off to Pineland four days a week while their parents work—or in some cases, just took a break. Much like our parents, Valerie and I were also in desperate need of a reprieve from the younger, whinier campers. So, we snuck off to find the spot where someone died. In retrospect, it was obscenely uncool of us, but I didn't have the perspective on death that I do now.

My second visit to the Old Wheel was also with Valerie, when we were thirteen. This time, to confirm if her then-boyfriend, Charlie Foglier, was cheating on her. He was. We found him macking on Grace Kidd, who had the obvious advantage of already being in high school. Valerie threw a whole box of popcorn at them—something I'm sure the birds enjoyed far more than the couple.

It wasn't until last summer that I went alone with a boy. An out-of-towner named Kyle. He was on vacation from Wyoming and the first boy I ever kissed. It was only okay. I didn't get his number afterwards, which was sort of the best part. I'd never see him again. There were no strings to sever.

Traversing the overgrown path with Dev is the last thing I ever expected to do. Maybe when we were younger, before I shut down any what ifs between us, it wouldn't be so much of a surprise. Our whole lives, people told us we'd end up together. They'd say longtime friends always made the happiest couples. I always wondered if that was because they were too afraid to leave and find their true love.

Or maybe, it really is that easy to fall for a friend.

"Do you know what we're looking for?" Dev whispers, his head craning up before we even reach the clearing. As if whatever it is, it might be looming in the shadowy branches hanging overhead.

I wonder if he's fighting the urge to reach for me as much as I am for him. As we creep through the woods, keenly aware of every twig snap and rustle of a branch, I could use a comforting link.

"Not a clue."

"Awesome."

With the only light coming from our phones, we trample through the darkness. I truly haven't any idea what we'll find, but if I were up to something—much like the two figures we saw on the security feed—this would be the time I'd enact my plan. We slow as we near the clearing, both instinctively turning off our lights as we approach. Slowing, we peer through the trees at the abandoned wheel.

There's no one in sight.

"Why did I kinda expect Ride or Die to be sitting in the ride, sharpening a knife?"

In the moonlight, Dev blinks at me judgmentally, turning his flashlight back on before stepping out into the open. Doing the same, I follow him, wading through the tall, untamed grass until we reach the base of the ginormous wheel.

"Don't forget," Dev reminds me, "we're on camera."

I can't seem to find it in me to care.

Knowing this, Dev moves on. "I can't believe Marty never had this thing torn down."

"Probably cost too much."

We both know I'm right. Why spend the money to tear down the cursed attraction when you could just let it rust in the wilderness? Marty Boone is lucky it was built in the back corner of the park.

Climbing up the creaking stairs to the loading platform, we carefully tread towards the cabin the figure crawled out from. Peering in, we find it completely empty, aside from some stray leaves that must've blown inside. There's no evidence someone was previously hiding inside. Or were they camping out? Whatever they were doing, they aren't anymore.

"We agree they were looking at one of the cabins up there, right?" I ask, pointing upwards.

"Yeah, seems most likely."

Glancing up, like the individuals in the footage, we study the curve of the wheel. Most cables appear to be intact but are littered with fallen debris and overgrown greenery. I didn't realize it was possible for vines to snake so high. There's not much else up there. A full moon. A smattering of stars. A–

"Oh my God," I breathe out when I see it.

Dev cranes his head. "What?"

I point to the highest cabin. It takes a second, but the moment he sees it, he curses.

At the very top of the Ferris Wheel is a faint blue light. As soon as it comes on, it vanishes. A moment later, it returns. It flashes once more and then disappears again.

We wait with bated breath for it to blink again, frowning at the sky when it doesn't.

"Wonder what's up there."

His head snaps in my direction. "Absolutely not."

"Oh, come on," I goad him. "It's like climbing a tree."

"Like hell it is!" Dev argues. "That's a rusting deathtrap. And I mean that literally."

"I know you do," I say under my breath, sizing up the best spot to begin my ascension. "We didn't trek all the way over here from Wetlands to just stare up at the thing. If it's not already over, the vigil will be soon. It's now or never."

His lips part as he studies me, trying to discern if I'm being serious. Unfortunately for him, he knows me too well to understand I am. "This is the worst idea you've ever had."

I grin, because fortunately, I know Dev well enough to understand this isn't a rejection of my idea. Just a clear disapproval. I can work with that.

"Okay," I continue as if I didn't hear him, "so I'm thinking the safest route is climb up the emergency ladder to the center—"

"Bad idea."

"The spokes crisscross enough, I'm sure I can make it to the top."

"And find what? Walker Andrew's ghost?"

"Don't be morbid, Dev."

"Don't be insane, Gwen."

"We have to see what's up there!"

"Why are you so certain something is?"

"Are we just going to ignore the light?"

A hand frustratedly runs through his hair, making his black locks stand on end. "It's part of the ride!"

"A ride that's been broken down for twenty years? Really?"

"If it's been broken, how did something get all the way to the top?"

We both stare back at the control stand. It doesn't appear to be operational, but what do I know?

"Today is not the day I'm going to get trained in attractions, Dev."

"Please," he grabs my shoulders, "stop and think for a second. You're basing this off of nothing. Less than nothing!"

But it's not, and I can tell by the way he's staring at me that he knows it. There's something up there and I'm far too stubborn to ignore it.

"Gwen," he says, finally earning my full attention. His long lashes rapidly blink as he searches for anything that'll convince me. Finally, he settles on a simple, "Please don't."

In any other world—one where my best friend isn't missing and a murderer isn't messing with me—I would listen to him. But I don't have the luxury of ignoring this.

"I'm going to be okay."

"You can't promise that."

"I promise you can call 911 if something bad happens."

He processes this, somehow his brow furrowing even more. "If you're climbing up there, I'm coming too."

"Absolutely not." My arms cross as his jaw drops. Before he can protest, I say, "This is my stupid idea. We can't both fall. Someone has to be ready to get help."

"Then I'll climb up alone!"

I bite back a smile at this ridiculous suggestion. We both know out of the two of us, I'm more athletic. Wanting me to follow in her footsteps, Mom signed me up for years of gymnastics. I only quit because I couldn't think of anything worse than cheering for Hathaway High.

"You're as funny as you are sweet." I sympathetically squeeze his arm. "Thankfully, I'm realistic."

Dev winces, knowing he's lost this battle. After all these years, we still concede the same way. With a disapproving look and our hands in the air. The moment his rise, I know I've finally won.

"Okay," I say, surveying the challenge before me. The Old Wheel suddenly feels much, much taller. "Let's see what's up there."

"Please don't slip," Dev pleads as I start for the ladder.

I laugh under my breath, "I'll try my best."

"Wait, Gwen," Dev says, grabbing my hand and turning me around. His eyes bore into mine, wide with concern. "I'm serious. Please, please, please. No stupid moves. No unnecessary risks. You can't fall."

"I won't."

"You can't," he says again, firmer. His eyes search my face, trying to find any glimmer of fear he can use to convince me to keep my feet planted on the ground. When he doesn't, his other hand presses against my cheek, making me suck in a surprised breath.

His lips part, and for a brief second, I wonder if he's about to kiss me.

An achingly long moment later, he says, "I need you to hold on tight. Please." His thumb rubs over my cheek once. Twice. It says everything his lips can't.

Heart pounding, all I can manage is a nod.

Get a hold of yourself.

That feels impossible with his thumb still caressing my cheek. I shouldn't be wondering what it would be like to stretch up on my toes and pull him closer. If he were anyone other than Dev, perhaps I'd bend my rules. Anyone else, I'd give in and face the consequences.

But this is Dev. Even after a year apart, he's back to being my best friend, like nothing happened at all. I've already hurt him once. I'm not sure I could live with myself if I did it again.

Still, it isn't me who steps away first. Giving my cheek one final stroke, Dev releases me with a sigh.

Wiping my suddenly clammy hands on my shorts, I stiffly approach the ladder that's along one of the two sturdy legs holding the wheel upright. Grabbing a rung that's eye-level, I test its sturdiness. Seems stable enough. Checking my foot on one, I kick down on it, pleased when it holds.

"That's a good sign," I chirp.

"Are you trying to stress me out more?"

Glancing up, I measure how far I have to climb. I'd estimate the ladder goes about a hundred feet up to the center of the wheel. Though, that still leaves me half of the wheel to scale.

"Here goes nothing," I say over my shoulder, causing Dev to curse under his breath.

Before I can come to my senses, I put all my weight on the ladder, freezing for a second to make sure it holds. When it does, I reach for the next rung. And then the next.

I've spent my whole life on janky roller coasters, so while this should terrify me, it doesn't. I'm not nervous I'll lose my grip. I'm not even afraid there isn't a cage around this ladder and a good gust of wind could get me.

No, the only factor that's making my heart pound in my ears is the darkness. Dev helpfully lights my path for as long as his phone flashlight can reach, but the higher I climb, the darker it becomes. At least it's a clear night. The moonlight cascading overhead is barely-enough for me to see the shadowy outline of the rungs before my face.

I'm moving slowly, carefully feeling for each metal bar before placing my full weight on it, but it's better than miscalculating and falling. Rung by rung, I ascend, praying I'm not the next Hathaway teen to become infamous for falling off a Ferris Wheel.

The halfway point, and the direct center of the ride, comes sooner than I'd like. It only gets harder from here. I freeze at the end of the ladder, contemplating my next move.

"Are you okay?" Dev calls up. Even all the way up here, I can hear the worry in his voice. It trembles like the surrounding branches in the nighttime breeze. I should know —all the way up here, I'm eye-to-eve with the tallest trees.

"So far so good," I yell down confidently, mostly so he doesn't call the fire department like I'm some cat stuck in a tree.

Peering up at the crisscrossing spokes, I try to map out my

route. There's one extending straight up, directly towards the cabin that's looming about a hundred feet up. Sweat drips down my temples as I start lying to myself. It's only a ladder with slanted rungs. Surely, it can't be that hard to climb. Between every one of these motivational thoughts, the truth pounds through my head.

I'm going to die up here.

Above me, the faint blue light flashes again. Only once this time, but that's enough for me.

Ensuring I'm steady, I reach one hand away from the ladder and stretch as far I can reach. After grasping at air, I finally grab a hold of the bottom part of the spoke. It's much thicker than the ladder, but I can still get a solid grip around it. Maneuvering myself to the tippy top of the ladder, I reach for a higher spoke, and once I grab it, I move my other hand to join it.

I slowly pull myself up until my feet are on the bottom spoke. Adrenaline races through me as I reach for the next bar that crosses overhead. And then the next. I'm going slower than ever, careful with every placement of my foot so I don't slip down the bars. I guess the only perk of the darkness is it's hard to process how high up I am.

My hands are beginning to grow clammy again, and more than once, I have to wipe one of them on my shorts before gripping the bar. No matter how much I want to shout for Dev to call for help, I refuse to give up. I've made it this far. Already risked so much.

It's time to find answers for myself, even if the only lead I have is a little blue light.

Nearing the bottom of the cabin, I realize I'll have to scale the bar that connects to the car. It's not that different from climbing a rope in gym class.

Keep telling yourself that.

The blue light flashes again, brighter now that I'm this close. There's no alternative. I need to see what's in there.

Placing both of my hands around one of the slanted bars that extends around the cabin and to the edge of the wheel, I carefully slide them as high as I can reach. Praying I don't slip all the way down like it's a fire pole, I twist my feet around the bar. My muscles burn as I inch higher and higher.

The edge of the cabin is only a few feet away, but reaching for it means letting go of the pole with one hand.

I just have to go for it.

Taking a deep breath, I release one of my hands and stretch towards the cabin.

"GWEN! NO!"

Startled by the scream echoing through the forest, I cling back onto the pole for dear life, doing everything I can not to slip to my death.

But it's not the warning that shocks me. It's the voice. A voice I'd know anywhere.

Valerie.

Too terrified to call down and lose my balance, I dare a peek below. It takes a moment, but yes, there. Right next to Dev. She's right there.

How the hell is she here?

The blue light flashes again. It's so close. Is this why Valerie suddenly appeared?

"Gwen, don't!" She screams again, confirming my theory.

In any other world, I'd scramble down the maze of bars and cables to finally see my best friend, but I can't yet. I need to know.

Emboldened by my beating heart, I shove away from the beam and reach for the edge of the cabin. By some miracle, I make contact. Fixing my grip, I dare to let go of the bar completely.

I expected the car to tilt slightly, as it would if someone stood up inside. But I know these things are built to not completely upend its passengers. Taking advantage of that momentum, I kick off from the bar and hurdle myself into the cabin.

I land on something that is simultaneously hard and soft. Though it isn't until I feel hair that I start panicking.

"Oh shit!" I shriek, realizing I just landed on a body. Judging by their limpness, I'd wager they're not alive.

Before I can pull out my phone, a smart watch on their wrist illuminates blue with an incoming text message. When I see his empty face, I scream.

Chase. Chase is dead.

"DEV!" I cry, the plea ripping from my throat. "Call 911. NOW!"

CHAPTER
TWENTY-TWO

BY THE TIME the police and fire departments arrive, locate a ladder tall enough to reach us, and manage the climb, I was trapped with Chase's body for nearly an hour. Between my trembling limbs and pounding head, I didn't dare try climbing down on my own. Then there would be a second corpse to sort out.

Like a driver passing a wreckage, I was incapable of averting my gaze from Chase's haunted face. The scream etched onto his lips. The emptiness in his cold eyes.

They can't claim 'natural causes' any longer. Not when Chase's body was stashed up here. He was killed.

Who would do this? The obvious answer toys at the back of my mind, but I'm too numb to linger on those kinds of thoughts.

The moment my feet touch the ground, I'm swarmed by medics and police officers. When they find I'm completely unscathed, but undeniably scarred, they drape a trauma blanket over my shoulders and focus their attention on Chase's corpse. Carefully, he's placed into a body bag.

My folks must have been called because they shove through everyone, squeezing me so tight I can't breathe. Have

I really been breathing this whole time? My lungs feel empty. Everything does.

Peering between their shaking shoulders, I finally spot Dev, who is relaying some version of the story to an officer. His black hair stands upright from grabbing it countless times. When those dark eyes meet mine, I see they're wet. Before my own tears can flow, I must know.

Dev reads my mind. *Where is Valerie?*

"Gone," he mouths with a helpless shrug.

Of course, she is.

That's when the tears finally come. Valerie couldn't even wait for my feet to safely reach the ground before running away again. Because, no matter what, she always comes first.

Where did she come from? How did she even know we were here?

God, did she do this?

Pierce approaches, hesitantly tapping my parents on the shoulder. "We need Gwendolyn to come down to the station."

No matter how polite the Captain sounds, it's clear this is not an option. My parents must realize this too, because after sharing a concerned glance, they nod understandably.

"Can we drive her ourselves?"

The woman agrees. "Of course. We'll meet you there."

"We?"

"Dev Vishwakarma will be driving with us."

"We can take him too," I say instantly. I barely recognize my own voice. It's dry and brittle. Hopeless.

Captain Pierce nods, like she expected this. "We've alerted his folks. They're already on their way to the station."

My mom waves Dev over, protectively putting an arm around his shoulder. "We're going to get you two out of here, okay?"

Dev doesn't take his eyes off me as he nods. They drift from my head to my toes, searching for any sign of harm, a wound. There are many, though none are visible from the outside.

We leave the clearing as Chase's mother appears. She sprints past us, fearful tears already streaking down her hollow cheeks.

My parents hurry us along, but it's too late. The mother's horrified, helpless scream echoes through the park. It grabs hold of my heart and squeezes so tight that I worry it might give out. My parents tremble as they walk and I realize it's because it could've been them roaring with pain.

Static fills my brain, but like a tuning radio, sudden realizations blare out.

Chase was never a Park Ranger. This doesn't follow the pattern at all. Why was he killed?

Valerie was in Pineland. She screamed for me to stop. I thought she was a hostage. Did she do this?

Whoever did kill Chase left his trackable smartwatch around his wrist. They wanted his body to be discovered.

The static is back. None of this is comprehensible.

It's easier to shut my mind off altogether and give into the numbness. But even after I push away the impossible questions, all I'm left with is the image of Chase's lifeless face imprinted onto my brain. At this rate, I'm not sure it'll ever leave.

I can still feel myself fall against him. My skin tingles at the memory. Itching like a thousand spiders are crawling over my body.

Stop. Please stop. But begging my brain is no use. I can't forget.

Dev and I slide into the back of my dad's car. It's older than I am, something you can tell the moment the key turns in the growling ignition. As we pull out of Pineland, red-and-blue lights begin to flash behind us.

Dad blows out a breath. "Whole town's gonna see."

"Jonah," my mom pleads from the passenger seat, though,

judging by the way her lips are pinched, she's not exactly thrilled by the police escort, either.

In another world, the lights would've bothered me too, but I barely notice now. Dev's eyes find mine across the backseat, also at a complete loss for what just happened.

It's my turn to read his thoughts. *How do we explain this to the police?*

My face must reveal I haven't a freaking clue what is safe to share with the cops because Dev's nostrils flare with nervousness.

His cellphone comes out of his pocket. After lowering the screen's brightness all the way and opening his notes app, he types a message and covertly holds it out for me to read.

This is our last chance to get our story straight.

He waits for me to nod before typing more. My mouth grows dry when he holds the screen up again.

I already told them about Valerie.

He hurriedly types more.

I'm sorry. She ran away when I called the cops. They heard me scream after her.

I take the phone from him and add my response.

It's ok. Her dad deserves to know she's alive. Enough is enough. I'm beginning to wonder if Ride or Die was trolling me the entire time. Convincing me they had Valerie captive in order to push me into doing their dirty work. Was she ever really kidnapped?

It's time to talk about Ride or Die.

Dev's eyes bulge. "Too dangerous," he mouths.

I shake my head. I'm no longer afraid of the account. I have no reason to play their game anymore. Better to cut ties before I'm in too deep. I'm not letting them ruin my life more than they already have.

Dev concedes with a nod.

We should mention Weston's name on the log, he goes on to type. *Make sure they know everything we do.*

I nod in agreement, reaching for the phone. *I'll tell them how Weston acted at Open Season.*

"Everything okay back there?" My dad calls from behind the wheel.

"Yeah," Dev says stiffly, shoving his phone back in his pocket. "I was texting my folks that we're pulling into the station."

Dad doesn't argue with this as he turns into the parking lot behind Hathaway Police Department, located at the heart of town. Mrs. Vishwakarma's minivan is already in the lot. They shoot out of it as soon as Dad puts the car into park, rushing across the pavement and throwing their arms around Dev. His mother cries into his chest, while his father's shoulders shake and tears streak down his cheeks.

Detective Weegan appears from the squad car that was following us, standing off to the side while Dev's parents check-in with their son.

Not wanting to be out in the open any longer, my dad waves to the detective. "It's getting late, yeah?"

"Yes," Mr. Vishwakarma agrees, pulling back from his son. "I'm sure I want to hear what happened as much as you."

This isn't the first time I've been in the back of the Hathaway Police Station. The first occasion was a harmless visit during a kindergarten field trip.

My second visit wasn't as charming.

Shortly before Gil was born, when I was nine, Dad moved back in because he and Mom were going to "give it another shot." I guess the neighbors heard them having it out one night, so some nosy officer brought me in to hear if things were "okay at home." Of course, I told her everything was fine. What was I supposed to say with my always-fighting-but-supposedly-back-in-love parents standing in the corner?

Then there was the time Valerie ran away. While the entire town organized a search party, I was doing my best to evade the cop's questions about my best friend's location. Though, after one look at the "Missing Person" posters coming in hot from the printer, I caved pretty fast.

This time is nothing like the others. The station is scrambling with officers dashing about, frantically barking orders over radios.

Through the chaos, I catch a glimpse of Marty Boone, sitting in Captain Pierce's office, his arms crossed as he slumps back in her desk chair. The moment he claps eyes on me, he moves to close the door with more force than necessary.

As expected, the officers direct us and the Vishwakarmas into separate interrogation rooms. It's probably the first time both are occupied at once. As we file into our respective rooms across the hall, I catch Dev's eyes, which are glazed with fear.

What if they think we killed Chase? Hopefully, if that were the case, they wouldn't have allowed my parents to drive us over. Not that we could've gone anywhere aside from the station with our escort.

His lips purse. *Tell the truth.*

I give him a slight nod. *As we agreed.*

Good luck.

The doors slam between us. Detective Weegan follows my parents and I inside, gesturing for me to sit at the heavy table in the center of the room.

"Before we start, Weegan," Dad says, his arms crossed in the corner, "do I need to call Hank Saunders?"

I balk at the suggestion. Can we afford to contact the best lawyer in town? Hank and Dad graduated around the same time. They still meet up once a month for a round of cards—the kind of affair where Dad leaves with lighter pockets and a pissy attitude. After all the dollars Hank has collected from my dad over the years, maybe he could give us a discount.

"That's not necessary," Detective Weegan says, his tone unreadable. "Your daughter isn't being charged. We're here to collect a witness report."

"I'm not a fool, Detective. I know you don't handle simple incident reports."

"This isn't a simple incident," Weegan bites back. "A boy is dead."

"I didn't do anything wrong," I pipe up. "Drag Hank over here if you want, but I have nothing to hide."

Mom's gaze meets mine, the corners of her lips just barely turning up. I can tell she's pleased I'm telling the truth. It's one trait I inherited from my parents—an ability to be bluntly honest, at the best of times and the worst.

Weegan's hands come to rest on his belt, shrugging at my father. Silently asking to proceed.

Dad fixes his attention on me, making it perfectly clear this is my last chance for him to call his buddy. If I choose to keep talking, that's on me. I'll have to face those consequences.

There's nothing to hide. Not anymore.

Giving Dad a nod, I turn to Detective Weegan. "What do you want to know?"

To no one's surprise, Detective Weegan wants to know everything. About the messages from Ride or Die and the notes seemingly from Valerie. Unable to meet my parent's ashamed expressions, I explain how Valerie and I used to manage the town's rumor account before it was hacked. After I'm finished detailing the whole tale, I unlock my phone, and slide the device across the table.

My parents share a puzzled look while Weegan reads my DMs with Ride or Die. As he scrolls, his brow grows more and more wrinkled.

"The prime suspect of a murder investigation has been messaging you for days and you didn't think to mention it to the authorities?"

I keep my eyes on Weegan. "They claimed to be holding Valerie captive. If I didn't do what they wanted, they were going to kill her."

"Valerie Ross was reportedly seen at Pineland not two hours ago."

"Nothing makes sense, but please, you have to believe me." My chest begins to heave as my eyes start welling up.

My mother squeezes my arm. "It's okay, baby."

"It's not. All this because of a stupid theme park? Ride or Die held my best friend's life over me so I would help them close Pineland. Now, I'm beginning to question if she was ever really kidnapped."

Weegan's expression is grave. "So, you don't know where Valerie Ross is now?"

"No," I say firmly. "I never knew where she was and I don't know where she is now."

The helplessness in my voice has Weegan putting his pen down on his notepad.

"I take it we're free to go?" Dad asks.

Weegan blinks at me, gnawing on the inside of his cheek, before clearing his throat. "Yes, but please stay close should we need anything else."

"Nowhere else to go," Dad grunts, nodding for me to get up from the table.

Weegan stays sitting, studying his notebook with his brow furrowed. "Did you say you saw Weston McCray's name on the access control log? Right after Luca went in?"

Halfway through the doorway, I turn back. "Yeah? Didn't you see Weston's name, too?"

Weegan doesn't answer—but the look on his face confirms otherwise.

CHAPTER
TWENTY-THREE

IT'S NEARLY midnight when my phone illuminates with a text from Dev. I'm so relieved I could cry, which isn't saying much because I've been a sputtering mess since we left the station.

DEV VISHWAKARMA

spot in 10?

GWEN GARDNER

see ya there

Pressing my palms into my eyes, I try to get a grip. It was easier to remain composed while methodologically answering Weegan's questions. All I had to do was pretend I was telling a story, rather than an account of actual events.

In my dark room, reality is pressing in from all sides. Images of Chase's face pound at the back of my mind, refusing to be forgotten. He's going to get his wish. I'll never, ever forget.

Seeing Luca's body was distressing, but feeling Chase's was life altering.

In the few hours we've been home, I've learned no number

of showers will rid my skin of the haunting itch left by Chase's skin against mine. Even as the water ran cold and my limbs grew raw from countless scrubbings, I came to realize that no matter how hard I try, I will always feel his body beneath me. An invisible scar forever imprinted into my skin.

It's made worse with the mind-numbing worry that the girl I thought was my dearest friend may be the reason he's dead. Why else would she have appeared and then disappeared so quickly? And why hasn't she reached out now?

As soon as we walked in the door, my parents sent me to bed before disappearing into their room. For once, they're quiet while they discuss my predicament. In the morning, I'm sure they'll tell me I have to quit Pineland and how I can never step foot outside of the house again. So, I guess I better enjoy the fresh air while I still can.

Sneaking out became tremendously easy after my parents installed a television in their bedroom. They can't fall asleep without it on. Even now, it's blaring some game show rerun, successfully drowning out their conversation.

The trick used to be leaving my phone behind, on the off chance my mom decided to check everyone's locations before falling asleep. I'm not stupid enough to do this now, so I'll just have to take my chances.

Tugging on my sneakers, I toe my way out of my bedroom and down the stairs, careful to avoid the third step from the bottom, which creaks louder than a grandmother rising from a rocking chair. Our front door is encased by a squeaky screen, so I opt for the sliding backdoor, swiftly slipping into the night.

Dev and I have been meeting at our spot, the playground in the center of our neighborhood, since we were kids. Though, as we grew out of the jungle gym and swing set, the hours in which we assembled grew later and later. It's a space for serious discussions. Ones that can't be risked over the phone. It's where I told Dev that my parents were getting back together and he tearfully shared his grandfather was starting chemo. Where I tried my best to explain why I could never risk getting caught up with anyone from Hathaway. This place has already hurt me too much.

Cutting through the Stuart's backyard, I sprint down the sidewalk once I hit the other side of their house. The park is on the opposite side of the street, shrouded in shadow because the neighborhood wants to discourage people from loitering after nightfall. They don't realize darkness is what we want.

I hold my house keys in my fingers, ready to impale anyone who might sneak up on me. It's best to keep my guard up—especially after I outed Ride or Die to the cops.

In the moonlight, I spy the outline of Dev sitting on one of the two swings. He sways gently, pushing around on his heels. My lips pinch at the sight. It's never a good sign when he doesn't choose the enclosed playhouse at the top of the jungle gym. The swings are too uncomfortable for long conversations, which means Dev wants to keep this short. But why?

"Hey," I say, traipsing over freshly laid mounds of mulch, the true mark that summer is officially underway. Sliding into the swing beside him, only the tips of my toes can graze the ground.

"Hi."

Something's wrong.

"How'd it go with HPD?"

"Fine," Dev responds. "Nice to get the whole truth out there."

Something about the way he says this puts me on the defensive.

"Is there something I should know?"

"I'm just curious if *you* gave the whole truth to the detective."

"Why wouldn't I?"

"Did you tell him you used to be Ride or Die?"

I fall into a stunned silence.

Shit. I should've known Detective Weegan would bring up my association with Ride or Die to see if Dev had anything to add. Now Dev knows, before he had the chance to hear it from me first.

Dev deserves the truth. Every day that I pretend I wasn't once involved with Ride or Die, the deeper my pit of lies grows. Secrets create chasms between friends. Pushing him away is the last thing I want to do. With that resolve in mind, I take a deep breath.

"Yes. Valerie and I started Ride or Die."

Dev's face is unreadable, so I press on.

"It was stupid and mean. Like unbelievably so. I don't even know why we made it in the first place. Hathaway is full of liars. I guess it felt nice to air some secrets. But that's no excuse. It went too far too many times and I hate that I was part of it."

Still no comment.

"But someone stole the account from us. Hacked it and changed the password. Whoever that is—they're the one messaging me and tearing the park apart."

"As opposed to mocking the people working inside?"

I flinch, even though I deserve it. When Valerie and I were in charge, no one in Hathaway was safe from Ride or Die. We scorned anybody and everybody. We even went after ourselves, with rumors about hooking up with guests and half of the hockey team, to throw anyone off our scent. It came with a few weeks of merciless mockery from our peers, but it also did the job.

Dev's not done. "You literally ruined my favorite ride," he mumbles. "I couldn't walk near *A Beaver Tale* without someone accusing me of 'getting it on' with Jenna on one of those boats." He shakes his head. "Like, really? That's disgusting, Gwen. How could you make that up about us?"

"I know," I moan, rubbing my hands down my face. "I was

so upset that you stopped talking to me, but that's no excuse. It was shitty of me."

"Beyond shitty."

"I'm sorry."

Finally, I dare to look over at him, my brow furrowing when I realize he doesn't look furious with me. Sure, there's disappointment in his eyes, but I know Dev. He's not one to let my confessions slide. So why isn't he hopping into an angry lecture? Articulating all the ways I went wrong and whatnot?

"Come on," I finally say, the waiting growing unbearable. "Let me have it. Rip me to shreds for being a horrible person."

"I don't think you're a horrible person."

"But I am one!"

"I thought you were a horrible person last fall when you posted that shit about me and Jenna, but I've had time to get over it."

I pause, digging my toes into the mulch so I stop swaying while I comprehend this.

"Wait," I say slowly, "did you already know the account was mine?"

Dev raises his eyebrows knowingly, making my jaw drop open.

"How long have you known?"

"Amanda told me last summer."

I blink dumbly, my head spinning. "Amanda knew too?"

Who else did she tell? Clearly, not many, or else I would've been burned at the stake by half of Hathaway. So then why tell Dev?

Reading my mind, Dev elaborates, "Amanda figured I was in on it too and confronted me. Needless to say, it was pretty shocking to hear my two best friends were running the town's gossip account."

"Why didn't you ever say anything?" I ask incredulously.

"I did." He pauses, side-eyeing me. "To Valerie."

I chew the inside of my cheek, trying not to be upset that

he went to her instead of me with something this massive. But I have no right to feel anything other than apologetic. "How did that go?"

"Took her a while to come clean, but once I said I was going to ask you instead, she caved." My brow creases as he continues. "She told me you two were going to shut it down soon and that was that."

That was our plan. To delete the account at the end of the school year, before either of us started applying for college. Then it was hacked and we never had the chance.

"I can't believe she didn't tell me you knew."

"Probably because it's 100% her fault that Amanda found out?"

I frown. Valerie should've never shared such a massive secret with a summer fling, especially when they happen to be our boss's granddaughter. But her betrayal feels more on-brand than before.

"Whatever," I say, "it doesn't matter how you found out. What matters is I did something horrible. I'm so, so sorry, Dev."

"I know you are," he says quietly, studying his feet while he chooses his words. "Honestly, I wasn't all that surprised when I heard. You've always hated it here. It was obvious Ride or Die did too. That account was savage, but we all followed it for a reason. Partly because we never wanted to see our name pop up, but mostly because it was entertaining as hell."

"Doesn't make what I said right."

"No, it doesn't. I wasn't sure I believed Valerie when she said you two were going to give up the account, especially after that video of your fight was posted. But obviously you haven't been messaging threats to yourself. I'm just relieved you finally admitted to it."

"I desperately wanted to tell you. It's been eating me alive."

The air around us grows warmer at this. I remember his hand in mine. How can a few hours feel like days ago?

"You couldn't tell me because I pushed you away last year. I really am sorry for not being strong enough to stay your friend," Dev continues after a long pause. "I wanted to respect your rules about Hathaway boys, but I didn't think I could be around you without trying to bend them, even a little. It was better for both of us if I stepped back. Had some time to move on."

After everything that's been said and done on this never-ending day, this is what finally shatters my heart.

Because all I want to do is reach out and grab Dev's hand again. To feel like I'm not alone, floating through space, without any tether to bring me back home—even if right now, that's freaking Hathaway. In a place where nothing is permanent and lasting, Dev feels indefinite. Almost inevitable. I don't want to move on from him.

I've been so afraid of hurting him again that I completely missed how I'm dying to bend my stupid rules and risk the consequences for him.

Mistaking my silence as the conclusion to our conversation, Dev rises from his swing. "We should get back before anyone notices we're gone."

"Wait," I say suddenly, rising too, "what does it mean if you're able to be around me now? That you don't want to bend my rules anymore?"

Dev stops walking towards the sidewalk and turns around. He hesitates, scratching the back of his head before shrugging guiltily. "Your whole world had just imploded. Figured you could use a friend, and that I could put my foolish wishes aside if you wanted that friend to be me again."

"I don't think it's foolish," I spit out, taking both of us by surprise.

I've ignored this—*him*—for too long. Wasted so much

time and potential. I've been so set on escaping Hathaway that I gave up an opportunity to make this place less miserable.

He remains a few feet away, his midnight eyes shining as they dart between mine. "Can you clarify what you mean by that?"

Taking a single step closer, I ignore the fear pounding in my heart.

"I take that back. There's a lot I find foolish." Before his face can fall, I hurriedly continue, "I was foolish to reject you. It was foolish to pretend that I don't feel the same. It's foolish to not think we're more than capable of navigating this—us—with care."

Dev takes a step nearer, but still says nothing. Waiting for me to make my intentions perfectly clear before doing anything.

"Why did you not take a job at Wetlands?" I ask, taking him by surprise.

A sheepish expression crosses his face, and finally, he says meaningfully, "Wetlands wasn't right for me. Pineland always felt more like home, all the risks aside."

"I don't think we're a risk, Dev."

He's quiet as he processes this. "Are—are you sure?"

"I'm sure."

I catch his gaze darting to my lips as he says, "I'll always respect your right to change your mind, but Gwen, it's going to be difficult to forget."

I tilt my chin even higher. "Let's forget everything else instead."

His deep eyes search mine for any doubts. Any misunderstandings.

Making it perfectly clear there are none, I rise on my toes. Dev's hand immediately finds my waist, keeping me balanced as I pull his chin down to my level. Not requiring any further convincing, his other hand curls around the back of my head, his fingers weaving between strands of my hair. And then, after years of resisting this urge, I finally kiss him.

I thought it would feel unfamiliar or wrong. I'm coming to realize I've been incorrect about a lot of things.

Kissing Dev is like finding the missing piece to a puzzle. Before this, our friendship was incomplete. As we fit into place, finding how we meld together, the buzzing in my brain instantly dissipates, leaving nothing but him.

Leading me to the matte-black playground stairs, which are still warm from basking in the sun all day, we settle with me on his lap. Our lips reunite, helplessly eager. I've known Dev forever, yet I'm making a hundred new discoveries. His hair is as soft as it looks. Surprisingly, his stomach is not. There's a spot on his neck that makes his breath hitch when I pass my lips over it.

We only pull away to catch our breath or resituate our cramped legs. Then, like magnets, we're connected again. Exploring. Appreciating. Sighing aloud, "*Finally*."

The world may be on fire, but if we've learned anything, there's nothing more important than to use what time we have wisely.

CHAPTER
TWENTY-FOUR

As EXPECTED, it's a fight to return to Pineland the following morning.

"What I don't understand is why would you even want to go back?" Mom shakes her head with disbelief. Her brunette locks loosely escape a claw clip while she fixes scrambled eggs for Gil.

Dad's not eating, claiming he doesn't have an appetite after last night. Instead, he's refilling Mom's mug with steaming coffee. My eyebrows raise at the gesture. Since when did acts of service become their thing? And since when did they have things? Up until recently, I wouldn't even call their relationship co-existing.

"I need to pay for college somehow! Unless you don't want me to go..."

I have them there. Almost everyone that graduates from Hathaway High goes on to college. It's always been the expectation that I attend, even if we can't afford it.

"There are a dozen other jobs you could work. There's Sal's Grocery, babysitting, Wetlands!"

"There's no way I'm working at Wetlands," I scoff. And

face Jenna after my night with Dev? Never. Not in a million years. I'd risk death over that awkwardness.

Dad helplessly shrugs at my mom. The laundromat can't afford to employ an extra body so he's out of ideas.

"There's no way you're going back to Pineland. Even if you're the Park Ranger."

"Let me get this straight," I bite back. "You want me to ruin my reputation after I fought to repair it." I definitely didn't fight but they don't need to know that. "Classic Gardner move, right?"

"Gwendolyn!" My dad warns as Mom stiffens at the stove.

"I thought we cared what people in this town thought of us." It's a low blow, but I'm over them pretending to be caring parents. I'm not quitting Pineland before I can figure all this out. Detective Weegan sure isn't making any big moves to do so on his own. If I want answers, I'm going to have to find them myself. I need to know what's going on with the girl I thought was my best friend.

Still, one look at my parents' hurt faces and I know I'm taking the wrong approach. "I'll come home right after work. You can track my location all day."

Before my parents can retort, the doorbell rings.

"God, please," Mom moans, moving her eggs around the pan. "Not more cops."

Dad squeezes her arm before heading out of the kitchen.

Seriously, what happened to them?

"Hey, Mr. Gardner!" A voice chirps as soon as the front door swings open.

I fight to keep the smile off my face. Right on cue.

"Morning, Dev," Dad says suspiciously. Makes sense. From his perspective, Dev hasn't been around for the better part of a year, and since his return, I've run into more trouble than ever before. "I'm not sure Gwen's going to make it to work today."

"Really?" Dev asks, his voice drenched with faux

concern. He's sure laying it on thick, but I'm not about to complain. "Because she asked me for a ride like ten minutes ago."

Mom turns around from the stove with an exasperated expression. She sees right through my plan. The wonderful thing is we both know it's going to work. My parents can say no to me all they want, but they won't utter the word to Dev. The last thing they want to do is appear too controlling and messy. That's their old image. Now, they're chill and in-sync. Or at least, they pretend to be. Usually that act only happens outside of the house, but their show at breakfast says otherwise.

I shrug innocently. "How was I supposed to know you didn't want me going in?"

"Because you have a brain." Mom scoops eggs into a dish for Gil, squirting some ketchup on the side, just the way he likes them. "Gwen, honey, a few days of pay isn't worth it. Not until they clear all this up."

"I'll give you a copy of my schedule. I'll text you when I get there and leave. We're ten minutes from the park. You can time me!"

Her head falls to the side, silently pleading for me to reconsider my choices. But we both know I won't. I get my stubbornness from her.

"My parents were only fine with me returning to work because of Pineland's statement this morning. They're heightening security at the park, particularly in backstage areas," my accomplice offers, following my frustrated father into the kitchen.

Dev's eyes immediately land on me, a hint of a smile playing at the corner of his lips. Scenes from last night push the current battle from my brain.

He's not done, apparently.

"I promise to escort Gwen to and from work safely," Dev concludes, batting his dark eyes sincerely. I have to admire his commitment. Even if it means looking like a fool in front of my folks, we're breaking me out of this house.

My parents share a helpless glance while Gil obliviously shovels eggs into his mouth. The game on his tablet beeps obnoxiously, heightening my need to escape.

"I promise not to die," I offer helpfully, earning an exasperated look from both of them.

"And I promise not to let her die."

"Seriously, who's going to kill us in broad daylight?"

"And why would anyone want to kill us?"

Dev and I innocently shrug at each other, as if we've made some incredible points.

"Your parents are really okay with this?" My dad asks skeptically, and I know we've won. The Vishwakarmas are scholars. Brilliant academics who would never make an uneducated decision, especially when it came to their only child.

"Completely," Dev answers quickly. Because he rarely lies, few know that talking swiftly is a humongous giveaway. I study my parents, waiting for them to call our bluff.

But they don't.

"Fine," Dad sighs with defeat. "But I want check-ins on the hour."

"I can't text at work," I start to argue, but Dad shakes his head.

"If you don't message me every single hour, I'm coming to Pineland and killing both of you myself."

"Sounds good." A small smile creeps onto my face. "We get off at 7:30 tonight."

"See you at 7:40," Mom says earnestly, hooking her hand around me and squeezing me close. "I mean it. No lolly-gagging."

"We would never."

With another tight hug from each of my parents and a forced "see ya" from Gil, we're finally out the door, skipping down the porch victoriously.

"I now understand why you never joined the drama club," I say, hopping into Dev's truck. "We're lucky they bought that."

Dev's jaw drops open with offense. "Please, my acting chops are the only reason you're out of the house right now."

"We both know it was your parents' astute reasoning that convinced mine."

"Speaking of, we better get out of here before they realize I brought my uniform to our brunch date."

My eyebrows raise as he backs out of my driveway. "You told your parents we were going on a date?"

His eyes cut over to me. "Is that okay?"

I spent all night mulling over this inevitable question. What now? We can never go back to being just friends. Not when I know what he tastes like.

And with that understanding, I can't help but think— why not go all in? If we can never return to the way things were, why not charge headfirst into what could be?

Dev knows me better than most. He understands why I have my rules. He knows why they mattered so dearly to me. By the way he's peeking over at me now—hesitantly, yet earnestly—I can tell they're echoing at the back of his mind. That's when I realize dating me is just as great of a risk for him.

Glancing at the clock on the dashboard, I'm happy to see we still have time. "Can you pull over for a second?"

I fight back a grin as his grip tightens on the steering wheel. He's bracing for the worst.

"Dev," I say calmly, not wanting him to worry while he parallel parks alongside the grassy square at the center of town, "of course, it's okay."

"Yeah?" He breathes out, failing to mask his relief. A warm smile stretches his lips as he shifts his body to me.

"Yeah."

"I wasn't sure you wanted to break any more rules."

Unable to resist any further, I unbuckle my seatbelt and

stretch across the center console, gently pulling his chin. With a click of his own seatbelt, his hand curls around my face as his lips reach mine, thrilled last night wasn't a fluke. His thumb pets my skin as he kisses me again, and again, and again. Promising it'll be worth it.

"Turns out breaking rules is kinda fun."

He whispers against my lips, "What about after gradua—"

"We'll figure it out then."

"Gwen," he pulls back, playing with the corner of my lips when I pout, "if we're going to risk everything, we need to be open. No matter what."

I nod in agreement. "We're actually doing this."

"About time, if you ask me," Dev laughs, pulling back and buckling his seatbelt. His hand stretches over to rest on my thigh as he continues what's left of our commute.

If Valerie could see us now, she'd lose her mind. Back before our year-long beef with Dev, she was adamant he would be the one to break my rules. I'd rebuke any such idea with a lecture on how boys and girls can truly be "just friends," which I still whole-heartedly believe, but will happily ignore in this case.

The rest of the drive is completely ordinary, like nothing between us has changed, aside from the fact that Dev's hand doesn't leave my thigh.

Then we pass Pineland's front entrance, where almost two dozen protesters are posted out front with signs. We grow silent, staring at the faces—some familiar, some not—of those congregated across the property line. One particularly large sign stands out among the rest. "When is enough bodies enough?"

It's not wrong. At the rate the bodies are appearing, Ride or Die is going to run out of Pineland employees before the end of summer. The park needs to address their security issue and the police need to catch a serial killer. Only then, can Pineland return to somewhat normal.

"You haven't heard from Ride or Die?" Dev asks, as if reading my mind.

I shake my head. "Not since we found Chase."

Not since we saw Valerie.

Dev shoots me a worried look and I wonder if we're still thinking the same thing. What if Ride or Die didn't want us to find Chase's body? It sure sounded like Valerie didn't.

There's a horrible part of me that wants to receive a new message from Ride or Die so I can stop assuming the absolute worst about my best friend. There's a part of me that wants to be all wrong. Maybe Valerie is actually Ride or Die's prisoner. Maybe she escaped last night.

But then why didn't she stay?

After we park, Dev pulls me back to him, covering my lips with his for a moment. "Try not to make any life-or-death discoveries today, yeah?" His thumb caresses over my cheek again, begging me to see past his brevity and understand he means his words. No bodies. No schemes. No danger.

I press my lips against his, silently apologizing for how I'm about to disappoint him.

"Gwen," he groans. Of course, he can tell I'm full of risks today, because with Valerie gone, he's the person in this world who knows me best.

CHAPTER
TWENTY-FIVE

It's scary how normal it feels inside the park. All the attractions have decent waits and every one of my shows collects a sizable crowd. Apparently driving past the crowd of protesters isn't enough to deter guests from quelling their summer boredom.

Without Chase, Sybil is also absent from the park. I half-wondered if they would have me step into the costume again, but clearly, Marty Boone deemed his prized Park Ranger more important than the mascot. Or perhaps, he was hoping people's minds would be off Chase and Sybil while they spend money in his park.

No one seems to have noticed Dev is without a character to attend, so he's wandering around the park until someone catches on. Without Hannah in charge, that may be a while. I find him frequently loitering around my programs, keeping a close eye on me.

As promised, between each of my forty-five-minute shows, I duck backstage to shoot my parents a "still alive" text. Then, while my phone is already out, I can't resist checking the news online.

That's how most of my morning goes. Perform a program, text my parents, doom scroll, repeat.

"The red squirrel is one of nearly three-hundred types of squirrels found worldwide. Fortunately, like our friend Sybil, many choose to call Michigan their home. This is thanks to our plethora of conifer, or evergreen, trees!"

GWEN GARDNER

Hi! I'm alive!

PINELAND FAN ZONE *@pinelandfanzone*
Another death?! This is devastating. Can the cops do their jobs already? Pineland better close to fix their security issues. While they're at it, maybe it's time to update some of those sketchy rides too.

"IF YOU ENCOUNTER an unfamiliar plant on your adventure, it's important to do your research! Coming in contact with pesky plants like poison ivy, hemlock, foxglove, and if you can believe it, mistletoe can cause serious reactions. Should you dare, you may discover more at the Preying Plant exhibit, located just past the *Deciduous Divers* gift shop!"

GWEN GARDNER

Still alive!

CHANNEL 8 OHIO *@Channel8OH*
News of a 4th death at a popular theme park in MI has many guests and employees concerned. Tune into Channel 8 for an exclusive interview with a friend of the latest victim.

. . .

 me, but of course Ride or Die can't stay out of the action.

Ride or Die *@RideOrDie*

Is anyone really surprised? It's business as usual for Marty Boone while the bodies pile up in his park. I thought the theme was nature not "natural causes?" As if we ever believed that lie…

The account has become the face of the cause, something I suspect they wanted all along. Even as the movement grows, one look at the park proves it's still not enough.

I can't think of why anyone would be so desperate to shut down Pineland. How could so many dead be worth it?

I crave for it to make sense, but fear what I will discover. *Who* I will discover.

I'm sure of a few things. Weston and Amanda aren't behind this. Amanda was at the vigil while Chase's body was stashed in the Old Wheel. And someone is trying as hard as they can to set up Weston, but not with the cops, which is what has me puzzled. Someone—presumably, Ride or Die— knew we would inevitably check the security log. For some reason, they don't want us to trust Weston. I don't know why yet, but I have every intention of figuring it out.

This is why I ask Dev, Weston, and Amanda to coordinate our afternoon breaks, so we can meet before the end of the day. I'd have asked Milly to join us too, but she isn't scheduled until 6:00pm, an hour before the park closes and I'm due home.

It took some finagling and begging other crew members to switch breaks around, but by mid-afternoon, we've claimed a booth in the corner of the cafeteria where no one can overhear us. Not that we'd have to worry about that. All other crew members in the break room are also huddled at tables, whispering about the horrors that continue to strike our place of work. I notice there are less employees than usual and immediately wonder how many quit this morning.

Dark creases loom beneath Amanda's eyes and Weston's shaggy hair appears messier than normal.

"Long night?" Dev asks, the last to join.

"It wasn't for you?" Amanda bites back, clearly not in the mood.

Best to get straight to the point. We only have so much time before we have to get back.

Weston must sense this too, because he mutters, "I swear, I never went into the Fake Oak the night Luca died." His sad eyes linger on me, begging me to believe him.

"Why would someone want us to think you had?"

"Ride or Die is trying to get us all mixed up. Besides, it's easy to pin Luca's death on me." His eyes fall to his lap, where I'm sure he's wringing his hands. "Everyone knew we were competitive and didn't always see eye-to-eye. But we all have people who push us like that. That doesn't mean we want them dead."

I nod with understanding. It makes sense. Weston is an easy scapegoat. Luca always was one step ahead in everything —hockey, girls, school. With Luca gone, Weston could finally achieve his full potential. Have everything that was once Luca's.

"There's something else too," Weston says, still fiddling with his fingers in his lap. He plays with the words on his tongue, as if debating with himself if he should come out and say it. Finally, after a painfully long pause, he whispers, "I think I know who killed Luca."

The table falls completely silent as we take in his words.

"You do?" Dev recovers first, blinking at me with surprise. How could Weston have an idea who's behind all this and not say a thing?

Weston nods, and when I notice the fear glazing his eyes, a

chill shoots up my spine. "It's only a theory, but I'd be willing to bet pretty much anything on it."

"Who?" I ask, terrified of the name he's about to utter.

"I guess it doesn't matter now," he says with a shake of his head. "It was Chase."

We all suck in a breath.

"Why do you think Chase killed Luca?" Amanda asks, her voice barely audible.

"It was the night of Open Season. I made it into HQ and Gwen told me about Valerie and Luca being together. That was obviously disappointing to hear—Luca knew how interested I was in Valerie, but just like anything else I wanted, he decided to take her first. The endless competition got old after a while. Luca always wins. I figured it was better for me to just go.

"I was almost to my car when I heard Chase screaming to someone over his phone."

"Screaming what?"

"I couldn't make it out at first." Weston's brow furrows while he thinks. "Then he calmed down for a second and I heard him say, 'they did what was necessary' and 'it wasn't her fault that he died.'"

"Her?" I breathe out.

Dev's caught up on a different word. "*They*? Chase wasn't acting alone?"

"All I know is that Chase saw me. He knows I heard him." Weston swallows hard, choosing his words carefully. "The next morning, right after Valerie found Luca's body, I started getting these messages."

My stomach drops.

Does everyone have a mine of secrets buried deep?

"From Ride or Die?" Dev's mouth falls open. "You are getting them too?"

I'm in such disbelief that Weston was also being messaged,

I don't even care that Dev revealed I was receiving threatening DMs from Ride or Die too.

After Weston nods, I ask, "What did Ride or Die want with you?"

"To keep me quiet." Weston pulls out his phone, pressing the screen a few times before scrolling for a moment. He turns it towards us and we all lean forward to read.

I'm morbidly disappointed to discover Ride or Die only messaged Weston twice.

@RIDEORDIE

We all know who really killed Luca. The boy who hated him most.

@WESTONMC46

idk who this is but everyone knows i'd never hurt luca

@RIDEORDIE

Are you confident about that? Don't talk to the cops and I'll make sure they don't suspect you.

@WESTONMC46

whats that supposed to mean?

hello??

"I always wondered if Chase was the mastermind behind that account," Weston grumbles.

"Did you share this with the police?" Dev asks, surely thinking about Weston's name suddenly appearing on the log.

"And let Ride or Die frame me for murder?" He scoffs at the irony. "I bit my tongue and they still screwed me over."

"But not for the cops," I mumble, my mind still reeling that Chase might be a victim of his own cause. This unlocks a whole slew of new theories. "Ride or Die didn't want you telling us that you heard Chase because they knew we'd figure something out."

"But what?"

I shrug, at a complete loss for what Chase's involvement could mean. He did speak pretty negatively of Ms. Sandy, but I never assumed he could be involved in her death over something as stupid as a failed grade.

"Maybe he was one of the two figures on the Old Wheel security feed?"

"Pointing out where his body would be found?" Dev shakes his head skeptically. "That's a little grotesque, don't you think?"

"Isn't all of this?"

"You say Chase was good with a computer?" Amanda asks. "Like how good?"

"Like he changed-my-hockey-stats-on-the-recruiting-site good."

"I wonder if he could have messed with the access control log," I ponder aloud.

"Chase would still need to have scanned an ID before changing the name on the log. Think he'd risk scanning his own to modify?"

My eyes squeeze shut as it hits me.

"My ID's been missing since Open Season," I breathe out, cursing my ignorance. "We'd definitely know if the police saw my name enter the Great Oak after Luca's."

"So, whose name did they see, if it wasn't yours or Weston's?"

Without the answer to Dev's question, we all fall silent. I return to what we do know.

"Regardless of who's name it was initially, someone had to know we were going to check the security log so they could change it to Weston. They didn't want us trusting each other."

Weston sits back, his arms crossing. "There's only one

person who was aware of our intentions to check the access control log. In fact, it was her idea."

We all share an uncomfortable glance, not wanting to say her name aloud.

"It's all over the news that Valerie Ross appeared at the crime scene and then took off. Did you really see her last night?" Amanda asks timidly, as if not wanting to believe it could be true.

Dev and I nod.

"She yelled up to me right as I was about to find Chase's body." My voice grows hollow as I remember the scene.

"And what made you two go to the Old Wheel in the first place?" Weston probes. "Was it Ride or Die?"

"We went on a whim. A total gut feeling. I don't think our suspect expected us to turn up at the Old Wheel. In fact, I don't think they intended for Chase's body to be found until much, much later."

Amanda is suspiciously staring me down.

Then it hits me. She still thinks I'm running that account. "Someone hacked the Ride or Die account. Valerie and I lost access to it after Open Season."

"What?" Amanda gapes.

"Hold up," Weston interjects, "You two used to run Ride or Die? For real?"

By the way his eyes are bugging out, Weston is likely recalling how we ruthlessly scorned pretty much every member of the hockey team after they convinced the whole school to skip opening night of our fall musical for a game.

"It was obviously a messed-up thing to do and I'm sorry we ever made the account. But I'm not the one who sent you those messages."

"Good going," Weston scoffs. "You lost a bogus platform to a serial killer."

"If it makes you feel better, they were harassing me too."

Weston frowns. "How so?"

I swallow, deliberating how detailed I want to get. "They wanted me to plant evidence that could turn the public's opinion on Pineland. Like Luca's autopsy."

"You were the one to leak that?" Amanda asks incredulously.

"They said if I didn't, Valerie would die!"

"Valerie's name is sure popping up a lot right now." Weston clicks his tongue. "Are you confident she lost access to that account too?"

"Yes," I say, hating how uncertain I sound.

Silence falls over the table, all of us wondering if we completely misjudged the girl who claimed a starring role in every one of our lives. I think of the mess we found in costuming. How frightened we were for her safety. Was all that a sham? Part of some show? I'm not sure Valerie is the victim anymore, but I'm terrified to start thinking of her as the villain.

Weston snaps the spell. "My break's almost done."

"Mine too," Amanda says.

I'm tempted to point out that there's no one around to get them in trouble for returning late, but maybe they want to escape this conversation. I can't blame them. We aren't getting anywhere and I'm confident we'll all leave feeling worse than when we started.

"I still don't understand how they got his body up there," Amanda says to herself, following Weston out of the booth.

"Maybe Ride or Die is also an electrical engineer," Weston grunts sarcastically, "and got the damn thing working again. Later, y'all." He doesn't wait for us to say our goodbyes before trudging out of the cafeteria.

After watching them go, I turn to find Dev lost in thought.

"How *did* they get Chase's body to the top of the Old Wheel? It's not like they could've carried him up there. The cops were under the impression that Chase died elsewhere and his body was hidden at the Ferris Wheel."

"Maybe Weston's right and they got it spinning again," I joke, my brow furrowing when Dev cocks his head to the side. "You can't be serious?"

"There was that weird power surge last night." Dev shrugs. "Sounds like a question for the maintenance team."

"Hey guys!" I mime, "Just wondered if anyone around here made the old, run-down Ferris Wheel start working for the first time in two decades to hide a body?"

"Maybe I'll do the talking," he says, nudging me to leave the booth. "How many people do you think care about your next show?"

"The one about natural pesticides?"

"Perfect. Skip it."

"And get fired?"

"Please," Dev scoffs, "we're more likely to die than be fired."

TWENTY-SIX

"Hey, Rusty," I chirp as casually as possible when we exit out of the stairwell and into the basement. "Long time, no see!"

"Miss Gardner!" The security officer beams at us, making my racing heart calm a little.

The space may be as shadowy as last night, but this sunny man's disposition warms the gloomy room. He's bald and stout, with a smile that could power half the property. The kind of employee who buys into the "Pineland saves the world" crap, Rusty has worked at the park for longer than I've been alive. "What brings you and dear Mr. Vishwakarma into my dungeon?"

"Can you believe this one lost her ID again?" Dev disappointedly clicks his tongue.

Rusty sighs, clapping his hands on the desk knowingly, though the smile doesn't abandon his lips. "You know what— I can. What is this, Gwendolyn, badge number three?"

"Yes," I admit guiltily. Two were 100% my fault. I accidentally sent the first through the washing machine and ruined whatever computer chip was on the inside. I'm confident the second fell out of my pocket during one of the loops on *Pine-*

ageddon, so I obviously never saw that sucker again. The third, well, I'm not sure how Ride or Die got their hands on it, but there are some questions I don't want answered because I know it'll just piss me off.

"I figured you were due for another trip down here after I sent last week's staffing log to payroll." He leans over his desk, raising his eyebrows. "You're lucky I assumed you were here and marked you as such."

"Thanks, Rus." I smile, relieved my gamble paid off. Rusty is far more agreeable than Hannah, and as we are still without an entertainment manager, I'll happily cut straight to asking the source for a replacement rather than go through the chain of command.

"Give me a few minutes and I'll print you a new one," he says, rising from his seat with a groan before shuffling into the back room.

The moment he's out of sight, Dev and I hurry to the other side of the basement, where the door to the maintenance office is barely cracked.

We debated if we should spend our time looking at the access control log for footage of the Old Wheel turning and someone stashing Chase's body but deemed it too great a risk. Surely, the camera feed was the first thing HPD checked. I wouldn't be surprised if the footage was destroyed.

Gently pushing the door into maintenance open, we poke our heads inside the dimly lit room. There's no sign of anyone, though perhaps that shouldn't be much of a surprise. Pineland is literally held together by its maintenance team. The toolbelt-clad folk who run around this park during all hours of the day and night earn their bad attitudes. Hopefully, I'm not about to piss them off even more.

With no one here to probe about how electricity works in the park, I resort to poking around the two desks on either side of the room. They must be shared between the department because the wall space above each desk is collaged with photos of numerous families, pets, and the maintenance team pictures from over the years.

Discouraged, my head shakes. "Let's just go." The mildew smell clinging to this glorified closet is making my stomach curl.

"Wait," Dev says from the back wall behind the second desk, "can you come here?"

"What is it?"

He's studying a collection of pictures in mismatched frames that have been screwed into the cinderblock wall. They're group photos, each featuring five or six people all wearing olive-green overalls and tool belts, standing before various attractions. Captions like "Deciduous Divers Grand Opening 1998" are pasted on the bottom of the frame, written in Sharpie on strips of masking tape.

"The team that helped bring each ride to life."

Most of the pictures are fuzzy with age and feature people who have likely retired. It may not look like it from their dominion in the basement, but it's widely known that Marty Boone takes care of his maintenance teams long after they work for him. Most positions are replaceable, but being able to make a broken ride work again is a skill high in demand around these parts.

As demonstrated in the hanging pictures, only a handful of rides have been added to the property in the last decade. It's a lot harder to get your picture on the wall when Marty Boone isn't desperate for ticket sales. Though, between the shiny, new park down the road and the bad press, I wouldn't be surprised if more pictures were hung over the next few years. If we can stay open that long.

Dev points to one of the older shots higher up on the wall. Craning, I stretch on my toes to get a decent look at it.

"Wolverine Racers Grand Opening 1988," I read aloud. "That's a year after the park opened."

"You don't think that's him?" Dev asks.

"Who?" My eyes dart around the picture, hunting for a recognizable face. It's difficult with the low-quality resolution and the knowledge these people are all decades older now.

But then my focus lands on a clean-shaven face with a familiar smile. I almost don't recognize the younger man without a cane, but upon further inspection, there's no mistaking him.

I suck in a deep breath. "Valerie's dad worked at Pineland?"

Add that to the growing list of things I didn't know about my best friend.

I instantly search the other pictures for Mr. Ross, but Dev stops me. "He's not in any others."

"He only worked at Pineland in '88?"

"I wonder why he left?" Dev's voice trails off, his brow wrinkling.

Valerie never once mentioned her dad had any ties to Pineland. Being a park legacy is a big deal around here. Children and grandchildren wear their family's longtime ties with Pineland like a badge of honor. Whether it's the annual legacy luncheon or first pick at job locations, Pineland is a fraternity and Marty Boone loves to reward loyalty.

"What are you two doing in here?"

We both jump at Rusty's voice behind us.

Shit.

We turn, immediately sporting innocent grins.

"You know me! Can't help but be nosy."

"Yeah," Dev chimes in, his voice shaking slightly as his eyes dart to the stack of nameplates on one desk, "we wanted to see if Marietta was around and got distracted by the old pictures."

A curious smile on his face, Rusty's bright blue eyes jump between us. After an agonizing pause, he finally says, "I've been telling them to start an internship. Kids are interested in how rides operate."

"Uh, yeah, that's a great idea," I agree. "Keep badgering them about it!"

"You know I will." Rusty grins, holding out my new lime-green badge. "I'm not writing you up, but don't count on the new entertainment manager to be as friendly. Try to keep track of this one."

I laugh dryly, "I'll do my best." Squeezing the card tight in my hand so that the curved edges press into my palm, I vow not to let this one out of my sight. Maybe I'll invest in one of those fancy, extendable badge holders that the way-too-into-their-job crew members sport around their waist for easy access. "Thanks again, Rusty."

"Anything for you, kid. You let me know if you need help with anything else, okay?" He says, giving me one of those smiles you only receive from an adult who pities you. You'd think I'd be immune to it by now, after receiving this sad-eyed grin from every single one of my teachers, coaches, and older colleagues. Behind those eyes, I can see each one of them wonder if my home life might actually be as messy as it looks.

It's not as bad as they think. At least, not anymore. I remember the tenderness in which my parents addressed each other this morning. I'm not naive enough to think it a fluke or hiccup to their natural state of general dislike, but perhaps they're inching towards tolerance. At this point, I'll take what I can get. It's better than them lying about being in love when I know they're not.

"I owe you one," I say, willing him to stop looking at me like that.

"You could never owe me," he says warmly and I know he means it. That's one of the best things about Rusty. He never cashes in. He doesn't keep score. He's just nice to be nice.

"We should probably get back," Dev says and Rusty happily steps out of the doorway, allowing us to pass. "Thanks for helping her out, man."

"Easiest part of my day," Rusty says and I believe him. His

chipper demeanor cracks slightly as we all share the same thought. This day started with the news of another death. "I better get back to the monitors," he adds soberly.

We nod understandably, selfishly relieved for the out.

I wave my ID badge, saying, "Thanks again," while dragging Dev to the stairs.

Just when I think we've gotten away, Rusty's radio crackles behind us. "Anyone know Park Ranger Gwendolyn's 20?"

We freeze at the bottom of the stairwell. My mouth goes dry as Dev's head whips towards me. Neither of us dare to say a word, hoping Rusty will forget we are even there.

Of course, he doesn't.

"Hold up, kids!" He calls after us, before speaking into his radio, "This is Rusty Porter down in the security base. I was just wrapping up with Gwendolyn down here."

He winks at me as we return to the basement, proving he'll keep the reason for my visit a secret. I'd appreciate the gesture more if I wasn't so stressed about why someone was calling for me over the radio.

The radio beeps again. "Marty Boone needs her in his office."

My heart stops ticking. What does Marty Boone want with me? Am I about to get fired for skipping one program? Is it because of Chase? Or Valerie?

Beside me, Dev is rigid. "Not me too?"

"Sorry, kid," Rusty says, as if Dev would want to pay Marty Boone a visit.

"Thanks for passing along the message," I manage after clearing my throat. Every meeting with Marty Boone feels like a death sentence. The last trip certainly was one.

"Later, kids," Rusty calls after us as we climb the stairs once more.

"What do you think Marty wants?" Dev hisses when we're out of earshot.

"Maybe he found out I skipped my last program."

"You believe he's that in tune with the hourly operations of the park?"

"You don't?"

We pass the opening to the main floor and keep ascending towards the offices above. Apparently, Dev is going to climb the whole way with me, not that I'm complaining about the company.

"What if it's about Valerie? Or last night?"

"Don't you think he'd want to talk to both of us?"

At a loss, Dev scratches the back of his head. "You're his precious Park Ranger, not me."

We near the top of the stairs, slowing with each step. Not yet ready to face what awaits. Silently, Dev reaches for my hand.

"Don't get in trouble for skipping more of your shift," I mumble, squeezing his hand.

His eyebrows raise. "Please, no one's noticed I'm missing. I'll be right out here."

The corners of my lips lift. I wish I didn't have to get used to him waiting outside Marty's office, but I have no intentions of making it a habit. Pecking Dev's lips, I leave him at the top of the stairs.

Before the anticipation can eat away at me any further, I knock on the wooden door leading to the president's office.

My mouth parts when it's opened by Luther Flannigan. The older gentleman frowns at the sight of me.

"I—"

"Have the appointment after me, apparently," he grunts. Thanks to me, this man has had to work overtime the last few weeks. Little does he know I've done more to damage the park's reputation than causing a scene at Open Season and finding Chase's body.

"Come on in, Gwendolyn," Marty calls from behind Luther. "We were just finishing."

Mr. Flannigan's scowl makes it quite clear they weren't "just finishing," but he excuses himself nonetheless.

His tongue clicking with amusement at his colleague's displeasure, Marty waves for me to close the door after him. "No one loves to work more than Luther. He'd sleep in here if I let him."

Not knowing what to say to that, I can only nod.

The curtains are drawn, leaving the office in murky shadows as sunlight presses against the windows, fighting to do its job and brighten the space. The only other light in the room comes from Marty's desk lamp, which just barely illuminates his face.

"I get my best work done at night," Marty explains before I can ask, "but alas, duty calls for me to be present during business hours, so I have to make do." His hand casually waves around the dark office. Between the miniature models of coasters and attraction props, if you squint, it's not impossible to pretend you're wandering the park at dusk.

The last thing I want to do is outright ask why the park president beckoned me to his office, but I'm not sure my anxiety can handle waiting much longer.

Again, as if he's reading my mind, Marty gestures towards the leather seat before his desk. "I'm sure you're curious as to why I asked you here."

His tone is unreadable. Am I about to be fired? Did they discover my best friend's body? Or did they find my best friend killing someone? Each possibility is worse than the last.

Swallowing, I slide into the seat.

"I'll keep this brief, as I don't want you missing too many of your afternoon programs," he tacks on knowingly.

I'm not dumb enough to out my prior antics without a proper accusation, so I only nod again. His eyes glint with amusement.

"I asked you here because I wanted to apologize."

I suck in a surprised breath. "Apologize?"

The leather on his chair squeaks as Marty shifts in his seat, clearly also uncomfortable by what he's about to share.

Oh God—did they find another body? Did they find her?

Marty clears his throat, folding his hands atop his desk. "I didn't fully understand the cause for alarm about your friend, Valerie."

He blinks at me like it's my turn to speak.

"Um, thanks."

When he realizes this is the best he's going to get, he continues. "I'm sure I don't have to explain to you how devastating the last few weeks have been for Pineland. It's difficult to sleep knowing perpetrators are targeting this property to carry out such horrific, unspeakable acts."

My mouth grows dry at his acknowledgement that the deaths are more than freaky coincidences.

"At first, I wasn't confident someone was behind the four devastating deaths that have occurred in my park. Unfortunately, tragic accidents are not uncommon in this industry, though most parks are better at keeping theirs out of the spotlight. But after it happened again and again, I began to doubt the coroner's claims of natural causes. This couldn't be natural. Not at my park."

His misty eyes crease with sadness. It's only now that I notice the glint of silver scruff covering his cheeks. Normally clean shaven, recent events have clearly taken a toll on Marty Boone.

"The Hathaway Police Department is stuck, and not due to a lack of support from Pineland. They've hit every roadblock imaginable: A criminal that's familiar with our property, grieving families who don't want to cooperate for fear of it making headlines, a hatefully anonymous social media account with an untraceable IP address." He trails off, pinching the bridge of his papery nose. "If I'd only believed the worst from the start, I wonder if we'd not be having this conversation."

"Why are we having this conversation?"

The question slips out before I can evaluate its bluntness. But why is he saying all of this to me? Marty Boone is a busy man. There must be some purpose to this meeting—and I'm beginning to feel like it isn't to apologize.

"Captain Pierce mentioned you saw Valerie last night."

"I only heard her, really," I mumble.

"Do you think she was abducted and then escaped her captor or—"

My head shakes with confusion. "I don't know."

Why is he asking me this? Surely, Nora Pierce shared the entire account of yesterday's events with her boyfriend. Dev and I already told the department everything we knew about last night, including Valerie's strange appearance and equally fast disappearance.

"Gwendolyn," Marty Boone says softly, "I remember the friendships I kept at your age. I grew up in Hathaway too. The town felt even smaller back then, if you can believe it. I remember having to keep secrets too. Though, in the end, the truth usually found its way out."

"I don't know where Valerie is," I say immediately. "I already told the cops this."

The corners of his eyes wrinkle with pity. "Are you sure?"

"Why would I lie?"

Leaning back in his seat, Marty studies me with a peculiar look on his face. It sucks to know he doesn't believe me. What's worse is I'm actually telling the truth. I want Valerie home safe. I need her to put my mind at ease.

"I swear," I say as sincerely as possible, "I have no idea where she came from or where she is now. I don't know if she's in danger or—"

"Or?"

Our eyes meet and I know we're both thinking the same thing. I don't dare say it aloud for fear of it coming true. He won't because he doesn't want to accuse a seventeen-year-old of being a serial killer.

"I don't know where she is," I say firmly. "Trust me, no one wants her home safe more than those who love her most."

He stares at me for a long while, determining if he believes me. I refuse to avert my gaze and let him think I'm anything but serious.

He eyes me for another moment before patting his desk with finality. "Well, let's not keep our guests waiting any longer, shall we?"

That's it? Marty Boone called me into his office under the guise of apologizing to pry about my best friend's disappearance? As if I was going to tell him something I didn't already share with the police?

"Yeah, we don't want to let them down."

"No, we certainly don't."

"It was kind of you to check-in." I almost sound like I mean it.

"I care so deeply for the people in this park."

"That's very apparent."

From the way he's smiling, I can tell he knows I'm lying. If given the chance to pick between the people working here, the planet, or the money earned by the park, I think it's clear which Marty would choose.

I rise from my seat, leaving certain of one thing: Absolutely nothing good can come of a man like Marty Boone suspecting Valerie is the one destroying his theme park.

CHAPTER
TWENTY-SEVEN

As promised, Dev is waiting in the stairwell. Sat three steps from the top, he startles as I approach. "Sorry, waiting for an important call about my—oh, it's you!"

"I take it you've been in the way?"

He waves my question off. "Are you okay? What happened?"

I recount my vague and uncomfortable meeting with Marty as we trod down the stairs, and by the time we're back on the main floor, Dev's jaw is slack at the stupidity of it all.

"What was the old man expecting? For you to come out and say where Valerie is hiding?"

"Apparently, I can trust him more than the cops!"

Dev shakes his head with disbelief. "So glad I worked myself into a state over that."

It does feel like a weird waste of time for an incredibly busy man. Did he think he could decipher if I was telling the truth or not by looking at my face? Because if I'm the sort who could convincingly lie to the cops, I definitely could fool an old park president.

"Yeah, I'm not sure what he was getting at," I say, wishing

it made more sense. I don't like how uneasy I feel after that conversation. Like I'm missing the point.

All I know is Marty Boone is the last man in town that I want to suspect Valerie and I of foul play. The longer she's away, the worse it looks for the both of us.

My lips pinch with frustration as we exit Crew HQ. It's a hellishly hot day. The kind where the warm air molds around you, without any hint of a forgiving breeze.

I guess it could be worse. I could be trapped in the Sybil costume.

My next program is in *The Glade*, towards the opposite side of the property, where many of the park's thrill rides are located. Outside the wooden coaster, *Everscream*, I teach guests about how Pineland "carefully and intentionally cleared only the necessary trees from the surrounding forest to make room for a theme park." Definitely no ulterior motive behind that program.

Making it perfectly clear he won't be doing any real work today, Dev walks in that direction with me.

"I looked up some stuff while you were in there," he says under his breath as I wave at a guest calling over to us. "I started with searching for Valerie's dad, Charles Ross. That was a bust. I was hoping for an online resume to document a bit about his time at Pineland, but nope. According to the internet, Valerie's dad doesn't exist."

"Who isn't online?"

"That's what I thought."

Passing the sounds of screaming guests flying down the steep hill of *Climate Coaster*, we head towards the Fake Oak at the hub of the park. The tree is back in business, hosting a singing troupe under its foliage. Guests queue for group photos taken by a park photographer with a wobbly tripod. Prints are sold at the front of the park for a pretty price. This evening, the hub will be crowded as guests view the evening spectacle, *Leaves of Light*, where various seasons are projection mapped over the Great Oak. It's the closest Marty is ever going to get to a nighttime firework display—something the Fire Marshall would never approve to take place in the middle of a forest.

The soothing scent of warm greenery fills my nose and I try to allow it to settle me. Though, I'm not sure the sweet air could ever make me forget where I am. What really goes on in this theme park.

Everyone here is a liar. The guests. The crew. We pretend all is well while sporting too big smiles and picking at cotton candy, but it's all a sham. Nothing at Pineland is okay.

But I guess that's how lies go. You spin them for so long you start believing they're true.

"I looked up Pineland 1988," Dev continues. Something in his voice shifts.

My eyes dart up to him with interest. "What did you find?"

"Not a lot at first. There isn't much record of what the park was up to other than a few articles about the environmental activist stuff, which happened a few years prior."

I nod, egging him to hurry up. "We have five minutes before I have to preach about Pineland."

"I'm getting to it," Dev says, throwing me a look to be patient. "Okay, fast forward a few sites, to this blog about small amusement parks."

"A blog?" I say with disbelief. "Who even blogs anymore?"

Dev's eyebrows wag. "Apparently, that reporter we met. Abigail Herron."

My jaw drops open. "What?"

So, Abigail has a thing for theme park drama. I guess I shouldn't be surprised considering how involved she is with this story.

"I think it was a passion project when she was younger. Maybe while in college? It hasn't been updated for years. But she wrote all about scandals that parks did their best to keep out of the news."

"How did she get her scoop?"

"Interviews with employees."

"Who weren't worried about the consequences of spilling company secrets?"

"She keeps her sources anonymous. And besides, we're talking about poorly paid, hourly employees. I'm sure a lot of crew members would open their mouths for a coffee and gift card."

I can't argue with that. I've seen crew members sell their souls for a cheap popsicle.

"What did she have to say about 1988?"

"Apparently, Marty was rushing to open *Wolverine Racers* because he was desperate for guests to return for Pineland's second operational season."

"Wouldn't be the first time he's rushed an attraction."

"This is worse than the cheap animatronics on *Sybil Saves the World*."

My brow creases. "What happened?"

"A cable snapped about a month after it opened. No guests were riding. Just a few maintenance crew members who were working overnight to keep the coaster running."

My eyes squeeze shut. I don't need to hear any more. I just can't believe Valerie never told me. Sure, neither of us were alive, but how do you say nothing? How does it never come up?

Dev's forehead creases and I know he's just as upset as me. "Valerie's dad isn't named in the post, but there's a vague mention that a crew member may have been injured."

"Can I see this blog?"

Dev passes me his phone. With one glance at the authentic Y2K layout, I can tell the blog is ancient. The background is fuchsia, cram packed with small, black text. My eyes strain to read the post entitled, "Theme Park Investigator: Pineland Edition."

Pressed for time, I skim to get the gist. Abigail had an anonymous source "extremely close to the situation" that was willing to go on the record about the tragedy. Apparently, an "undisclosed employee" was working overtime, trying to get the park's latest attraction running reliably. They were not using the correct safety gear while climbing the ride and fell. According to the source, they were seriously injured.

Not wanting to read any more, I return Dev's phone. He hastily stuffs it into his back pocket. Either he doesn't want to be caught with it on-the-clock, or more likely, he also wishes the puzzle wasn't coming together this way.

I think about Charles Ross, who has used a cane for as long as I've known him. When we were younger, Valerie mentioned he's always had it and I wasn't the type to rudely pry about her father's medical history.

Pineland suddenly feels quieter. The sounds of area music and energetic guests grow muffled as blood pounds in my ears.

I've never wanted to be wrong more in my life.

"You okay?" Dev asks softly. I sense him wanting to reach for me.

"Do you really think she's capable of all this?" I whisper.

Dev spares me a knowing glance. We both know Valerie's taste for revenge. She's the type to let nothing slide.

We silently pass through the hub and head for the far side of the park. The Glade is themed like an old campground, complete with an RV park, fishing carnival games, and a sing-along around a faux, forest-friendly campfire. My mouth grows dry as we pass *Wolverine Racers*, where a green train clicks up the lift hill. The snaking queue out front is packed with guests, most who have no idea Ms. Wade wasn't the only accident to occur at this attraction. Mr. Ross's life changed here too.

"Why did Valerie never say anything?"

Dev's concerned gaze darts to me. "Maybe she couldn't? Maybe Marty paid them to keep quiet or something?"

"Even so, Mr. Ross stopped working at Pineland immediately after the incident. Surely someone in Hathaway put two-and-two together with the timing. It's too small a town for no one to bring it up."

"Yet no one except Abigail did."

"Maybe Valerie had enough of everyone letting Marty get away with it," I murmur, my heart aching as I piece it all together. "She might not have been able to outright say what happened, but—"

"What if she decided to get back at Marty?" Dev's concerned gaze meets mine.

"Enough of this," I say, pulling out my phone. I don't care if there are hundreds of guests around. I'm done.

My message to her is simple.

GWEN GARDNER

> I know you need help. 8:00. Safe space.
> Just us.

If I'm right—and honestly, I really hope I'm not—she'll see it.

Maybe it's all a misunderstanding or maybe my best friend is a serial killer. Regardless, it's time to learn the truth for myself, no matter how much it hurts.

CHAPTER
TWENTY-EIGHT

"THIS IS SUCH A STUPID IDEA," Dev groans, anxiously tapping his fingers on the wheel as we sit parked in the school lot.

It took another round of convincing my folks to let me back out of the house after our shift ended. Dev swore we were just going to grab a scoop of ice cream (lie) and that he would be by my side the whole time (another lie, no matter how much he hates it). After almost ten-minutes of pleading, promising, and puppy-dog eyeing, my parents finally caved. Honestly, I wasn't confident they would, but once Dev put his arm around my shoulder, something in them changed. Maybe they saw a glimmer of their past lives. Grabbing sweet treats on summer nights. A time when they were actually happy and not just pretending to be. They let us drive off after that, saying we had an hour before they were calling the cops to come find us.

Pulling up to school in summer feels like a sin. It's been a little over a week since we were freed for the season. The time simultaneously crept along like a curse and transpired in the blink of an eye.

"She won't hurt me."

"You can't be certain." Dev helplessly shakes his head at me. He spent the whole drive pleading with me not to go inside. I know he doesn't expect me to change my mind; otherwise, he wouldn't be driving me here himself. "She's going to see my truck. At least let me come inside with you."

"Kinda defeats my promise to come alone."

"You don't even know if she's coming at all!"

"She'll show," I say firmly. I have the horrible suspicion Valerie hasn't been that far off this whole time. Watching and waiting—for what, I'm not sure. More victims? A chance to come home?

She may be keen on revenge, but she's also quick to recognize when she's in too deep. That's what's happening now, I'm sure of it. Valerie went too far and is desperate for a way out.

Reaching for the handle, I freeze when Dev squeezes my arm. It's not a firm grip, but a pleading one.

"Gwen, please."

"She came out of hiding for me once before. She'll do it again."

"And do what?"

"Hopefully not kill me because Hathaway High is the last place I want to die."

Dev sighs gently tugging me towards him. While he knows I'm going inside regardless, he also understands how to keep me in this truck a little while longer. Any force missing from his grip is found in his lips. They firmly press against mine, dizzying and desperate.

"Stop acting like this is the last time," I whisper against his lips.

He only kisses me harder, his fingers curling past my cheeks to wind around the short strands of my hair.

"I have to go."

"Stay with me."

It takes all my power to pull away. "I'll be okay."

I stare into Dev's deep eyes, finding them glossed with fear.

God, I hope I'm right.

When I push open the truck door and hop down, I'm surprised to hear Dev doing the same. Before I can protest, he waves me off. "If you think I'm sitting in the car, you've lost your mind. I'll wait outside the door, just in case—"

"I scream?"

He winces, jaw clenched. Although I'd never admit it, I'm fine with this plan. The closer Dev is to me, the better.

The school parking lot is empty, but it's not like I was expecting Valerie to pull up in her beat-up Corolla.

A victim of countless snowplows, the pavement has seen better days. Dodging rubble and potholes, we hurry around the side of the building, towards the performing arts wing. There's no better place for Hathaway's misfits to hide. Valerie will know to meet me here.

Each summer, the community uses the school's auditorium to put on a pretty-rough rendition of whatever musical has affordable rights. Hathaway's thespians are passionate for their craft and they're sure to leave the stage door unlocked for anyone wanting to rehearse early.

Yanking on the metal handle, I'm pleased to find I'm correct.

"You'll be here?"

Dev nods, his forehead wrinkled with worry. "Right out here."

I squeeze his hand. "See you soon."

With a nod that I hope conveys confidence, I slip inside, letting the heavy door swiftly slam behind me, but not before Dev calls, "Good luck."

I sincerely hope I don't need it.

Rapidly blinking so my eyes adjust to the consuming darkness, I freeze until I can get my bearings backstage. Thankfully, I don't need long. After serving on the crew for several school productions, I'm more familiar with the wings in the dark than when the work lights are on.

Maneuvering around a ginormous paper-mâché cow and half-built tower, I cross the stage. Rehearsal ended a few hours ago and even the most loyal of theatre nerds have called it a night.

The ghost light, a single bulb on a tall pole on wheels, offers a weak glow from its station at center stage. Scanning the rows of plush chairs for any signs of life, I'm keenly aware of every shapeless shadow and phantom creak.

I'm not afraid of Valerie. I don't want to be. But the bodies don't lie.

This is why a can of pepper spray is stuffed into my pocket. Mom got it for me when I turned thirteen. At the time, I thought it was ridiculous. What could possibly happen to me in the middle of nowhere? I now know. Even the smallest town can be unsafe.

Valerie never answered my message—not that I expected her to—but I know where she'll expect to meet. The only place at Hathaway High that truly understood her potential. Where Valerie felt seen. Valued.

That is, until she became the Park Ranger.

Crossing to stage left, I exit through a doorway in the wings to the main hallway connecting all the performing arts classrooms. The theatre room is the first one, located directly across from the auditorium.

Calling it a classroom is certainly a stretch. There aren't any desks or uncomfortable, plastic chairs. Instead, the windowless room is scattered with couches and armchairs, amassed by Ms. Deborah Stintson, the blessed theatre teacher with an affinity for garage sales. She's commanded the dominion for decades and is a fan favorite by any student she instructs. Ms. Deb, as she implores us to call her, refers to the room our safe space. The name caught on among the students. Here, we're free to make bold choices and nervous confessions. Be wholly ourselves. If nowhere else, at least we are safe here.

I pray that sentiment is still the case tonight.

Sucking in a breath, I twist the handle, already knowing it'll be unlocked. It's pitch-black inside. Before anything can jump out at me, I flip the switch beside the door.

Exhaling sharply at the empty room, my eyes dance over the tattered furniture for any signs of life. My heart pangs with disappointment. I was so sure she'd show. Valerie is no coward.

The couches and armchairs form a ring around the center of the room. A casual theatre-in-the-round. Students frequently take center stage to perform a monologue or scene for the class.

Settling into a once plush sofa covered in faded velvet the color of a plum, I don't take my eyes off the door. Adjusting my back so a spring isn't poking my spine, I cross my arms and wait. Junior year, this was our usual seat. Everyone knew this couch belonged to Valerie and me.

The same thought plays through my head on a tedious loop. *I shouldn't be here.* My best friend is fierce with an affinity for getting even, but she would never endanger someone—least of all, me. If Valerie was capable of taking not just one life, but four, maybe I never knew her at all.

Where is she?

I type a quick update for Dev, letting him know I'm still alone. Clearly staring at his cell, he responds almost instantly.

DEV VISHWAKARMA

Give it two more minutes, then leave.

GWEN GARDNER

I'll give her five.

DEV VISHWAKARMA

She knows how important this is. If she was going to show, she'd be on time.

I hate that I agree with him. Valerie abides by the old theatre mantra, "To be early is to be on time, to be on time is to be late, and to be late is a sin."

My attention settles on the couch directly across from mine, eyes-narrowing when I spy something out of place. The couch is royal-blue leather and squeaks horribly whenever anyone gets up from it, though it's not the ancient furniture that's of interest, but what's resting beneath it. *A laptop.*

Flying across the space, I bend to reveal a computer I'd recognize anywhere. It's plastered with her personality. Stickers from her favorite Broadway musicals and concerts. There's a disco ball, purple cowboy hat, and a globe.

Holy shit.

Is this where she's been hiding out? We all know from experience it's not a bad place to fall asleep. Plus, barely anyone comes into the classroom once school is out. Even the community production rehearsing on the main stage prefers to loiter in the audience or lobby, lest they miss a cue. Did she leave this by accident? Or for me to find?

Settling into the leather couch, I hastily open it, my mouth growing dry when I see the familiar lock screen. A picture of Valerie and me from a few summers ago. We're backstage, taking a selfie with Sybil's head, which is definitely against the rules.

Praying she hasn't changed her password, I type, "*hell-awayfromhere.*"

The screen flickers to Valerie's desktop. There's no way Valerie would've kept the same password if she had any worry that I would tell someone. If she suspected I would turn on her.

Or maybe she wants me to see something.

Her texts are logged in, but she hasn't sent a single message since she disappeared. Valerie wasn't the type to waste time texting loads of people. There are a few drama club group chats—all that I'm a part of. Other than that, it's mostly me, her dad, Weston, Amanda, and before he died, Luca.

A quick skim of her messages with them reveals nothing interesting. Honestly, the conversations are rather boring by her standards.

In fact, the only message of note is the one I recently sent her. There isn't a blue dot next to my request to meet up, so I know she read it. The cops are tracking her phone, so she likely opened it on this laptop. A chill runs up my spine. Where is she now?

There are countless messages from her dad. Begging for her to come home if she can. Each one makes my heart squeeze tighter and tighter until it hurts. How could she do this to him? To all of us?

Valerie isn't the type to save files onto her desktop. Too much clutter for her taste. So I'm surprised to spot one at the top right of the screen, labeled ICE. Clicking on it, I'm annoyed to find it's locked. Trying a slew of Valerie's usual passwords, I blink with frustration as it refuses to open. I shouldn't be surprised. We clearly stopped sharing everything long ago.

I open a web browser and head to her online files, thinking she left me a note there. But I'm disappointed to find nothing but papers for school and college research. Nothing I haven't seen before.

Suddenly, there's an itch in the back of my mind. The way I'll be able to confirm or deny every horrible assumption. I need to know if Valerie's laptop is still logged into the Ride or Die account.

It'll be blocked on the school Wi-Fi, but that doesn't mean I don't have my ways of checking. Using a trick we learned freshman year; I change the Wi-Fi to a hotspot on my phone. I'll have to work fast, otherwise, my parents will kill me for running up the bill on our family plan. Now, I'm able to access the site I need.

A few clicks later, I blink at the laptop, not wanting to believe my eyes.

The screen illuminates with the damning profile. The devilish mask mocks me. Laughing at me for missing what was right in front of me all along.

We weren't hacked at all. Valerie locked me out. All this time, I've been talking with her. Pleading with *her* for her own safety.

My insides twist as I take it all in. There are countless posts riling up the masses and DMs to myself and Weston. There are messages to others too. Most names I don't recognize, but then I see one that I do. A name that makes the knot in my stomach drop completely.

Valerie has been feeding information to Abigail Herron. Tips about poor worker conditions, the blatant lack of care for guest and employee safety, and evidence about Luca, Ms. Wade, Ruby, and Chase. She even gives up information about herself, the beloved Park Ranger who went missing.

I keep scrolling, through unanswered messages from supporters, stopping at a message from Ride or Die to Chase.

RIDEORDIE

You're going to die if you keep ignoring me.

Weston was wrong. Chase wasn't the villain, but another victim.

And that's when the tears come. Valerie threatened to kill Chase and then she followed through. The sobs shake my whole body, ripping at my throat. Unable to see through my tears, I shove the laptop away from me.

If I don't know Valerie, maybe I don't know anyone.

At the sound of my cries, Dev dashes inside. Feeling his arms curl around me, I helplessly sink into him. He reads the open laptop on the floor and squeezes me tighter. It only makes me cry harder into his chest.

My head begins to pound with the same thought over and over. How could she? *How could she?*

I should've seen this coming. If I had, four people would still be alive.

"Gwen," Dev whispers, lifting my chin and rubbing my streaking tears away with his thumbs, "I have to tell you something."

I hold my breath. How much more can I take?

Dev must know this too because he quickly says, "They've made an arrest."

My lips part. "They found Valerie?"

It's only then that I realize Dev's eyes are red. He's been crying, too. He swallows before shaking his head.

"No. They arrested Jenna."

CHAPTER
TWENTY-NINE

R EPEATEDLY WIPING HIS EYES, Dev speeds through town, not caring he's running at least four lights. It doesn't matter if we draw the attention of a few cops when we're driving straight to the police station.

We have to tell them they have the wrong girl.

Valerie's computer rests in my lap, still hot from being run back at the school. It should contain enough evidence for them to free Jenna and start a manhunt for my best friend.

I should feel guilty for backstabbing Valerie, but instead, all I am is empty.

Silent tears of betrayal trickle down my cheeks and onto the laptop.

The station is a madhouse. It's like the whole town is tail-gating the arrest. Abigail and her cameraman are out front, delivering the news of Jenna's arrest.

This is just what Valerie wanted. More bad press for Pineland. How much more can the park take before it shuts down for good? What'll happen to Hathaway then? When half the town is out of a job and the rest of the world stops driving our way? Just when I didn't think this hellhole couldn't get much worse. I don't want to imagine Hathaway without its cornerstone.

With the station lot completely full, Dev has to parallel park far down the street, which is a feat in his massive truck. As we dart towards the station, I try to steady my emotions by gulping in the warm air. This is not the time to be hysterical. Jenna deserves our composure.

"You've got the computer?" Dev calls over his shoulder.

"Yeah," I breathe out, clutching it tighter to my chest and allowing the corners to dig into my skin while I run.

Valerie may be a minor, but she won't get away with murdering four innocent people. By handing this evidence over, I'm ruining her life.

No. Valerie ruined her own life, along with that of countless others.

Her father's accident was tragic, but trying to close Pineland by massacring crew members? In what world could she ever think that was the best way to avenge her father?

Even more unsettling—I still can't figure out how she picked her targets. Sure, she seemed to go after Park Rangers at first, but Valerie adored Luca. She used to say that in an alternative reality, one where she stayed in Hathaway, they were "endgame." How could she hurt him? Is anyone off-limits to her?

We push through the throng of people. Unsurprising, no one has anywhere better to be. It doesn't get much more interesting than the daughter of Hathaway's newest hero getting arrested for sabotaging the other attraction in town.

Over it all, Abigail bellows in her most official reporter voice, "The impacted families will see the closure they deserve and the people of Hathaway can sleep soundly knowing the murderer haunting their town is apprehended."

There's an officer posted on the front step of the station. Officer Sarah Mulligan, or neighbor, pretends to barely recognize us.

"No one's going in the station," she says, hands on her hips. We both notice her left hand creeping towards the taser on her belt, like we might pull something funny.

"Jeez, Sarah," Dev objects, "we're not trying anything."

"It's Officer Mulligan." Her blue eyes plead with us to take her seriously. Unfortunately, we know her too well for that.

"Officer Mulligan," I say with wide eyes, "are you seriously going to tase the kids you used to babysit?"

"We have something Detective Weegan is going to want to see," Dev says, nodding towards the laptop pressed against my chest. "Trust us."

"Captain Pierce doesn't want anyone unrelated to the investigation inside."

"They've been interviewing us nonstop about this case!" I protest.

"Sarah, please," Dev pleads, taking a calmer approach. "This is too important not to share."

Sarah's hands rub down her face. "I figured you two would grow out of being so obnoxiously persistent."

"Never." I squeeze the laptop even tighter.

Her shoulders droop with exasperation and I know we've won. It's the same expression we saw on her countless times as kids, like when we wanted ice cream for dinner or to watch an R-rated movie.

"Thank you, thank you! We owe you!"

"If anyone asks, you snuck around me," she hisses, waving us past her. "I swear, if you get me fired..."

"Good thing you know where we live!"

We hurry around Sarah, yanking open the door and barreling inside.

And I thought it was wild *outside*.

Relatives of anyone impacted are sitting in the lobby, nursing cups of coffee while they cry. I don't spy Jenna's mom, but I suspect she's being kept far from these families. They're probably questioning her alongside her daughter.

"You shouldn't be in here," an officer says behind a desk, waving us away. "I don't care if it's your friend. You two gotta go."

Not wanting to upset any of the grieving families, I lean over the desk and hurriedly whisper, "There's been a mistake. Jenna didn't do anything. I have proof." I hold up the laptop.

The officer, a middle-aged man named Daryl Hicks, widens his hazel eyes. They dart between me and the computer.

"It's true," Dev whispers. "You need to see this."

"Will you two have a seat?"

Dev and I hastily nod. At least they're not tossing us out.

Officer Hicks radios to the back, speaking so quietly we can't make out his words. His eyes don't leave the laptop in my grip. We only wait another minute before Weegan appears.

It's clear the detective has had quite the day. The edges of his brown mustache are turning in lopsided directions and there are dark circles under his eyes. His jaw clenches when he sees us, but nevertheless, he waves us down the hall and into an empty interrogation room.

Weegan closes the door behind him, sighing, "I'm sure I don't have to explain to either of you how this is truly not the time."

"Jenna didn't do anything."

The detective doesn't budge. "We have concrete evidence that connects her to multiple murders at Pineland."

"What evidence?"

"Do your parents know you're here?" Weegan asks instead. Dev and I share a nervous glance, which is enough for the man. He sighs again. "I'd really like your parents present, kids."

"We don't have time for that," I insist, "and you're not questioning us. We're informing you."

Weegan looks unsure of this, but when his eyes dart to the laptop, I know we've got him. "Whose is it?"

"It belongs to Valerie Ross."

His face remains expressionless. "And how did you come across this?"

"I found it at the school."

My pocket vibrates. I doubt Detective Weegan will mind me pulling out my phone. If it's my parents, I need to warn them I'm here.

My heart stops when I see the sender. It's her.

The back of my neck prickles. Valerie must know we're here. I think of the locked file. Why keep it hidden then, only to reveal it now? What does she want the cops to see? Proof it's Jenna? Showing the cops fake evidence that'll only help Valerie's case is the last thing I want to do.

Another DM lights up my screen. This one makes my mouth grow dry.

What the hell is that supposed to mean? Sorry for what? Murdering people? Being a shitty human being? Or is it something else I'm completely missing?

One thing is for certain—I'm opening that file.

Whether I like it or not, Valerie understands me better than anyone. She knew I'd wait on our usual couch and placed her laptop in my sightline. She figured I'd immediately confirm she was Ride or Die. She knew I would come straight here.

But why is she making it so easy? Why leave the laptop? Why stay logged in? Why message me the file password?

What am I missing?

All our lives, Valerie has always been one step ahead of me.

She was the first to kiss someone. The first to get asked to a school dance. The first to get a phone, have a later curfew, and know what she wanted to do with her life. She was the one to get the Park Ranger role.

Even now, it feels like she's still outracing me, calling for me to hurry up behind her. Guiding me like I'm a plaything.

Screw her. I'm done playing her game.

"I thought we'd been hacked, but I was wrong. Valerie is still Ride or Die." Opening the computer and logging in, I slide it towards him. "There's a locked file on the desktop."

"And you don't know what's in it?"

Swallowing, I shake my head. "She waited until we were here and with you before sending the key."

"I don't like playing along with the vague DMs of a teenage girl." The detective grunts, but still, he carefully begins typing in the passcode.

We wait with bated breath as the folder opens, revealing only one file inside. It takes all my self-control not to sigh with relief. I half-believed the password wouldn't work. That this was just another test I was going to fail. A way to prove I was a traitor.

"Is that a video?"

"You two are lucky it didn't explode. Would've ruined your lives," Weegan says.

"Hard to ruin our lives if we're all dead," I point out, before hastily adding, "which we're not!"

Weegan waves me quiet, clicking open the video, which seems to have its original file title. A bunch of letters and numbers followed by ".mov."

It takes a second for the video to load on Valerie's ancient computer. The fan's running again, challenging the department's strong AC for the loudest sound in the room.

Finally, it loads.

It takes me a moment to register what I'm looking at.

Someone is filming on their cell phone, keeping the

camera face-up as they place it on a flat surface. They're making very little sound as they flutter around the space, which I suddenly recognize.

"This is inside the Great Oak," I whisper. I'd know those rounded walls and cement stairs basking in fluorescent lights anywhere.

We wait for something to happen, and about thirty seconds of silence later, it does.

"Seriously, Jenna?" A male voice says. "What the hell are you even doing here? And what are you wearing on your hands?"

"Luca," Dev breathes out, shooting me a concerned look. I know what he's thinking. *Are we about to see Jenna kill Luca?*

"Do you know how much rat and roach poison they spray inside this tree? I'm a violinist. I'm not accidentally touching those chemicals with my bare hands."

"Yet another reason why you shouldn't be here."

"You left us no other option, you idiot. Someone had to give you a wake-up call," we hear Jenna hiss. No one is in view of the camera, but we can see their shadows dancing on the wall.

Jenna keeps talking, her voice high pitched with exasperation and stress. "You've gone off the rails, Luca. What you're doing is criminal."

"What *we're* doing is criminal," he corrects her. I barely recognize his voice, which is dripping with snide arrogance and cruelty. Long gone is the golden boy with the power to charm an entire town.

"Screw that," Jenna spits back. "You're the one killing people."

We all suck in a breath. Everything I thought I knew flies from my head.

"Don't get cold feet now," Luca says in a low voice. "You wanted Pineland gone just as much as the rest of us."

"Not because people are dying!"

"You and Valerie's weak ideas weren't working. You two really thought bad reviews of the new Sybil ride and a few technical difficulties were enough? We needed to step things up if we wanted Pineland to actually get some bad publicity."

"They would if you just gave them time."

"Online warfare is petty," Luca scoffs. "I took real action. That's what they wanted us to do. Drastic measures to take down the park."

"I doubt they want to be linked to a string of murders. None of us want to be. Which is why you need to stop. Now."

"It's too late," Luca laughs.

There's a pause before Jenna finally asks in a small voice, "What's that supposed to mean?"

"I told Val that she involved too many people."

"So what?" Jenna says, and I can tell she's doing her best not to sound concerned. "You're going to kill us off until it's just you and Valerie? Or is she not even safe from your insanity?"

"I'm sorry you won't live long enough to find out."

I gasp when Jenna screams for help. We hear the two scuffle and wrestle off camera, fighting to overpower the other. Beside me, Dev's lips are parted with horror. Detective Weegan isn't blinking.

"Get off me!" Jenna shrieks.

Finally, after a painfully long minute of listening to our classmates claw at each other, we hear Jenna start to sob while Luca begins to cough and sputter in the background. It continues for an agonizing length of time before there's a horrible cracking sound, followed by a sudden, chilling silence. Jenna begins to cry harder.

Holy shit.

Jenna killed Luca, but in self-defense. He went after her first.

The distraught girl grabs for her cell phone, revealing a

hand covered in a plastic glove. No wonder they didn't find any prints on Luca.

It's like she forgot she was recording, because one second, we see her horrified expression as she fumbles around the Great Oak. The next, the phone is turning in her grip and we're granted a glimpse of Luca's body. Wide-eyed, head bleeding. Gone.

The video ends there.

We're all still for a long while, processing what we just watched. Waiting for someone to break the spell.

Weegan finally does, closing the laptop, and tucking it under his arm as he rises from his seat. It causes us to take a step back, though we don't return to the other side of the table. Instead, we stand awkwardly, unsure of what happens next.

"I need to show Captain Pierce."

We nod in agreement, both our brains a storm cloud of confusion, raining white noise over our thoughts.

"Call your parents and have them pick you up. Let them know you aren't in any trouble, but we'll likely have you come back tomorrow morning to collect further statements."

"What happens until then?" My voice sounds raw.

Weegan pauses at the interrogation room door, his eyes darting between the two of us. "We're going to get to the bottom of this mess."

"Mess" feels like such a simple word for all of this. A mess is when you tip over a glass of juice and have to mop it up with paper towels. A mess is when your pencil sharpener opens at the bottom of your backpack, littering it with shavings and lead.

This isn't a mess. It's a fucking nightmare.

"Oh, and Gwendolyn?" Weegan says. "Let me know if you hear from your friend again."

To no one's surprise, our parents are pissed. They didn't even bother to take separate cars so they could chastise us together in the back of Dev's family minivan. Mr. Vishwakarma drove Dev's truck home, trusting his wife and my parents to give us the earful we deserved.

"What were you two thinking?"

"You lied to us!"

"You could've been killed!"

I barely hear a word of it, still processing the video we just watched.

Valerie isn't the only one we thought we knew. We can now add Jenna and Luca to that list.

I'm positively sick by the time Mrs. Vishwakarma pulls into our driveway.

"We'll continue to speak about this inside," my mom says, more to Dev's mother than to me. I fight back an eye-roll. Maybe if they were a decent parental unit, they wouldn't have to try so hard to look like one in front of his folks.

Whispering "good luck" to Dev, I climb out of the minivan, my parents at my heels.

A window rolls down. "What do you think you're doing?"

At Mrs. Vishwakarma's exclamation, I turn to find Dev exiting the van as well.

What *is* Dev doing?

"Saying goodnight," Dev retorts in a tone that surprises everyone. "The way we went about tonight was wrong, but it needed to be done. So yeah, I'm going to say goodnight to my girlfriend because I'm thankful she's safe."

At the use of "girlfriend," everyone pauses, including Dev. We'd yet to put a label on us, something he seems to be remembering as he blinks guiltily at me.

The shocked adults stay silent, all except my dad, who is incapable of that sort of thing. "You two are... *dating*?"

Dev gapes at me and I realize it's my turn to decide. Are we an official couple? Or am I about to reject him again?

My usual reaction begins to simmer inside me. Don't put down roots. Don't get hurt.

But then I look at Dev—at the hope glinting in those midnight irises—and my fears dissipate. There's no one else I can fully trust. It's only him.

And so, the answer comes far easier than I ever expected.

"Of course, Dev is my boyfriend, and thank goodness for it because it's probably the reason I'm still alive today."

Now I've truly shocked them. I'm sure my folks never thought they'd see the day where I'd wind up with a boy from Hathaway. Even Dev looks slightly surprised as a pleased grin stretches across his face.

Shortly after, both of our mothers mimic his gleeful expression. Mrs. Vishwakarma leans out the window, shrugging helplessly at my parents, her tone completely shifting. "What they did *was* very brave."

"They've always made quite the team," my mother agrees. Even she can't keep the excitement out of her voice. "Perhaps we can grant them a moment to say goodnight before we continue our conversations inside."

Dev's mom is already rolling up her window. "No more than five minutes," she says before it closes and she's backing out of the driveway.

Meanwhile, my own mother is pushing Dad towards the front door. "Agreed. Five minutes max. You're still in trouble."

"Really seems like it," I mutter under my breath while Dev cheerfully waves them inside the house.

With one last skeptical look from my father, it closes shut and we're alone.

Dev instantly swivels towards me, a coy smile still on his face. "So, I heard you got a boyfriend."

I pinch the dip at his waist where I know he's most ticklish. He twitches, but nothing can wipe that smirk off his face. "Stop acting like you just won a marathon."

"I kinda did."

I stop fighting back my smile. "Come on, it didn't take that long for me to come around."

He scoffs. "Uh, yeah it did. I was beginning to think you never would."

"Yeah, after recent events, it turns out my greatest fear isn't becoming a lifer."

It sounds silly to say aloud, but it's true. After finding countless bodies and facing the reality that the people I love most aren't who I thought, the idea of having a boyfriend—someone I can trust—doesn't sound like a life sentence.

And so, with that sentiment in mind, I rise onto the tips of my toes to press my lips against his.

His arms immediately wrap around my lower back, and as he draws me closer, I feel him finally relax after a long, stressful evening. The idea of being that person for him makes my insides simmer.

"We're almost out of time," he whispers against my lips. Chuckling as he kisses my pout, he finally pulls away.

Who am I? I opened the floodgates a smidge and look at me now. I barely recognize myself, with my cheesy smile and inability to take my eyes off my best friend. "Fast five minutes."

"Too fast."

He hugs me close and I eagerly stretch back up on my toes so my chin rests in the crook of his shoulder. I nuzzle him there, wishing we didn't have to say goodnight. Over his shoulder, my porch lights blink on and off. A signal that time is indeed up.

As I reluctantly stare at my family home, my eyes land on something that makes my heart stop. An unfamiliar shadow looms on the other side of my bedroom window, backlit by golden light. Too large to be Gil, but too slight to be either of my folks.

Whoever it is—they're waiting for me.

CHAPTER
THIRTY

IT TAKES all my strength to not scream when I say goodnight to Dev and slip through my front door. My parents don't have much more to lecture me about—Mrs. Vishwakarma took care of most of it for them. Not before long, I'm sent up to my room to think long and hard about my foolish decisions. Little do they know walking into my room is just that. Possibly the most foolish decision I'll ever make.

There's precisely one person who knows how to sneak into my house as well as I know how to sneak out.

At the end of the hall, the crack between my closed bedroom door and the floor reveals a beam of yellow light. My parents are strict about turning off lights after we leave a room, but with everything going on, I'm not surprised they didn't see it. Meanwhile, Gil wouldn't notice a burglar unless they stole the tablet out of his hands. As I pass my brother's room, I hear the wretched thing blaring high pitched explosions. It reminds me to fiddle with my own phone before it's too late.

Blood pounds in my ears as I approach the door. I know who's waiting on the other side, so I brace myself the best I can. For once, I need to be in control. Not her. I can't let her twist this into a story with a happy ending.

What if I've got it all wrong? What if it's not her?

Sucking in a deep breath, I muster my courage as I creak open the door. I hate how something inside me swells when I clap eyes on the girl that I used to consider my dearest friend.

I wish my initial reaction wasn't relief. It's the kind of emotion that'll get me killed.

She's sporting a knowing grin that punctures a hole in my heart. "I always knew you and Dev would eventually hook up."

"Why are you here, Val?"

To my sinful dismay, Valerie Ross appears perfectly healthy. Maybe a slight shadow under her eyes, but I guess not sleeping well is the price you pay when becoming a criminal. She's in the exact outfit Dev described her to be wearing when she appeared at the Old Wheel. It also matches the description given by Weston and Amanda on the morning she went missing. A pair of torn black denim shorts and an off-white crop top that's definitely mine.

I offer her the best glare I can muster, repeating my initial question. "Valerie, what the hell are you doing here?"

She cocks her head to the side, that coy smile still on her face. "Didn't you miss me?"

"Enough of the bullshit," I whisper frustratedly.

Valerie knows me enough to drop the casual antics. Arms crossing, her chocolate eyes harden. "Jeez, what else am I supposed to say?"

"Everything, Valerie," I hiss. "You owe me an explanation for everything."

I can't believe she's in front of me. After all my frantic texts and pleading voicemails—how can she return so easily?

We remain standing on opposite sides of the room, my bed between us, dutifully keeping us a safe distance from each other.

"If you don't talk, I'm screaming for help. Then I'm keeping you here until the cops can come pick you up."

Valerie winces. "That's how you think of me?"

"Were you expecting a welcome home party?"

She bites the inside of her cheek, eyeing me hesitantly. "I guess I deserve that."

Valerie deserves a lot worse than I'm giving her right now. I don't even feel guilty for thinking about it. I'm horrified by the girl standing before me. She might as well be a stranger. Not the girl to whom I once bared my soul.

"Gwen—"

Our eyes meet and I'm surprised to find tears welling in hers.

She should cry. She ruined everything.

"I'm so sorry."

"Are you?"

"What happened to you?"

"To me? Seriously?"

This girl faked her own kidnapping and has the audacity to vibe check me? I'm fully confident her disappearance was not caused by some outside entity.

And yet, she has the nerve to look shocked by my reaction to her return.

"What do you expect?" It's difficult not to raise my voice, but I can't have my parents dashing upstairs. Not until I hear what I need to learn. "Why return now?"

"Because I want to come home."

"Why leave in the first place?"

"I had to go," she insists. "It was too risky to stay."

"And it's less risky now? Because things look a whole lot worse than when you left."

"I'm here to explain."

I cross my arms, nodding at her to go on. "By all means."

Her entire being plummets, like I've sucked every hopeful ounce of a happy homecoming from the room. She's blinking like she barely recognizes me, but I don't care. I'm tired of wondering and worrying. What did she expect after disappearing for a week and then sneaking into my bedroom? For me to run into her arms and squeeze her close? To welcome her home with no questions at all?

"I don't even know where to start."

"How about with a big one? Did you help Luca kill them?"

"No!" Valerie says firmly, imploring me to believe her. "I swear, I never wanted anyone to get hurt."

We're quiet for a long moment, her eyes glistening as she silently pleads with me to accept this as the truth. After everything I've seen tonight, I do believe Luca went off the rails, but I'm not letting Valerie know that.

"Prove it."

"You watched the video on my laptop, right?"

I nod once.

After a long pause, Valerie says in a small voice, "We were trying to create enough scandal to close the park, but I never expected Luca to take it so far."

"We? Who all does that entail?" I want to know who Valerie trusted more than me.

"Luca, Jenna, and Chase," she says guiltily.

I want to ask, "why them?" but I resist. No one other than my ego benefits from that question. It's better to hear more about their plan to destroy Pineland.

"Did you want to close the park because of what happened to your dad?"

She grows quiet, glancing at the old stuffed animals in the corner of my room, as if they'll give her the right words to say.

"Listen, Val. If you can't come out and be completely transparent now, it's not going to be good for you."

"Stop acting like a cop, Gwen."

"Funny because your only allies are either currently at the station or they're dead."

Her lips purse at the line I've drawn in the sand. "Point taken."

I'm silent until she speaks again.

She concedes with a patronizing eye-roll. "This has nothing to do with my dad."

I blink with surprise. I was certain Valerie was doing all of this to avenge her father's accident. Though, I guess I should know better. The only person Valerie cares about is herself. With every passing day, that becomes abundantly clear.

"Then what was the point?" My question bites, but I can't hide my disappointment. The girl standing in my bedroom may as well be a stranger. Sure, the Valerie I knew was full of brazen risks and bountiful confidence, but this is too far. People are dead.

"Because someone said if I ruined Pineland, they would pay for me to get the hell out of here."

And that's the damning blow that knocks any remaining speck of hope from my body.

"That's it? For money?" I ask incredulously. "You already have money."

Her eyes squint as she tries to correct me, "My dad has money."

"Just stop," I snap.

I've had enough of Valerie Ross insisting she and I are as equally pressed for money. Her dad can pay for her to go to college, plus live in a decent dorm and have a full dining plan. Mine can barely afford community college. I had to drop out of gymnastics because the "Pay-to-Play" was growing too costly. I buy all my clothes secondhand. School supplies come from the dollar store.

She already took my scholarship from me. How much more money could she need?

"Don't act like you wouldn't have done the same," she snaps, a knowing look on her face.

I push past the accusation. "Who wanted you to ruin Pineland?"

A helpless expression crosses Valerie's face. It's such an

unfamiliar look for her that my stomach squeezes nervously. "I have no idea. And that's the truth."

The sincerity in her voice pulls at something inside me. Growing up with a front row seat to her schemes, I have a solid barometer for when she's lying and when she isn't. I should feel relieved that she's finally telling the truth, but I'm only left all the more unsettled.

Valerie must not think I believe her, so to further prove her point, she fishes in her pocket, pulling out a smart phone I don't recognize.

"I couldn't have anyone tracking my location until I knew it was safe to be found."

I can't help the snort that escapes me.

Unlocking the phone, she opens an app before holding the screen out for me to see.

Leaning over my bed to get a better view, my eyes flit up to her when I see she's logged into Ride or Die and has a DM pulled up with an account I don't know. The profile is so unassuming that I didn't bother clicking in when I scrolled through the account on Valerie's laptop.

"I can explain the Ride or Die stuff too."

"You will." I return my gaze to the phone. "What am I looking at?"

"@account120346, that fucker."

"How anonymous." I reach out and take her phone. Valerie gives it up easily for a criminal. Studying the screen, I realize I wasn't far off with my initial assessment. The strange account has no profile picture, no name, and no clear identifiers. There are only two messages to Valerie—both sent shortly after she was promoted to Park Ranger.

@ACCOUNT120346

You want out of Hathaway. I need Pineland to close. Think we can help each other?

"That's it?" I say, glancing up at her with shock. Some stranger on the internet offers her money and she takes it without question? I was expecting blackmail. Threats to her life. Something worthy of this extreme of a reaction.

"Don't act like you didn't initially fall for the 'cash in exchange for content' line too."

"But I didn't! I played along to keep *you* safe! Meanwhile, you were the one playing me!"

"You should've taken the cash, Gwen. The Account gave me enough funds to keep the park in the headlines by any means necessary. It felt wrong not to give you a cut of that."

Again, I can't find it in me to speak. Good thing Valerie's always been the star of the show. Let her have center stage. This is her big monologue.

"You more than anyone know how horrible this place can be. Everyone likes to pretend that Hathaway is this happy bubble full of sweet, small-town folk and roller coasters, but we're all rusting away. Pretending to be satisfied when no one is remotely close to it."

"Better off pretending to be happy than to be dead."

Her face darkens. "I didn't kill anyone. That was all Luca. I brought him in to help and he went out of control."

"Why him?" I can't resist asking. I tell myself it's for the voice memo secretly recording in my pocket, but I need to know why he could be trusted more than me.

"Because I knew he'd go along with tearing down the park without question. He hates Pineland."

My eyebrows pull together with skepticism. "Yet he chose

to be a Park Ranger last summer and then return to work this season?"

"Last summer, I guess Hannah was out of town, so Ruby trained him to be a Park Ranger. According to Luca, she came onto him strong, which he thought was gross because he was only sixteen and she was twenty-one. But when he reported it to Marty, nothing was done."

"What?" My jaw drops open with disgust. "That's so messed up."

Then I connect the dots. Luca took things into his own hands by killing Ruby.

Valerie watches this train of thought reach the station. "Luca puts on a decent nice guy act, but he was a fantastic hockey player for a reason. He's not one to shy away from physicality. I just never realized he could be so aggressive off the ice."

Valerie was never the murderer. She just enabled him.

Reading my mind, she says, "I know. It's a fucking nightmare. I had to get out of here until I could figure out a way to explain. I'm guilty of generating some bad publicity, but not hurting anyone!"

"You hurt me!" My voice cracks. "You blackmailed me by thinking you were in danger. You bribed me to help with your stupid plan!"

"We needed everyone to see Luca's autopsy! People needed to know about the scratches on his body and wonder if someone was fending him off. Otherwise, no one was going to believe he was the killer and not me. Or Jenna."

"And your hat in Jenna's locker? If you were looking out for her, why did you have me steal incriminating evidence from her locker?"

"Jenna didn't want to go to the cops with the truth. I figured you and Dev would find my hat in her locker and turn her in. I was wrong, but that's okay. The cops found different evidence instead."

"What evidence?"

"I had a back-up plan. Her confession in Chase's pocket."

Even Valerie's accomplices weren't safe. The girl before me serves betrayal like it's Thanksgiving.

"I thought you said you didn't kill anyone?" I demand. "Luca wasn't around to kill Chase. So, who did?"

"Just because Luca wasn't around doesn't mean he didn't do it."

"How the hell could Luca have killed Chase from beyond the grave?"

"When they get the autopsy back, they're going to find hemlock in Chase's system. Luca stole some from the *Predatory Plants* exhibit and gave it to Chase. It seems like a harmless herb, only it's anything but. We tried to warn Chase, but he didn't believe us until it was too late."

"What idiot would knowingly eat hemlock?" I ask skeptically.

"It looks a lot like parsley. I bet Luca said his mom grew it in her herb garden."

Stricken, I recall the last time I saw Chase alive. He was in the cafeteria with Dev and I, eating spaghetti with something green on top.

"Chase was never a Park Ranger. Why would Luca kill him?"

"Chase was getting cold feet and wanted to confess by way of throwing Luca under the bus," Valerie admits. "He was helping us hack into some of Pineland's systems. I caught him changing his grade when I worked in the office. I figured he could help us with—"

"Pineland's access control system," I finish, holding my hand out.

Guiltily, Valerie fingers through the cards hanging in a lanyard pouch around her neck. I know what she's digging for before she pulls it out. But when she does, I bite the inside of my cheek with anger.

I refuse to take my Pineland ID from her hand, so she throws it on the bed between us. She stole it from me. She used it to scan into backstage areas and changed the names to point the blame at anyone but her.

"How did you get past security?"

"We didn't."

At this, my lips part. "Did Milly help you?"

Valerie shrugs meekly as my head starts reeling.

Milly was helping Valerie this whole time. We trusted her and she was two-timing us. She knew exactly whose name we were going to find on the Access Control Log and had the audacity to act shocked. It was Milly who showed us the footage of the hooded figures at the Old Wheel. She's also probably responsible for the missing footage from the wheel turning with Chase's body.

Forget being an influencer. Milly Dillard should be on Broadway.

"What? You're not going to throw Milly under the bus too?"

"Milly turned a blind eye in security, but that's the extent of her involvement."

"Not exactly. She showed us you and Jenna at the Old Wheel? At least, I assume that was you two."

Valerie ducks her chin. "We needed Chase's body found. Not as soon as you did, admittedly. You're quite the go-getter nowadays."

My face scrunches at her assessment. I had no choice but to become this person.

"Since when did you and Jenna become friends?"

"It was a fluke. Jenna caught me still logged into Ride or Die before school let out."

"That's a convenient fluke."

Valerie shrugs. "Jenna wanted in so she could help boost her mom's park."

"Something tells me she's regretting that right about now."

"We agreed to tell the cops everything together. Nothing good will come from waiting it out any longer."

She came back for Jenna. Not for me. Not for her father. Only because the trouble had finally caught up with her.

"How did you get Chase to the top of the Old Wheel?"

"I'm my father's daughter. I know a thing or two about how basic rides operate. Especially on a grid as basic as Pineland's."

"You returned power to the Old Wheel." I scoff.

Valerie shrugs like this isn't a ridiculous revelation.

"How did you even know Chase died?"

Her cool exterior falters briefly. "Don't ask me how or where, but the Account found Chase's body. They messaged that I was out of my depth and were taking back the reins after I *disposed* of Chase's body." She tucks a long strand of hair behind her ear. "So, time ran out. They were going to frame Jenna and me for something we didn't do."

A chill runs down my spine. This Account is the real puppet master here. The true star of the show.

My brain is spinning as I piece what I can together.

Desperate people do dangerous things. Someone wanted to close Pineland so badly that they outsourced their dirty work to a bunch of stupid teenagers. Valerie faked her own kidnapping to take the blame off herself and buy time to fix the mess she made. Now the Account is taking back control of their operation.

I can't help but feel a little sorry for the two girls. Things spun out of hand. It's clear neither of them wanted anyone to die.

"You need to go to the police."

"I know," she agrees, "but I wanted to come here first. I needed you to hear it all from me before you saw it on the news."

Ducking my chin, my heart doesn't soften as much as she'd like. But I can't help the hurt that beats inside me.

I can tell Valerie is itching to move around the bed. To hug me close and regain any semblance of the home she ran from. But she doesn't, because as much as I hate to admit it, Valerie still knows me better than anyone. She knows I'm not ready.

"I'll go with you," I hear myself say.

Her face rises with hope. "Really?"

"Don't get too excited," I say with a wary shake of my head. "I'm only making sure that you turn yourself in."

Her expression hardens, but after biting her lip, she gives a slight nod. "Desperate people—"

"I'm not desperate, Valerie. I'm done."

CHAPTER
THIRTY-ONE

BY THE TIME I clock in for my shift the following morning, it's all over the news. A story that—to my relief—is pretty on par with the one Valerie described to me last night. How she, Jenna, Chase, and Luca tried to stir up a scandal around Pineland. That Luca was the one to take it too far. How Jenna acted in self-defense and Valerie was so afraid she ran away. Somehow, Milly's name is left out of the tale, but I wonder if that's more to do with her father than anything.

Though, there's one detail no one, not even Abigail, seems to be reporting: Why they did it. There isn't one single mention of an anonymous account who set this horrible plan in motion by bribing Valerie. While the scandal of Hathaway's golden boy being a murderer and the involvement of the daughter of Pineland's greatest competitor does make for a saucy headline, this is the last piece of information I need for true closure. We can't move forward without knowing who wanted to close the park.

After her grand confession in my bedroom, Valerie and I descended my creaky stairwell together and startled the hell out of my parents, who were watching TV on the couch. I might as well have walked into the living room with a monster.

But Valerie is no killer. Not really.

My folks drove us to the station, and after an emotional phone call with her father, he insisted on meeting us there. It was late enough that the media frenzy had dispersed, so only a few cars remained in the lot.

My heart spasmed when Valerie dashed out of the car before my dad finished parking, only to calm once I realized she was running to embrace her father.

The cops took Valerie in immediately. After a brief questioning of me and my folks, they asked us to leave, saying they didn't want anyone loitering and encouraging the crowd to return.

I received another lecture on the way home, but I didn't listen to a word. My head was too numb from trying to process the evening's events.

I hoped Dev wouldn't be mad that I faced Valerie without him, but I knew it was me she needed to see. I was the one who had to get her to the station.

Walking into Crew HQ with him now, I can tell he's still debating on how he wants to react. It was too much to text, and I couldn't call, because I knew my parents would now be listening for anyone else who might sneak into my room. I'm only lucky he picked me up for work today because I had the whole car ride to explain everything.

He still hasn't said anything when we reach the locker rooms, his face twisted into an unreadable expression. We loiter between the two doorways, allowing people to pass around us as we wait for him to find the words. It appears the weight on everyone's shoulders has lifted. All their questions have been answered, so Pineland can go back to being their safe-and-happy place. They have no idea there's still one glaring hole in this story.

Finally, just as I was beginning to worry that I'd miss my first program, Dev says, "So we were completely wrong?"

"Kinda, yeah."

I should be relieved to know Valerie was never capable of something so horrible. I guess I am. But it leaves such a glaring question in its wake, I'm left almost as unsettled as before.

Who goaded her and the others into all of this? Who was the enabler?

Dev shakes his head and I can tell he's wondering the same thing. Who is behind everything? It's someone with the utmost desperate desire to close Pineland, who clearly understands this town's secrets well enough to correctly target Valerie into doing their bidding, and has the means to make it all happen.

To our left is the sound of a throat clearing. Dev and I turn to find Weston and Amanda standing there with wide eyes. Amanda holds out her phone, which displays one of dozen news articles about Pineland's latest scandal.

"We need to talk."

"I'll miss my presentation—" I start to say, but Amanda shakes her head like it's the most preposterous thing she's ever heard.

"Priorities, please. If you get in trouble, I'll talk to Grandpa."

And so, despite the fact I'm definitely going to get in trouble and Dev is supposed to be escorting the new Sybil recruit around the park, we follow them into the mostly empty break room. There are only a few crew members hanging around, sipping their coffee while scrolling on their phones. Probably reading the news. No one attempts to mask their stares when I enter the room. I was the best friend of the girl behind everything, or so they think. As I pass, I hear one mutter, "Your friend failed, sweetie. The park is packed this morning."

We slide into our usual booth in the back, all leaning forward to speak in hushed whispers. Before they can bother asking, I fill them in on everything. I gain nothing from hiding a single detail.

They're a captive audience—even Dev, who's hearing it all for the second time. They nod knowingly when I reveal Valerie was still Ride or Die. Amanda gasps when I share that Jenna killed Luca out of self-defense, while Weston curses his teammate's name. When I explain how they were using my lost identification card to switch the access control logs, Weston's fists tighten.

"Milly played us?"

"Everyone played us. They all tampered with evidence and deserve to be punished for that."

His eyebrows raise with surprise. "Doesn't sound like you and Val made up."

"We didn't."

Forgiving Valerie feels impossible. I'm not sure there's any way for us to ever move forward from this. In a way, it feels like a part of myself has died. A void that I'm not yet sure how to fill. I recognize that our friendship was toxic, but who am I without Valerie?

I guess I have plenty of time to figure it out.

"I want to go back to this anonymous account," Amanda says, her brow furrowed with concern. "Does that mean there's still someone out there who wants Pineland to close?"

"Desperately," I confirm. "But who?"

"I've been thinking about it," Dev says, "and I think we can rule out Ms. Thatcher. There's no way she'd ever support her daughter being implicated with a murder investigation."

"Agreed," I say. "She may benefit from Pineland's downfall, but not if people are too afraid to visit Hathaway."

"No, this feels personal," Amanda says, her voice brittle with worry.

"Very personal."

And then it hits me.

Despite everything, Pineland is somehow thriving during a summer it was expected to suffer. In fact, over its decades of operation, I can't think of a time where bad press has ever negatively impacted the park. I'd be willing to bet there's data demonstrating consistent spikes in attendance and revenue during the summers where Pineland is in the spotlight—positive or negative.

"What is it?" Dev asks, seeing my horrified face.

I meet Amanda's eyes, and before I can utter my theory, she muses, "You think Grandpa wanted this to happen?"

It feels too terrible to admit aloud, so all I do is nod.

"Jesus, Gwen, that's crazy," Weston scoffs. "Why would Marty Boone want to sabotage his own park?"

I glance helplessly at Dev and am relieved to see it starting to snap into place for him too. "Even with the new ride, everyone was predicting it would be a slow summer, thanks to Wetlands. Yet, miraculously, we're making headlines and are still packed every day."

"Who's to say Marty didn't learn from the past?"

We both turn to Amanda, because only she can green light this theory. Give us permission to suspect her grandfather of foul play.

Before she can say anything, Weston interjects, "No offense, but isn't Marty a little old to know how to slide into someone's DMs?"

"Oh shit," Amanda breathes out, her lips parting with horror.

"What is it?"

"Last summer, long before I knew who was behind Ride or Die, Grandpa asked me to help him set up an account of his own." Amanda chokes on her next sentence. "He said it was wise to 'keep an eye on your enemies.'"

"You don't think—"

"I do." She frantically looks at me. "You saw the DMs to Valerie? Can you remember the handle?"

"Um," I say, "It was 'account' with a lot of random numbers."

"Was it 120346?"

My jaw goes slack as I remember. "How do you know that?"

Amanda looks like she's been punched in the gut. "Those numbers aren't random. That's my grandma's birthday."

Oh shit.

"We have to tell the cops," Dev says, reaching for his phone.

"I figured Jenna and Valerie already brought it up—so why isn't there any word of it on the news?"

"They must have a reason for withholding this information," I insist.

"Who cares?" Amanda snaps. "That monster needs to answer for what he's done."

We're all taken aback by her harshness. She only shrugs, clearly over it.

"Call HPD," she says darkly. "Tell them we'll leak everything to the media if they don't arrest Grandpa. Let's end this."

I pause, silently asking if she's sure. Only after she nods do I fish my phone from my pocket.

I jump as it vibrates in my hand. A call from a number I don't recognize. Glancing nervously at the others, I answer.

"Gwendolyn Gardner?"

"Yes?"

"This is Officer Annmarie Grint with HPD. Will you please come down to the station? There's a few more questions Detective Weegan needs to ask you."

Not caring that I'm completely ditching my shift, I hastily say, "I'll be right there."

"We've already made your parents aware and they will be meeting us at the station."

"Sounds good. See you soon." Hanging up, I find the whole table blinking at me with anticipation. "Their ears must be burning. HPD needs me in. I'll tell them our theory."

"I'm coming with you," Dev says immediately, already scooching out of the booth.

"I'm coming too," Weston insists, also rising to stand beside Dev. "Like hell am I hanging around here."

Only Amanda and I remain in the booth now. I glance at her. "I know this is a lot to process. It's okay if you don't want to join."

"I need to stay," she says. "Grandpa wanted me to stop by his office before I head into the park. If I don't go, he might get suspicious and do something drastic."

"Are you sure?" Dev asks. "What if he—"

"My grandfather can't hurt me. I'll keep an eye on him until the cavalry arrives."

The look of betrayal on her face feels familiar. I'm sure it's how I appeared with Valerie last night. The people we hold dearest have the power to hurt us the most.

"I shouldn't be surprised," Amanda mutters. "He ruins everyone's lives." Her disappointed eyes meet mine. "Hurry."

Nodding hesitantly, I finally slide from the booth. "Text me if anything comes up," I say to her before following the boys out of the break room.

"This is so messed up," Weston groans as we hurry through the atrium and out the front door, not caring in the slightest we'll all likely be fired for this. Soon, there won't be a park to fire us from.

"What isn't in Hathaway?"

Neither of the boys can disagree with me now.

When we walk into the station, I balk at the last person I expected to see. I almost didn't recognize her without her signature bun and fake smile.

"Hannah Flannigan?" Dev gapes. She hasn't shown her face around town since she quit.

When she turns to us, I'm taken aback to find her cheeks wet from tears. "Are you okay?"

Choking back a sob, the young woman pushes past us, hurrying to a waiting car in the lot.

The three of us share a concerned look. Hannah Flannigan is always composed.

"Your folks aren't here yet?" Detective Weegan asks when he appears.

We don't have time to wait for them to arrive. Every minute Marty Boone is out there, this whole town is at risk. He's like an invasive weed, choking the life out of Hathaway. I don't like Amanda being alone with him. Even if he never hurt anyone himself, I don't trust a desperate man.

"They'll be okay if we start without them," I say hurriedly.

Weegan raises a bushy eyebrow but is clearly on a tight schedule of his own, because he doesn't push it. After asking the boys to wait in the lobby, he leads me back into an interrogation room. On the way, I glance through the window into the room across the hall, not surprised to see Valerie, her father, and a lawyer sitting inside. My eyes meet Valerie's for a second before I turn my back on her.

"This shouldn't take long. I just have a few follow up questions for you about the account that was messaging Valerie." He flips the page on his yellow legal pad, reading, "Account120346. Just like Ride or Die, they're hiding their IP address."

I don't even want to know how Marty figured that one out.

"I know who runs it," I say, relieved that Weegan is already barking up the right tree.

The detective's eyes dart up to me with surprise. "You do?"

There's a knock at the door. The kind of knock that doesn't wait for permission to enter.

It's Captain Pierce. My insides curl at the sight of her.

Does she know? How am I supposed to blurt out that her boyfriend is behind all of this now?

"Looks like I made it just in time," she says, leaning against the wall behind Weegan.

"Gwendolyn was just saying she knows who runs the account."

The Captain's face brightens with interest. "Do you now?"

Screw it. What do I have to lose by telling the truth?

"It belongs to Marty Boone."

Weegan's brow furrows. "Excuse me?"

"Of course, it does." The Captain laughs sarcastically, rubbing a kink in the back of her neck as she heads for the door. "I have someone waiting in my office," she pointedly says to Weegan before disappearing.

"I'm not lying!" I call after her, willing the woman to stay. "I know it's hard to hear, but it's true. Mr. Boone was worried no one would come to Pineland this summer, so he created this whole publicity stunt to put the park back in the spotlight. He was the one who told Valerie to stash Chase's body at the top of the Old Wheel and—"

Captain Pierce doesn't even let me finish before closing the door behind her.

"She needs to come back! Even if it's hard to hear, this is too important to ignore."

"Gwendolyn," he says, shaking his head, "I'm sorry, but I think you're mistaken. Marty Boone didn't find Chase's body."

"How can you be so sure?" I all but shriek. "Because he said he didn't?"

"No," Weegan says calmly. "Because Hannah Flannigan just admitted to finding Chase's body in her office at Pineland the day before you, erm, stumbled across it."

"Excuse me?"

Valerie said the Account found Chase's body. There's no

way Hannah is behind this. Surely, she must've told somebody a body was in her office. Her father, Donald? Marty?

All leads point back to him.

"Marty Boone isn't Account120346," Weegan says, reading my mind.

"Yes, he is!" I say, my voice raising slightly as I beg someone to take me seriously. "I know it sounds absurd, but it's true. Go search his work computer! I'm sure you'll find him logged into the account."

"Marty Boone has been cooperative with our investigation from day one. We would know if he was running a secret account to extort his employees."

"Amanda Boone said she made it for him!"

Detective Weegan sits up straight. "What did you just say?"

"Wait," I cut in, thinking about what Nora said before she departed, "is Mr. Boone here now? In the station?"

"Not that it's any of your business," Detective Weegan says, "but yes."

"Oh my god," I breathe out, a chill running up my spine. "We need to get to Pineland right now."

"Why?"

The blood drains from my face. I can't believe I didn't see it before. She was always right there. Asking all the right questions. Pretending to be on our side.

Is everyone in this town a fucking liar?

"Because Amanda Boone is Account120346."

CHAPTER
THIRTY-TWO

IT'S ALREADY a quick drive between the station and Pineland, but when you're in the back of a squad car blaring its sirens, the trip is over in the blink of an eye.

My mind is reeling as I question everything Amanda has done over the summer. She hated her grandfather and yet chose to return to work. She was insistent that we trust Milly. No wonder she was so desperate to find my best friend. With Valerie a wildcard on the run, Amanda's whole agenda was at risk.

But what was her agenda? To ruin her grandfather? How could she do that to her own family?

Dev, Weston, and I are all squeezed into the back of Weegan's squad car. There's something incredibly unnerving about sitting back here. I know we're not in trouble, but between the heavy barricade separating us from Weegan and his squawking walkie, the situation could not be more tense.

"Sirens off as soon as we reach the park! We will not disturb the guests. I repeat, we will not scare the guests."

Dev and I exchange a look across the backseat. Even in a crisis, Marty Boone won't have the atmosphere of his park shattered.

"Too late for that," Weston says while he reads something off his phone. Whatever it is, it has him going pale. "Uh, excuse me, detective, but according to one of my teammates, *Wolverine Racers* just stopped at the top of the lift hill."

"So?" Dev asks. "That ride breaks down at least once a day."

Weston holds out his phone for us to see the picture that was just texted to him. "Yeah, but not with Amanda Boone aboard and standing on the wrong side of the lap bar."

"What?" Weegan roars from the front seat, daring a look over his shoulder to see the blurry photo. "Suspect is on the stopped ride, *Wolverine Racers*!" He bellows into his radio. "All units approach, but do not engage!" He waits for his team to confirm before calling over his shoulder at us, "How could she get out of the safety restraint?"

The three of us share a guilty look in the backseat. There's only a simple lap bar that pulls down over each seat in the train. Anyone looking for more air time could keep a bag on their lap or raise their knees when pulling down the bar. We're all prone to doing it and the ride operators are too tired to care. Weegan curses when we explain this.

We skid into the parking lot, not bothering to pull into a spot as Weegan unlocks us from the backseat and we all race through HQ and into the park.

Like bees to spilled pop, the entire park seems to draw towards the coaster. Everyone is running in the same direction, unable to tear their eyes away from the girl standing on the top of the lift hill. There aren't evacuation stairs lining that portion of the track, so Amanda is balancing in the ride vehicle. Between screams of horror, guests on and off the ride beg for Amanda to return to her seat before anyone gets hurt.

Of course, she won't. Desperate people do dangerous things. This is the greatest scandal she could have ever wanted. The granddaughter of Marty Boone dangerously teetering over the top of his most infamous ride? I'm sure it's trending already.

"Get her down from there!" Marty Boone cries as he runs alongside Captain Piece. He's petrified, tears leaking down his wrinkled cheeks.

Captain Pierce is all business as she orders crew members to open the tall gate surrounding the ride. Thankfully, a leader is ready with the key and law enforcement swarms the grassy space below the track.

"How the hell did she stop the ride while on it?" Dev gasps, panting heavily in between words.

I was thinking the same thing. The ride had to have stopped before Amanda slid out of her likely loose lap bar.

Weegan must be wondering the same because he immediately cries into his radio, "Two units to the ride's control room! Find who stopped the ride!"

"I pick up shifts at *Wolverine Racers* all the time," Weston offers. "I can show them where to go!" He races off before waiting to hear otherwise.

Too focused on racing through the open gate, Weegan lets him go.

I'd be willing to bet money Milly found her way into the control booth this morning. She's the only one not at the station or dead.

Milly Dillard has no reason to be a lackey, but maybe she hates her father too. Or perhaps she really did it for the content. I'm sure she'll plead that she was forced into helping. I can practically see her posts now. *"A serial killer blackmailed me?!"*

"You kids stay back!"

We pretend not to hear the detective. He doesn't stop us from following the officers through the gate and into the untamed grass beneath the lift hill. Crew members stand at the ready with a tall stairwell on wheels that's used to evacuate guests from the ride.

"Please don't jump," I plead under my breath.

"She won't," Weegan says knowingly, squinting up at Amanda. I silently pray it's the worst she has in there.

It's clear she is prepared for the scene she's causing. Now that she's taken center stage, she's ready to capture the world's attention.

"Marty Boone doesn't only pollute our planet," she screams as loud as she can. "He pollutes every life he promises to change."

"What is she talking about?" Marty cries as he blinks up at her.

Someone hands Captain Pierce a megaphone and she calls up to the girl, "Amanda, please reconsider what you're doing!"

The crowd quiets to hear Amanda's cries. "Don't you think it's convenient that after years of knowing Marty Boone, he suddenly realizes he's in love with you? Just before things start to go wrong around here?"

"That's preposterous!" Marty gasps, turning to his girlfriend.

But judging by the frown on Captain Pierce's face, she's suddenly not so sure. Sirens begin to wail in the distance.

"He's a fraud!" Amanda bellows over the park. "He acts like a family man, while tearing our family apart. He pretends to adore the planet, while extorting it for cash. He doesn't care about safety. All he cares about is success."

Captain Pierce's lips disappear as she purses them tightly. Marty begins to protest, but she holds her hand up. "You'll let me handle this! She's the one in danger. Don't you dare fight with her now."

Though shaking with anger, Marty silences immediately. Even he must realize this isn't a scandal he can come back from.

Amanda isn't close to being done. "Marty Boone destroyed this community by taking advantage of your economic reliance on his park. He pays you minimum wage, overworks you, doesn't maintain facilities—and the worst part? He knows he can get away with it because you need him.

"What's most disappointing is Grandpa entrusts your lives in the hands of his shady operating partners. Partners who think they can pay teenagers for publicity stunts!"

The crowd falls in a confused silence.

"Who is she talking about?" I whisper.

Amanda knows she has everyone's attention now.

"Please!" Captain Pierce bellows into her megaphone, "Let us evacuate you and the other guests from the ride so we can talk this through together."

"Even now," Amanda screams, "you want to give him what he wants! A clean image!"

"What do you want?" The Captain calls up. "I know you don't want people to get hurt. Not really."

"Of course, I don't!" She cries. "I never did! You know who doesn't care if people die? My grandfather and Luther Flannigan!"

My jaw drops as blood begins to pound in my ears. We were wrong.

"What is she talking about, Marty?" Nora demands. We all snap our attention to him.

"I haven't the faintest idea."

"I thought you knew everything happening in this park," I hear myself say.

Marty waves me off like I'm a pesky mosquito.

"Luther isn't here," Dev observes.

He's right. Shouldn't the head of Pineland's PR team be concerned with such a serious matter?

Captain Pierce nods at Weegan, who runs out of the restricted area flanked by a few officers. They are likely heading for Crew HQ, hoping to track down Luther Flannigan before it's too late. God, I hope it's not.

It's all beginning to snap into place. For real, this time.

Amanda wasn't the one messaging Valerie. It was Luther

Flannigan, cooking up the next PR scandal that would put the park back in the headlines. Maybe Amanda did make the account for her grandfather, but he wasn't the one using it.

Of course, Hannah would report a dead teenager to her father. Then Luther Flannigan decided enough was enough. Attendance was booming, but too many kids were dead.

Captain Pierce swivels her attention back to Marty. "Did you know?"

"No!" He says immediately. "Of course, not!"

"But you adore Luther. You trust him. He's been with you since the start. He cleans up your messes."

"And now I'm going to have to clean up one of his!"

Nora stares at Marty with his disbelief, her jaw clenched. "I don't believe you."

"Excuse me?"

"Tell them, Grandpa!" Amanda yells from above. "Tell them the truth or I'll jump!"

"No!" Marty screams with panic. "Amanda, please!"

She holds her arms out like she's about to dive from the ride vehicle, earning screams of terror from the onlooking crowd.

"Fine, fine!" The man bellows, wildly waving his arms, like he can hold Amanda in place. "It's true! I knew."

"Knew what?" Captain Pierce demands.

"I encouraged Flannigan to create bad press, but I didn't think anyone would get hurt!"

"Marty," Captain Pierce says, her voice devoid of any emotion, "you're under arrest."

"Nora," he pleads, his voice breaking, "please, not in the middle of my park."

"You should've thought of that before partaking in criminal activity in your park." She unclips the handcuffs from her belt.

As soon as they snap around his wrists, we hear Amanda call from above. "I want to come down now."

Waiting for a nod from Captain Pierce, the crew members wheel over their evacuation walkway and begin assisting the guests from the attraction.

I can't tear my eyes away from Marty as Captain Pierce leads him away from the ride. The man who gave our town everything before dragging us into hell.

The president leaves his park in handcuffs. It's the kind of scandal he would've loved to see in the headlines, as long as it was anyone but him.

OF COURSE, my parents want to argue about me staying at the park after work.

"Technically, I'm not even staying late!" I explain for the umpteenth time. "Ms. Thatcher is letting the student crew members get off early so we can enjoy the park before school starts next week. I'll be home at the same time as every other night!"

"Can you blame us for being concerned parents? We don't like what goes on in that park after dark."

The last two months, "we" has become their new favorite word. *We* want you to be safe. *We* want to know where our daughter is at all times. *We* are going to start acting like a proper family because clearly this town needs a few of those.

After Marty Boone left town for the state prison, my parents found their calling to step up and reclaim the identity of what it means to be a citizen of Hathaway. It may be obnoxious, but they've been worse.

"Please!"

"Is this because it's Valerie's first shift back?"

Valerie, Jenna, and Milly spent their summers performing community service for not immediately going to the cops and saying anything. Jenna's mom, the new president of Pineland and Wetlands, preferred to speak of it as a "life lesson," and promised that the girls would keep their jobs in the parks. I heard Amanda received the same punishment but was granted permission to carry it out back in Texas. I doubt we'll ever see her in Michigan again.

I haven't spoken to Valerie since we dropped her off at the police station. She's tried to reach out a few times, but I've ignored every attempt. After a while, she took the hint.

Although I'm not sure I'm ready, there's a part of me that wants to face her today. Not to rekindle, but to prove that I don't need her. I can make my own way without her.

"No," I assure my folks. "This has nothing to do with her."

My parents share a pleased look, which makes me wonder if these were the magic words they were waiting to hear all along. That shouldn't surprise me. It may come from a loving place, but my family likes to communicate with passion.

"We want you home as soon as the park closes," Mom says in a knowing voice.

"Emphasis on *you*. No visitors in your bedroom after the fact."

They haven't forgotten about the night Valerie snuck into their house. I'm lucky they haven't caught Dev doing the same every other night this summer.

The doorbell rings.

My parents offer me exasperated looks while I grin. My back-up is here, not that I need him anymore.

"I'm getting the door," Dad says, rolling his eyes as he walks from the kitchen. I offer Mom a guilty shrug and she tries not to smile.

"Hello, Mr. Gardner. Would you please consider allowing Gwen and I to stay la—"

"We already said yes, kid."

"You did?" Dev chirps from the hallway. He pokes his

head into the kitchen, already dressed in his uniform. "You could've warned me before I started begging to your dad!"

"But it was so cute!" My mom says and I nod in agreement.

Jumping up from my seat at the table, I kiss her on the cheek. "Love you. See you all later."

"On time tonight," my dad warns Dev. "Sitting in your car in my driveway does not count as getting her 'home' on time."

Dev's ears turn red as he smiles sheepishly. "Yes, sir. Noted."

Grabbing his hand, I pull him out of the house before he goes full tomato.

Dev opens the passenger door for me, helping me hop into his high truck. "I can always trade her in."

"Who? Me or the truck?" I call as he closes my door.

He laughs, sliding into the driver's seat. "Fair question."

When my jaw drops open with offense, he pulls my chin over the center console, pressing his lips to mine. "Please," he whispers, resting our foreheads together, "I'm not giving you up that easily."

We have no idea how senior year is going to play out. Sure, the obvious stuff feels certain. We'll have lunch together every day. We'll work at Pineland on the weekends until the park closes for the season. We'll go to prom. But the rest is a mystery—and I'm in no rush to figure it out. I'm not giving him up that easily, either.

"Good answer," I say against his lips.

"Oy!" My dad's voice bellows from the front porch. "What did I say about loitering in the driveway?"

Dev jumps, grinning guiltily as he waves at my dad. "Sorry!"

"Sure, kid! Get to work!"

Dev turns the key in the ignition. "Let's go have a super save-the-world day."

In the few short weeks that Jenna's mom has overseen

Pineland, the mission of 'saving the world' does feel all the more sincere. She's already made the company more transparent about how we donate our money towards active conservation funds. She's cleaned up backstage a lot too. The cafeteria now serves food, and the AC works everywhere again.

It's obvious she's trying to save face after her daughter's scandal, but I'm not going to complain about the better working conditions.

When Dev and I walk into the HQ, I spot Valerie instantly, wearing all but the head of a Winston Woodpecker costume. She lost the role of Park Ranger, but Ms. Thatcher said she could keep a job in entertainment. Only Valerie could find a way to pull off a black-and-red fursuit.

I should've known she'd be waiting for me.

Everyone gives her a wide berth as she stands in the center of the atrium, balancing the woodpecker head on her hip. As soon as she claps eyes on me, her lips pull into a hesitant smile. It sends a confusing warmth through my body. There's a part of me that missed her, but I've enjoyed who I became while she was gone. Someone who isn't afraid to put down some roots.

"Do you want to see her?" Dev mutters under his breath.

But it appears that I don't have a choice because Valerie is hurriedly crossing the room to meet me.

"Welcome back," I say, keeping my voice even.

"I figured this place would go to shit without me around."

Dev snorts at the irony.

"Yo, what ride are we hitting up first tonight?" Weston says, strutting over. Then he glances towards Valerie, pretending to have just noticed her. "Oh, hey Val. Didn't see you there."

"Of course, you didn't," she agrees with a bat of her eyelashes. I wonder how long it'll take for her charm to win him back over.

"What do you think, Gwen?" Dev asks, pulling the attention from Valerie. "What do you want to ride?"

"Anything but *Sybil Saves the World*. I can't get that song stuck in my head again."

"Am I invited to join?" Valerie asks shyly. The nervousness in her voice is almost unrecognizable.

The boys turn to me, making this my call.

I meet the eyes of the girl I used to consider my best friend. I'm a different person without her in my life. Better. More content. But isn't this what I wanted? I need to prove the version of me that blossomed over the summer won't wilt in her presence.

"You can hang with us if you want."

"Cool," she says eagerly. Maybe she wants me to see a new side of her too. "Wanna ride something that'll make us scream our heads off?"

I cock my head to the side. "That shouldn't be too hard around here."

ACKNOWLEDGMENTS

LIARLAND doesn't exist without a theme-park-sized team of support. It's an honor to recognize a few of them.

To my Marmee. Your Jo finally published her book! Thank you for reading every single story I've ever written. It means more to me than you'll ever know. You are a brilliant editor, and an even more precious friend. I am so blessed to have you in my corner, Mom.

Dad, I am a storyteller because of you. Thank you for teaching me to make anything and everything into a story.

Adam, you're the best brother in the world. It was cool of you to let me steal your books when we were kids.

Taylor Maloney, you're the greatest friend I could have ever dreamed up. Thank you for listening to every last one of my schemes and helping me make them better.

A tremendous thank you to my incredible editor and friend, Andie Smith. We are living proof that sliding into a stranger's DMs works.

Thank you to Katt Phatt for creating this absolute vision of a cover, and to Nancy Moore for helping make it happen.

This sounds silly, but I'm going to thank my dogs, Holly and Elwood. This book was written with them snoring in the background. While I hope it's not an indication of the story, I did appreciate their company.

Lastly, here's a fun fact: I met the love of my life in a theme park. This book is real because of you, Taylor. Thank you for pushing me to believe in my wildest dreams. I love you endlessly.

ABOUT THE AUTHOR

MADISON RUPP
grew up surrounded by books and theme parks. It was only a matter of time until she combined the two. Based in Orlando, Madison is frequently found scribbling in a quiet corner of a theme park. She is a firm believer that riding a roller coaster cures writer's block.

You can connect with her online at madisonrupp.com.

 instagram.com/madisonrupp
 x.com/madisonrupp